Praise for
LAURA WOOD

"I Capture the Castle meets Gatsby. It's absolutely delicious!"
Laini Taylor on *A Sky Painted Gold*

"Heady, sun-drenched and achingly romantic"
Guardian on *Under a Dancing Star*

"Irresistible... gorgeous escapism"
Guardian on *A Snowfall of Silver*

"Pure escapism... a wildly romantic, delicious indulgence"
Observer on *A Sky Painted Gold*

"The perfect comfort read, the kind of lovely, absorbing
novel that is not published any more. I loved it"
Ella Risbridger on *A Sky Painted Gold*

"A brilliant, beautiful book. I loved it"
Louise O'Neill on *A Sky Painted Gold*

"Think Dodie Smith's *I Capture the Castle* set in Italy and
revolving around a summer romance, and you'll understand
the joy of Laura Wood's *Under a Dancing Star*"
Stylist

Also by
LAURA WOOD

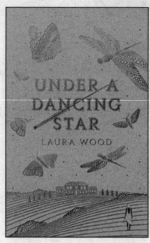

A Single Thread of Moonlight

LAURA WOOD

SCHOLASTIC

Published in the UK by Scholastic, 2021
Euston House, 24 Eversholt Street, London, NW1 1DB
Scholastic Ireland, 89E Lagan Road, Dublin Industrial Estate,
Glasnevin, Dublin, D11 HP5F

ISBN 978 07023 0323 4

A CIP catalogue record for this book is available from the British Library.

Printed by CPI Group (UK) Ltd, Croydon, CR0 4YY
Paper made from wood grown in sustainable forests
and other controlled sources.

1 3 5 7 9 10 8 6 4 2

www.scholastic.co.uk

To AJ, one of my very
own fairy godmothers.

"On what slender threads do life and fortune hang...!"
– Alexandre Dumas, *The Count of Monte Cristo*

PROLOGUE

Once upon a time there was a girl whose life was a dream, spun from golden thread.

She lived in a vast and rambling house in the countryside. It was a house that had been in her father's family for generations, and she loved it. She loved the jumble of hallways and rooms knotted strangely together, the huge Georgian windows, and the old Tudor beams.

It was a big house, and her father was a big man. Nobody could ride like him or shoot like him or throw her up into the air like him. She had no memory of her first time on a horse; it was as if she was born knowing how to gallop across open fields. Her father would take her around his estate, telling her thrilling stories of daring adventures.

The girl's mother was a haze of honey-coloured hair and blue eyes. She was a gentle voice and soft arms. "Delicate" – that's what the girl's father called her – which meant no loud voices, no running, no tumbling about. Her mother's rooms were as quiet and sleepy as any belonging to a fairy-tale princess under a spell.

The girl knew all about fairy tales, because her mother read them to her while she combed her blonde curls with her fingers. Her mother also taught her how to sew, how to create beautiful things out of nothing but cloth and thread, and this seemed like another kind of magic to the little girl.

All was well, and the days fell like neat stitches in a beautiful tapestry.

Then, when she was nine, the golden life began to unravel.

Her mother died – one day she was there, and the

next she simply slipped away, like a candle that had been burning lower and lower as the months and weeks passed, finally extinguished.

But the girl still had her father, and she held him closer than ever. He was her whole world, and she was his shadow, following him wherever he went.

Then, less than a year after her mother died, the girl's father remarried.

At first she was excited about gaining a stepmother and two new stepsisters, but her new family were cold and cruel. Her father started to disappear, staying away from home from morning to night. He did not take his shadow with him.

It was only a year after the marriage that the unthinkable happened. The girl's father – the greatest horseman in seven counties – had a riding accident on his way home. *A rabbit hole*, they told her. He fell from his horse and was killed instantly.

It was impossible. Her father rode the same path through the woods every day – there was not a chance that he could be thrown from his horse so easily. The little girl knew a convenient lie when she heard one. She saw the satisfied smile behind her stepmother's black veil, and deep in her heart she knew the truth: that she was living with a cold-hearted killer.

But she had no proof, no one to confide in.

And she had an ominous feeling that she might be next.

So the girl did what any self-respecting young heroine would do.

She vowed that one day she would have her revenge.

And then she ran away.

Part One

London
October, 1899

CHAPTER ONE

Not a lot of people knew when they were going to die, but I did, right down to the minute. At the stroke of midnight, on the twenty-fifth of November 1899, Iris Penelope Scott-Holland would die. The letter in my hand told me so.

I sighed, closing my eyes and crumpling the sheet of paper between my fingers.

I hadn't been *Iris Scott-Holland* for a long time now. It had been almost seven years since I had run away from home, and – according to the investigator that I had scrimped and saved to hire – seven years was all the time that you needed to be missing before you could be declared legally dead.

It was no surprise to learn that my stepmother had been counting the days.

The final sentences of the letter danced behind my eyelids like sunspots.

I regret to inform you, Miss Grey, that time is not on your side. If you wish to act, it must be soon.

Seven years since I had been home. Seven years since Father had died. Seven years of questions left unanswered. Perhaps it was time for that to change.

"There's no time for moping over love letters." Annie bustled in. "Madame wants that embroidery for Lady Flintlock's gown finished today."

Annie was not exactly how one might picture a guardian angel. She was short and seemed permanently angry, with grizzled grey hair and a frighteningly hard stare. She was not warm, she had never expressed one word of affection towards me, and yet, when I was eleven years old, she had saved my life.

I had arrived in London alone, a pretty, spoiled child,

4

with no idea of the real world. Fortunately for me, Annie took me in – temporarily, she said – and when she found out that I could stitch like a dream she got me a job at Madame Solange's, the 'dressmakers' where she worked.

I had an instinct for colour, an interest in the latest fashions, and clever fingers. After Annie showed her some of my embroidery, Madame Solange took me on as an assistant dressmaker, and when my new employer asked for my name, I gave her my mother's maiden name instead of my own. So, Iris Scott-Holland became Iris Grey, and I shed my old name and my old life gladly, like a winter coat on the first sunny day of the year.

Seven years later, Madame Solange's designs were in great demand. The dresses that I created were beginning to change hands for a lot of money – not that I saw much of that. My job was to be grateful for the opportunity. And I was, really.

Every day I sewed in the small workroom, surrounded by bolts of fabric in all the colours of the rainbow. It was work that I enjoyed, and it was the perfect work for someone who wished to remain a shadow – no one wanted to think about the fingers that stitched their dress, and that was exactly how I liked it.

"I've almost finished," I told Annie, folding the letter briskly into quarters, and sliding it under a length of rich red silk. "It will be done in time for her fitting tomorrow."

"Is that Lady Flintlock again?" Claire, the shop's model, drifted in. "I can't stand showing the clothes for her – she's a nasty old thing. Last time she came, she said that lovely blue dress would probably look well enough on someone built less like a work horse." Claire's eyes widened in distress. "*A work horse.*"

Claire was seventeen and sweet, with enormous doe-like brown eyes and masses of dark, curling hair. She hadn't been at the shop for long, and she was still trying to be my friend. I was as discouraging as possible.

Fugitives didn't have friends.

Which is why, instead of commiserating with Claire over Lady Flintlock, I schooled my voice to be cold when I replied, "Lady Flintlock is one of our biggest customers, Claire." *And a mean old bat*, I added to myself.

Claire flushed and mumbled an apology.

I turned back to the piece of embroidery that I had laid across my desk. It was for a morning gown of pale lemon silk, and I was embroidering hundreds of tiny yellow butterflies across it. It was a bit fussy for my taste, but Lady Flintlock had never met a flower, a feather, or a ruffle that she didn't like. *Butter upon bacon*, was her philosophy.

At her last viewing she had demanded the addition of hundreds of crystal beads. Madame Solange had praised her keen eye for fashion, added several guineas to the price, and then told me to get to work.

Claire moved closer, her fingers hovering above the embroidery, not quite touching the fine material.

"So beautiful," she murmured. "I couldn't understand at first – why Madame kept you hidden away in the back room, with your looks. It's because you can do this. How did you learn?"

"My mother taught me," I replied, my eyes on the stitches.

That, at least, was a small truth in a sea of lies.

Mother had taught me to sew as soon as I was old enough to hold a needle. She was an artist when it came to embroidery, and I had spent my whole life trying to capture some of the magic she had in her fingers. In another world – one where women's work was taken seriously – my mother's art would have hung in galleries. I thought with a pang of the beautiful wall hangings that had adorned my bedroom. Images from fairy tales brought to life: Rapunzel with her golden hair tumbling from the tower window; Red Riding Hood followed by a shadowy wolf – a shiver of silver fur and gleaming amber eyes.

I wondered what had happened to them after I ran away. Helena had probably burned them.

I gave myself a shake, forcing my focus back to the piece of silk in front of me. Thankfully, Claire had taken the hint and gathered her things, heading home for the night.

"She's right, you know," Annie said from the corner of the room where she too was getting ready to leave. "It is a waste, you being stuck back here. Think of the fuss you and Claire would cause together, her so dark and you so fair. People would buy anything you put in front of them. We'd sell hundreds of gowns."

"And who would make them?" I asked tartly.

Annie only made a huffing sound and pulled on her coat. She knew I was right, and that was a good thing. If it hadn't been for my usefulness back here, I have no doubt Madame would have wanted me parading about out front, and that was a risk I could not take.

If things had turned out differently, perhaps I'd be a smartly turned-out customer, looking for a wardrobe to suit my social calendar – the daughter of a wealthy marquess probably had need of a great number of gowns. But I had left that life behind on the night I ran away from home and caught the night coach to London.

I had spent my first night in the city huddled in the doorway of Madame Solange's shop – drawn by the words painted in neat golden letters: *DRESSMAKERS OF QUALITY, THE FINEST STITCHING IN ALL OF LONDON*. I sat there for hours in the dark, increasingly afraid of the noises around me. The country had noises too, but they were different: the sharp bark of a fox, the insistent tap of a tree branch against the windowpane. Here, there was a constant, cresting wave

9

of voices, and crashes, and horses, and footsteps. By the time the sun rose I was half-dead with fright.

That was when the door opened, and I fell flat at Annie's feet.

For almost seven years after that, I had hidden away in London, saving what little money I could to hire investigators. I had hired three so far to look into Helena's background, her life before marrying my father, her first husband (Samuel Weston, a mere baron) and his death – anything that could help me uncover a truth that I was certain of in my heart: that she'd played a part in my father's death. All three had come up empty-handed.

I tried not to think about home too much, or the large inheritance that was owed to me, but this latest letter was clear: in just a few weeks' time I would be declared dead, and the woman who had killed my father would have won.

I rubbed my temples. It was late now, the lights low as I set my final stitches in place. The moon shone through the window; it was time to go home.

I packed up and let myself out of the shop, carefully locking the door behind me. It was a cold night, and the blanket of London fog tucked itself snugly around everything in sight. A nearby streetlamp struggled valiantly, managing to cast a dim silver halo of light that diffused into the darkness like perfume from a glass bottle.

"Hello, darlin'," a voice slurred from over my shoulder. "Aren't you a pretty piece?"

I turned. A man was weaving his way towards me – older, dressed in a worn suit, and clearly the worse for drink.

"Anyone ever tell you you've got the face of an angel?"

"Yes," I replied. "It's not an imaginative compliment. Now, excuse me, please."

His brow furrowed. "I'm only trying to be friendly."

He reached out and put his hand on my arm.

That was his mistake.

In a flash I had the thin silver blade of my pen knife against his neck.

"Let. Go."

His hand leaped from my arm like I was a burning-hot coal.

"Now, now," he said, his voice coming out in a thin whine. "There's no need for that, just being friendly, just being friendly."

"I'm not looking for a friend." I stepped back and the man exhaled. I kept the knife pointed towards him, moonlight flashing wickedly across the blade.

"I thought you was a nice girl," he grumbled, backing further away, his hands held up in front of him.

"I suppose you were wrong."

With a shake of his head, as though I had let him down, he finally turned and walked away.

A nice girl. More fool him. My mother always told me that appearances could be deceiving. Well, I was living proof of that. I had learned a lot during my years in London.

You see, people always assume that I'm the pretty little piece of embroidery.

But I'm not.

I am the needle.

CHAPTER TWO

Three days later, I was no closer to a decision about what to do.

I couldn't just go home and reveal that I was very much alive. At best, Helena hated me and at worst, Helena was a ruthless murderer. Who was to say what lengths she would go to conceal the truth?

The city was hardly safe, yet the thought of living with Helena felt riskier still. If my father had been unable to survive her, then I wasn't sure I liked my own chances.

But I was no longer a naive child. I was a force to be reckoned with. And I would *not* abandon my father's memory without a fight. Helena couldn't win.

It wasn't simply justice that I wanted. It was revenge. I wanted her to suffer as I had suffered. To lose.

These thoughts chased each other round and round in my head.

Then, as so often happens in stories like this, fate stepped in and everything changed.

* * *

Madame Solange's shop was a smart building in the West End of London. These premises had been acquired two years ago, when the success of our dressmaking made moving to more luxurious surroundings a possibility. Now the words in Madame's window were no idle boast: we really did produce the finest stitching in London.

Madame was a whip-smart businesswoman, and over the last two years the shop had become increasingly popular with the aristocratic set – the kind for whom money was no object. The kind who enjoyed the plush red velvet seats, the shining walnut and brass fittings, and the tea from fine china served with lemon shortbread from Fortnum and Mason. They enjoyed the heady, Turkish-delight scent of the rich roses that spilled out of dozens of vases, the exclusivity.

You had to make an appointment with Madame, and then she lavished you with her full attention. The clients liked her creations, the ones made to their exact requirements. No request was too difficult or extravagant, no demand too outrageous.

The back room where I worked was cramped and much less smart, but it was clean and neat, and when I bought Madame's roses I always spent a farthing or two on something small and cheerful, like a bunch of daisies to sit in a jam jar on the side. It had two large windows – artists needed good light, Madame said.

Autumn sunlight filtered through them that morning, the kind of sunlight specific to this time of year – heavy, dancing, golden – like a breeze streaming through ripe wheat.

Last night, I had dreamed of a dress, woken up with the idea for it so clear in my mind that I could almost feel the cool slip of the material through my fingers.

A deceptively simple gown of opalescent cream silk and layers of airy tulle, stitched all over with a silver thread so pale that it was only when the light hit it that the pattern emerged. I pictured hundreds of small glass beads sewn across it and hanging from the shoulders to form short sleeves that moved and sparkled as the woman who wore it danced in a beautiful ballroom.

I had begun sketching my plans, when Claire came steaming into the room, her cheeks pink with excitement. "Madame says we need everything worth showing, quick," she said. "There's a lady here, says her daughter's going to marry a prince!"

Annie and I leaped to attention. Annie began pulling gowns out and rummaging through hat boxes. I was already lacing Claire into a beautiful sage-green day dress.

"Can you imagine?" Claire asked, sucking in a breath as I tugged on the laces. "Marrying a prince, I mean?" She clasped her hands together. "It's like something out of a story. She must be the luckiest girl in the world."

"I suppose it depends on the prince," I said, around a

16

mouthful of pins, as I carefully fluffed the folds of ivory lace at the neckline of the dress.

"Come on, girls." Madame Solange appeared, clapping her hands together. She was a formidable woman, tall and generously curved and dressed head to toe in black. "This is a customer worth having. If we get this right, we'll be set for next season." Her dark eyes were gleeful, her cockney accent at its most pronounced.

Madame Solange was about as French as a Yorkshire pudding, but all the most fashionable establishments boasted a modish French designer, and Madame Solange did not care to disappoint her customers. Her false accent was slathered on, thick as butter on bread, the kind that left tooth marks behind.

She called herself a widow too, though there was no evidence of that. That was the thing about the city. Here you could be anyone you wanted. You could let go of your history, as easily as if it were a feather on your palm – unclasp your fingers and off it flew.

"Iris." Madame's voice was brisk, a world away from the honeyed tones she used on clients. "Make sure you send out the pink silk. It will work well with the young lady's colouring, and Lady Scott-Holland specifically asked for pastel shades."

The world slammed to a stop.

I froze.

Madame kept talking, but the pin cushion fell from my hand, bouncing and rolling across the floor and under a table. There was a sound in my ears, like a swarm of angry bees.

I lurched forward, my legs almost going from underneath me.

Claire reached out and held my arm.

Her mouth was moving, but it took me a moment to understand what she was saying. "Iris ... Iris? Are you all right? You've gone white as a sheet."

"Just a dizzy spell," I managed. "Did you say Lady Scott-Holland?" I was pleased that my voice was almost steady.

Madame's clever eyes narrowed. "That's right. What do you know about her?"

"Not very much." I bent down to retrieve the pin cushion, taking a moment to school my expression into something more like indifference. "Only that she has

18

two daughters." I straightened up, my breathing now under control. It seemed Madame Solange's reputation had finally reached my stepmother.

"Yes," Madame agreed, clearly losing interest. "And she's unhappy with the work her usual dressmaker has done, so let's not waste any more time – here's a pigeon ripe for plucking!" On that note she swept from the room.

Claire trotted out after her.

"Glide, Claire, *glide*!" I heard Madame scold under her breath. "We don't want any more bloody horse comments, do we?"

Claire's pace slowed and she did something droopy with her arms which I supposed was meant to imply elegance.

I hesitated for a moment, and then, on silent feet, I followed, keeping myself well hidden behind the sumptuous red velvet drapes that separated the back and front rooms.

"Ahhhhh, Madame Scott-'Olland!" I winced as Madame Solange's heavily accented words pierced the quiet. "'Ow delighted I am to 'ave you 'ere een our 'umble établissement."

"I have heard great things, Madame."

That voice. That cool, musical voice. Suddenly, I was ten years old again.

I edged further along, pulling back the corner of the drape and clinging to the shadows.

Helena was facing away from me. She was tall and clad in a sophisticated gown of apricot silk. Her hair was coiled at the back and still as dark as I remembered. Not a grey hair in sight. When she turned slightly and I saw her in profile I was startled by how young she looked. I suppose as a child every adult seems older than the hills, but Helena could not have been much more than forty now, and she looked younger than that. Her face was regal, with a definite set to her chin and mouth. Her dark green eyes were framed by long black lashes. She was still a beauty.

Something seethed inside me.

"My daughter must have the best of everything," she was saying. I saw Agatha, standing to her side, running her fingers across the bolts of fabric Madame had already pulled out for them. There was no sign of Cassie.

Agatha was no longer the child that I remembered. She was a young woman, almost twenty-one. I would not have recognized her, except that she looked much like her mother, though her mouth was softer, her eyes smaller and more grey than green. She smiled at Helena's words, a self-satisfied smirk that made my toes curl in my sensible boots.

"Of course, of course!" Madame Solange agreed. "Mademoiselle will be very well looked after 'ere. Your special guest will not be able to take 'is eyes off 'er."

Agatha gave a pleased titter and Helena smiled.

"Naturally, I hope for your discretion," Helena said in a low voice, and Madame nodded seriously. "But when one is preparing to welcome royalty into the family home, one must put on a bit of a display. We're hosting a house party at our estate in Kent which is to be quite the affair. That will last a fortnight; there will of course be a large ball, as well as another formal reception, dinners, luncheons, excursions ... all the usual entertainments." Helena's eyes gleamed. "Most urgent, though – before we get to all of that, there's a ball being given here in town at the end of the week, which we are to attend, and Agatha must look her best."

I thought fast. We knew all about the Devonshire House ball; we had several customers who were planning to attend. It was being given in honour of the visiting Prince Stefan, a member of the royal family of a small Austro-Hungarian principality, distantly related to our own Queen Victoria. His visit had caused quite the stir among the matchmaking mamas who visited Madame Solange.

So, he was the prince Agatha was to marry.

"We expect there to be an announcement any day now," Helena added, the words heavy with meaning. "*All* eyes will be on Agatha. Then of course the prince will be our guest at Holland Hall for two weeks, alongside several other important visitors."

I knew what Helena was saying. If Agatha – a future princess – showed off Madame Solange's work while spending time with the cream of society, then it could mean big business. Helena might be rich, but she wasn't above trying to make a deal on a new wardrobe.

Madame sucked her cheeks in for a moment and then smiled. "Eet will be our verrrry great pleasure to dress your daughter, Madame. I think that we can come to an arrangement that ees très agreeable to us all."

With a flick of her wrist Madame gestured Claire forward.

"Now thees particular design ees very suitable for a luncheon..."

I let the drape fall from my fingers and backed away into the sewing room where Annie was hard at work.

"Where have you been?" she snapped.

"Sorry," I muttered. "I was dizzy. I just needed a bit of fresh air."

"Gawping at the customers isn't going to help with that," Annie retorted. She peered at me closely. "Are you all right now?" she asked, reluctant concern creeping into her voice.

I nodded.

"Then press this gown quickly, will you? Claire will be through any second."

I did as I was told, letting the familiar monotony of the work steal over me. I needed to focus on something else while I caught my breath.

Now that the shock was starting to wear off, I found

23

that what I was actually feeling was anger. Hot, violent, crimson-silk anger.

Helena and Agatha both looked so carefree, so pleased with themselves, the picture of health and prosperity.

They'd built a nice life for themselves – or rather, they'd stolen it. Stolen from my father, stolen from me.

Agatha was going to marry a prince, was she?

Over my dead body.

CHAPTER THREE

One thing was clear: I needed to go to that ball.

It was at the ball that Helena was hoping to secure a proposal. Something had to be done about that.

The plan started to take shape in the long hours that I spent working on Agatha's wardrobe over the next several days. Finally, the opportunity for revenge had presented itself and I wasn't going to throw it away. It wouldn't be enough … nothing ever could be, but it would mean something to Helena, and it would be a beginning. I would stop that marriage if it was the last thing I did.

It was a strange thing, labouring over Agatha's clothes. The first priority was obviously the dress she'd be wearing to the ball here in London, but as Helena was also throwing a small house party for Prince Stefan and some friends, Agatha had to be dressed in a way befitting a future princess for the entire fortnight.

Helena had clearly thought this through. If Stefan proposed at the London ball, then the house party became a celebration – but if he did not? Well, then there would be plenty more opportunity to throw Stefan and Agatha together until he did.

There was not enough time to build a wardrobe from scratch, but fortunately we had several items already made up that would work with some clever alteration. Some of these had originally been destined for other customers – "If they can't pay their bills on time then that's their fault." Madame had shrugged, a mercenary spark in her eyes.

What this meant for me was three nights in a row of falling asleep at my workbench and waking with a stiff neck. It also meant fighting every urge to line the gowns with pins or choose a fabric that would make Agatha look bilious. I knew a nice pea-green trim that would make her look like she had a nasty case of the flu.

I didn't do it. Madame Solange had taken me in, taken a chance on me, and I owed her my loyalty.

Besides, the clothes were sacred. It wasn't their fault that they were going to be worn by the second most loathsome woman on the planet. I took as much time and care over the alterations as I usually would. I tried to forget that Agatha would be slipping her arms through the sleeves or smoothing down the skirts that were spread across the table in front of me.

But there was one thing I couldn't bring myself to do, and that was to turn over the dream dress. I worked on it in secret, snatching odd moments to dedicate to it wherever I could. It was far from being finished but I could already tell that it was going to be special – perhaps the best thing I had ever made – and I couldn't stand the thought of Agatha owning that.

It would be the perfect dress for a princess, but then Agatha wasn't going to *be* a princess. Not if I had any say in the matter.

The London ball was in two days' time. It was a

masked ball, which was all the rage, a gift to someone trying to sneak in unseen – someone like me.

It was being held at Devonshire House in Piccadilly, the site of the notorious fancy dress ball two years earlier. Getting in was not going to be easy. My best hope was to try and sneak in as a servant. At events like this, where each guest was examining each other for clues to their identity, it was the staff who became invisible.

These were the thoughts that occupied my mind when Madame appeared, unusually flustered.

"Claire's been taken sick," she said shortly. "There's a woman here looking for something to wear to the ball at Devonshire House. I need you to model for me."

"You know I don't model the clothes," I said, laying down my work.

She put a hand on my arm. "She's brought someone with her ... Nicholas Wynter."

These last two words were breathless, her tone one of mingled horror and delight.

Nicholas Wynter.

I had never met the man, but even I knew his name.

Everybody did. Nicholas Wynter was an earl, a title he had inherited from his father almost three years ago. He was, I suppose, what you'd call a tastemaker. If you met with his approval then you were bound for success, but more often than not people encountered the cutting cruelty that he was famous for. He could put Madame Solange on the map, or he could just as easily destroy her.

"Get that green lamé that Lady Huntingdon hasn't paid for yet." Madame's voice was shrill. "And I don't care that you don't model, Iris, this is too important. If you can't make yourself useful at a time like this then there's no job here for you. You can pack your things." She crossed her arms and glared at me.

I wasn't fooled. We both knew that I could walk out of here and get a job with one of her competitors. It was hardly the first time she had threatened to give me the sack.

Still, the note of panic in her voice gave me pause.

I pressed my lips together.

"Fine," I snapped. "But you're paying me double. If I'm going to have two jobs, then you can pay me two wages."

"You'll take what you're given and be grateful," Madame snapped back, but her shoulders eased, betraying her relief.

On that note she sailed out to the front of the shop again, and Annie began to help me dress.

I stood in front of the mirror as Annie laced the back of the gown. It was a beauty. Green lamé, shot through with gold threads, and a sheer silk overlay that added to the shimmering effect. It was low cut, with full, trailing skirts. It would be perfect for the Devonshire House ball.

While Annie fiddled with the fastenings at the back of the dress, I tried to tidy my hair. I had inherited my mother's colouring, though I didn't think I looked much like her otherwise. My hair was blonde with a natural curl, and my eyes were the same deep blue, but my brows and lashes were darker than hers had been, my nose more snub, my mouth fuller. I was shorter than her, and less willowy – I remember her as a slim, graceful reed in a long gown.

I knew that I was beautiful. I suppose it sounds hopelessly arrogant to say as much, but enough people had told me so that I had accepted it as a fact.

Personally, I thought my looks were a bit on the insipid side, but it was that which made so many people underestimate me. People never thought the pretty little milkmaid would be the one holding a knife to their throat.

I pinched my cheeks, trying to add colour. Spending all my days in this room, slaving over a sewing machine, had not done my complexion any favours.

"Right," Annie said. "You're in. There's a bit more to you than there is of Lady Huntingdon."

That was true. The dress might be lovely, but at the moment it felt like a lovely cage. The bodice was so tight that it forced my spine absolutely straight – there was no chance of slouching.

In a way, it helped. I felt made of steel, and I lifted my chin to match my posture.

"All right, Queen Victoria," Annie murmured. "Don't go getting any ideas."

The corner of my mouth tugged up, but I forced my face to stay serene.

I swept through the curtains, my steps as gliding as Madame could wish.

31

"Ah, 'ere is Iris now," Madame cried, and the indulgent look she gave me would have fooled most people into believing I was the daughter she'd never had. I pinned a smile to my face, even as I fought the urge to stare at Nicholas Wynter.

It was extremely difficult.

He stood in the corner of the room, one elbow propped up on a cabinet. His tall body possessed a certain grace even when he was standing still. He gave the impression of a big cat – a leopard, perhaps – poised to unfurl himself. He was not a large man, but he seemed to take up a lot of space. I was surprised by how young he was – he must have been only in his early twenties. I had assumed a man who commanded such authority over society would be older, more established.

He wore a beautiful dark blue jacket, perfectly cut, and a waistcoat that was a trifle too ostentatious for my taste, embroidered in heavy gold thread. In one hand he held a polished wooden cane with a gold handle. There was a white rose in his lapel. His hair was very dark, and he wore it slightly longer than most. His features were a series of hard, sharp lines. From the cut-glass

32

cheekbones to the square jaw, he looked as if he had been sketched by a decisive hand.

But it was his eyes that made him impossible to ignore. Ice-cold blue eyes, their touch a shiver across the skin. Those eyes were older than the rest of him, full of the sort of lazy amusement that I could easily see would cause people to wilt.

It had the opposite effect on me.

Despite my intention to remain inconspicuous, I lifted my own gaze and met his assessing stare full on.

I did not smile.

For a moment it was as if the rest of the world fell away. The lazy look disappeared, sharpened, until all that remained was the challenge in those cold eyes. His face was still, but after a long moment a small pucker appeared between his brows. Whether it was because he disliked what he saw I wasn't sure, but he turned away, and the spell was broken. The room rushed back in, and I realized that my pulse was racing.

I pasted a vapid smile on my face, and shook out the skirts of the dress, ready to be admired like a china doll.

"Well, Teresa," Nicholas Wynter said, "I think you

might actually have found something after all." His voice was a dry rustle of autumn leaves.

I finally noticed the woman he was with – curvy, dark-haired and a little younger than him. She had risen from the sofa where Madame had plied her with tea and biscuits, and she stepped closer, her face wreathed in smiles.

"And you thought I'd never get a dress so late as this," she exclaimed and turned to Madame. "I hadn't planned to be in town for the ball, but then my husband got detained on business and I thought why not stay a little longer? Lord Wynter offered to come and help me choose a dress." Her eyes returned to Nicholas, as if seeking his approval. "It's very beautiful, isn't it?"

"Very beautiful." Nicholas too moved forward. There was still more than an arm's length between us, but it felt as if he was closer. "Though not, I think, the right colour for you. Blue or purple would be best."

Teresa pouted, but Madame swept in, effusive. "The gentleman 'as a verrrry good eye." Madame clicked her fingers. "Iris, we weel show the purple silk next, I think, for Madame."

It was a dismissal and I picked up my skirts, glad to escape even temporarily, though determined not to show it.

Madame and Teresa continued to chatter, but Lord Wynter was silent.

Even with my back turned, I felt him watching me as I left.

CHAPTER FOUR

In the end, Teresa took the purple silk. Lord Wynter was right; it suited her perfectly. She also ordered a lilac day dress, and a pale blue evening gown for delivery at a later date.

I thought Madame's Cheshire-cat grin was going to split her face. A future princess ordering a new wardrobe, and the approval of the most fashionable man in London – it had been quite the week for her.

That fashionable man himself, though, had seemed largely bored throughout the whole affair. Only once did he become truly animated, and that was when he vehemently rejected Teresa's suggestion that she buy a hat with an ostentatiously dyed-green ostrich feather curling at the front. I couldn't blame him for that – the hat had been sitting in the shop for months.

While Madame and Teresa disappeared to measure her for the necessary alterations, I took the opportunity to slip away. The purple gown was less constricting than the green one, but I was still finding it hard to catch my breath in Lord Wynter's presence.

"One moment, Miss…" His voice stopped me in my tracks. I turned reluctantly to face him. I let the silence hang heavy in the air for a moment longer. He lifted an eyebrow, making it clear he was in no hurry and could wait as long as it took. I resisted the temptation to roll my eyes.

"Grey," I said finally.

"Miss Grey." His voice was smooth, and he sketched an unhurried but beautiful bow.

I did not respond, forcing myself to be still. I adopted an expression of blandness, returning his look of enquiry with all the indifference I could muster.

"May I ask how long you have been modelling here?"

I saw no harm in answering honestly. "Today is the first day," I replied, smoothing the skirts of my dress.

He nodded, as though I had confirmed a suspicion he had. I was not sure why – I thought I had done a perfectly acceptable job at showing off the clothes. Still, I kept my mouth shut. The less information I gave him the better.

"And prior to your employment by Madame Solange," he asked, "what were you doing then?"

I stiffened. "I do not see what concern that could possibly be of yours." As an afterthought I added the word, "Sir." I had meant the word to get us back on to polite, distant ground, but instead it came out like a taunt.

Those mesmerizing blue eyes blinked lazily. Again, I was reminded of a cat before it pounced.

He moved to sit down on the red velvet sofa that Teresa had vacated, and swung one ankle across his other knee, his fingers drumming against the side of his boot. I noticed that his boots were polished to a higher shine than I had previously believed possible – dark mirrors, in which I could see a distorted image of my own pale face reflected back.

"Indulge my curiosity."

I didn't bother trying to hide my annoyance then. His high-handedness made my hackles rise. I could think of only one direction in which these questions could be leading. It was wearyingly predictable.

"I am not usually a model at all," I said, as evenly as I could manage. "I'm a seamstress. I work in the back of the shop."

Something flickered across Lord Wynter's face, something that looked curiously like satisfaction. "Better and better," he murmured. "Hidden away, as it were?"

"If we're done, sir…" I said, turning away and hoping to avoid the inevitable scene that would follow.

"Actually, there is something else I wanted to ask," he called.

Fine. Let's get it over with.

I turned to face him again.

"I have a proposition for you," he said, his voice a lazy drift of smoke curling towards me.

I folded my arms. "I'm not interested."

His eyebrows rose. "You haven't heard what it is yet."

"Yes, I have. Not from you, perhaps, but from several

39

other self-important, entitled men who think all they have to do is snap their fingers and they can buy a girl as easily as the gown she's wearing."

Amusement leaped in his eyes. "I see," he said. "So, you already know what's on offer?"

"A nice little house in the best part of town, jewellery, fine gowns." I ticked them off on my fingers. "I believe one gentleman thought a caged canary might sweeten the deal."

"I hadn't considered a canary," Nicholas murmured.

"And you're worse than the rest of them, when you've already come here to buy another lady's clothes ... and a married lady at that! Good grief, sir, how do you expect to juggle us all?" I threw the words at him – a challenge, like the sharp sting of a glove across the cheek.

"Ah," Nicholas said thoughtfully. "Now if *Teresa* is the problem, that is easily resolved..."

My mouth dropped at that. The cold lack of concern, as if a woman was an expendable object, easily thrown aside when she became inconvenient or a better proposition came along. "You ... are ... insufferable!"

"My dear, you have no idea." His mouth curled up at the corner, almost a smile, though one that got nowhere near his eyes. "But I actually meant that I could clear up the misunderstanding. Teresa is my cousin, and I was helping her to choose a gown – which I certainly won't be paying for – because she, tragically, does not possess an eye for colour. Last season she developed an unfortunate passion for puce, and my eyes have still not recovered." He shuddered.

"Your … cousin?" I managed. "Not your…"

"No." Nicholas shook his head. "*Not* my…" His smirk made it clear that he understood me perfectly.

I was momentarily thrown, but I gathered my wits together and pulled myself up to my full height. "That changes nothing. I hope that I have made my own position clear."

"Oh, extremely clear," Nicholas said politely. "You do not care for canaries."

"I do not care for canaries or ungentlemanly oafs."

"I don't think I have been called an oaf before," he mused.

"I find that hard to believe."

He laughed then, and I could feel the colour rising in my cheeks.

"Better and better," he said again, and I began to cast my eyes about for a suitable weapon. It was entirely possible that the man had lost his wits, and I didn't have my pen knife on me.

"I think," he said, "that we had better start again."

Fortunately, we were interrupted by the arrival of Teresa and Madame Solange.

"Oh, Nick." Teresa beamed up at her cousin. "Madame says the gown will be ready first thing tomorrow."

Does she now? I thought. *That's another night at the sewing machine for me then.*

"Fine," Nicholas Wynter replied, uninterested.

"We weel send ze parcel around just as soon as possible," Madame nodded. "I 'ope we weel see you 'ere again."

"Oh, you may count on it," Nicholas said. His eyes never left Madame's face, but somehow I knew that the words were aimed at me. I just couldn't decide if they were a threat or a promise.

CHAPTER FIVE

I had much bigger problems than Nicholas Wynter. The following morning, I feigned illness and begged Madame for a couple of hours off work.

"A headache. I think I just need some fresh air, perhaps to go and lie down for an hour," I murmured weakly.

"It is a very bad time for you to be ill, Iris," Madame huffed. "Not at all convenient. Claire might be back, but she still looks terrible!" Madame glanced over to where Claire was wilting in the corner, her skin tinged slightly green. She was going to clash horribly with most of the dresses.

Annie stepped in. "She's been staying up all hours the past few nights," she said to Madame. "She'll get more done after a short rest. Probably overtired." Annie sniffed, making it plain what she thought of people who got "overtired". Clearly she did not want me to think she'd gone soft.

"Fine." Madame threw her hands up. "You can take two hours."

"Thank you," I murmured, the picture of meekness. Two hours should be enough time to gather the information that I needed, but I didn't want to waste a minute of it.

I wrapped myself in my sensible coat of navy wool and bustled out into the October sunshine. It had been days since my face had seen the sun – I'd been arriving at the shop before it came up and leaving long after it went down – and I tipped my head back, my eyes half-closed, enjoying the feeling of warmth on my skin.

The road was typically busy, seething with people, a sea of dark coats and bowlers and the odd higher and more elaborate lady's hat drifting into view. Hackney carriages wove through the wide street, and horse-drawn omnibuses followed steady tracks, their brightly painted sides calling out at passers-by to purchase Nestle Milk or Champion's Vinegar. It was full of noise and colour and life, and I could feel my body coming awake as I darted through it all.

I made my way briskly along Regent Street, in the direction of Piccadilly. Skirting the edge of Berkeley Park, I noticed that the trees had begun to adopt their autumn colours in earnest now, stubborn patches of green leaves hanging on amid a sea of yellow and orange. A blackbird sat on one of the railings, his rich song following me down the street like another greeting from this daylight world.

The entrance to Devonshire House was guarded by a pair of tall, wrought iron gates, heavily emblazoned with gilt and topped with a swirling design of leaves. Two bronze sphinxes sat on stone pillars, one either side, gazing impassively at any visitor who wished to pass through to the house beyond.

Typically, the gates were shut, and you could

glimpse the huge, austere house only by pressing yourself up against the bars, but today – the day before a royal ball – the gates were open, and a stream of carts and coaches were passing through with deliveries of everything from tablecloths to elaborate floral arrangements. There were two burly men hovering near the gate, checking anyone who wanted to enter.

I hesitated for a moment near the gates, pulling a small notebook from my pocket and pretending to leaf through it as I observed some of the comings and goings. If I wanted to sneak in as staff tomorrow, then I was going to need to know a few things, including what the staff would be wearing.

A young man with a handsome, freckled face emerged from the gates, gesturing to one of the carts waiting nearby to move forward. He was wearing the smartly cut jacket, the breeches and stockings, and the superior smile that could only belong to a footman.

"Excuse me," I said, stepping towards him with a tentative smile. "I wonder if you can help me?"

The man looked at me and interest flashed in his eyes, but his countenance remained professionally aloof. "I certainly will if I can," he said.

"This is Devonshire House, isn't it?"

He nodded. "That's right."

"Only," I carried on breathlessly, "I'm supposed to be working here for the ball tomorrow night, and I can't find the instructions that I wrote down. The agency sent me, you see, and it's my first job for them. I'll be in such trouble if I'm not where I'm supposed to be."

I had found that if I pinched the back of my hand hard enough, I could make my eyes well convincingly with tears. This trick had got me out of several scrapes in the past, and its effect here was unsurprising.

"Now, now, miss," the footman said, his expression softening, "you don't need to worry."

"Thank you," I sniffled, trying to hide how pleased I was with myself. Unfortunately, his next words rather dispelled my triumph.

"There's no chance of you missing anything because this agency's sent you on a wild goose chase," he said. "I don't know what they were thinking, but all the staff are here already. The duke and duchess have so many, and the rest are hired by Mr Jones the butler directly. He'd never hear of using an agency."

"Oh," I murmured weakly. "I wonder how such a mistake can have been made."

The young man scratched his head. "Which agency was it?" he asked. "I can have a word with Mr Jones. That's no way to be treating such honest employees as yourself, miss."

I cast about for an employment agency name. "It was … Sphinx and … Blackbird."

He frowned. "Never heard of them."

"They're … new."

"Not going to stay in business long if this is the way they conduct themselves," the footman said.

"Thank you for your help," I said, giving him one of my best smiles. "It must be a misunderstanding. I'll go and speak with Mr, er … Sphinx."

The footman nodded, looking dazed. "Yes, miss." He treated me to smile of his own. "And if you happen to be in the neighbourhood again—"

"Goodbye!" I sang out, and then I turned and hurried off as quickly as I could.

As soon as I rounded the corner I slowed to a ponderous trudge, falling in with the stream of other pedestrians.

Well, that had not gone to plan at all. It seemed that sneaking in was going to be a lot more difficult than I had anticipated. I would have to think of something else. The most important thing was going to be keeping Agatha and the prince apart, and to do that I really needed to get inside.

The short walk back to Madame Solange's did nothing to inspire me. I made my way around to the back of the shop, kicking my feet across the cobbled yard in frustration. There *had* to be a way. How could I let Helena's plans fall neatly into place, when I had been given such a clear opportunity to thwart her? It had been years and I was no closer to making her pay for what she had done.

It was then that I noticed a large white box, leaning against the back door to the shop.

It had the words MISS IRIS GREY written across the front in black ink.

I frowned, approaching the parcel slowly as if it were

a wild animal, likely to snap if I got too close.

Why would someone leave a parcel for me at the shop? For that matter, *who* would leave a parcel for me at all?

I picked the box up gingerly. It did not hiss or burst into flames or behave in any way that a large cardboard box should not behave.

I struggled with the latch on the door and made my way inside, through to the workroom, where Annie was sitting at a sewing machine, turning up hems on the dresses I had altered for Agatha.

"Oh, you're back," Annie said, in a tone of voice that was meant to convey I hadn't been missed. Sometimes I thought that Annie's utter determination to show how little she cared about me was the most obvious way of letting me know that she did.

"Do you know who left this parcel for me out the back?" I asked, dropping it on to my workbench.

Annie glanced up, indifferent. "No idea. I've got better things to do than to act as your personal post mistress. Madame wants the bodice on that purple silk finished by this afternoon."

"Of course she does," I sighed. I shoved the box into a corner.

The rest of the day passed in a blur. By the time the clock struck nine at night, my fingers were stiff and aching, but the enormous pile of work in front of me had decreased dramatically.

Annie left for the evening and so I allowed my eyes to drift, as they had every few minutes, over to the box in the corner. Jumping down from my stool, I rolled my shoulders, hearing the bones crack in my back.

I picked up the box again. It was heavy. I placed it on the workbench and tugged at the knotted string.

I don't know what I had been expecting, but my breath caught when I lifted the lid. Nestled inside was the green dress I had modelled yesterday. On top of the dress was a mask made of fine gold lace with a gold silk ribbon. There was also a gilded invitation, printed on stiff white card. In swirling calligraphy, it read,

The Duke and Duchess of Devonshire
Cordially invite
Miss Serena Fox

To a masked ball at Devonshire House
On the evening of twenty-eighth of October
Given in honour of His Royal Highness Prince
Stefan Franz Albert Karl August of Saxe-Illyris

Guests are requested to arrive,
masked, from nine o'clock.
Carriages at dawn.

My fingers brushed across the fine print, the ink dark and heavy, pressed firmly into the paper. The scrolling gold design around the edges framed the Devonshire family crest.

With a gown and an invitation, I'd be able to walk right through the front door to the party. But who could possibly know that I needed to be there? Who was Serena Fox? I wracked my brain. Had I met her? Was she a customer, perhaps? I was sure I had never heard the name before.

I shivered. I knew that life was no fairy tale, but it felt as though my fairy godmother was about to appear and declare that I *should* go to the ball after all.

I frowned at the dress, my fingers running absently over the green silk. Who had bought this dress and left it for me? That, I suppose, was one mystery I might be able to solve.

I put the lid back on the box and made my way through to the shop. Madame Solange was still there, sorting through an enormous display of ribbons. It was one of the things that made the long hours bearable – no one worked harder than Madame herself. She was as tough as they came.

"Still here?" she asked, without turning. "I thought you'd have pushed off with Annie."

"I just wanted to finish the Scott-Holland order so that it can go over first thing in the morning."

She nodded, pleased.

"I can't find the green lamé," I said hesitantly. "Did someone buy it?"

"The green ... oh, yes, this morning. A lady's maid arrived and asked for it. It was strange actually, because she didn't want any alterations, said it was fine as it was ... though how she could know that I've got no idea. Still" – she heaved herself to her feet – "I wasn't about to argue. Easiest sale I've ever made, didn't even quibble on the price. Must be another one of these fine ladies desperate for something to wear to tomorrow's ball."

"Do you know who it was that bought it?" I asked.

"The name will be in the accounts book." Madame waved a hand dismissively, her interest already waning. "But I don't think it was anyone I recognized."

I ducked behind the counter to pull out the heavy accounts book, bound in soft black leather. I flicked through the pages until I came to the right one and ran my finger down the list. There it was: one green lamé silk evening gown, paid in full.

And the name on the account was Serena Fox.

CHAPTER SIX

The next evening, I stood in my room, staring at the mirror.

The girl in the expensive dress staring back at me could not have looked more out of place in my dingy rented rooms.

I lived in a shabby but respectable boarding house about two miles from the shop. It was owned by my landlady, Mrs Turnbull, and I had been there for almost two years now. Before that I had lived in a small box room above Madame Solange's shop along with Annie.

Compared to that, my rooms here were positively palatial, and I loved the feeling of independence it gave me to live alone, and to pay my own way out of my wages. I had worked hard for that feeling.

Mrs Turnbull was a widow in her forties who seemed perfectly happy to have seen the back of her husband. She liked to talk about the various torments her vicar assured her were going on in Hell and how Mr Turnbull would be enjoying all of them. I had the impression he had treated her very badly, and so I did not at all mind hearing about Mr Turnbull being strapped to a burning wheel or swimming through a river of fire and blood.

Apart from her keen interest in her husband's fiery afterlife, Mrs T was a gentle soul and a terrible cook. Various grey, lumpy meals were included in my rent, though I tried to eat there as little as possible, and I frequently snuck in greasy packets of chips wrapped in newspaper for Mrs Turnbull's twelve-year-old son, Tommy – a gesture which had earned me a level of chivalrous loyalty one might typically associate with a medieval knight.

My room was clean, but impersonal. I didn't spend a huge amount of time there, so I had never seen the need to change things much. The floorboards were bare, and a pair of pale blue cotton curtains hung at the window. There was a small bed with an iron frame and a thin mattress, a large cupboard, a battered but comfortable old armchair in front of the fireplace, and a shelf containing a stack of fashion magazines and novels from the circulating library.

As of today, there was also a long, slightly tarnished mirror that I had borrowed from Mrs Turnbull, and I stood in front of it now, moving from side to side, the low light from the oil lamp catching on the fine gold threads in my skirts.

I had washed my hair and braided it into an intricate crown on top of my head, several loose curls resting against my shoulders, which were left bare thanks to the cut of the dress. There had been a pair of gold silk slippers in the box underneath the dress; these were slightly too big, so I had stitched ribbons into the sides and tied them tightly. I held the lace mask at my side, the silk lining cool in my too-warm hand.

I suppose that the girl in the mirror was Iris Scott-Holland. The girl I could have been. In another world it would have been my name on the invitation. My shoes, like everything else, would fit perfectly. I would fit perfectly.

But tonight I wasn't Iris Scott-Holland. I wasn't even Iris Grey.

No; tonight I would be Serena Fox.

For the thousandth time I wondered who she was, wondered why she had left me a dress and her invitation. I wondered if I had ever met her. I imagined her, auburn-haired with a cupid's-bow mouth and dancing sable-brown eyes. Was this some sort of prank? But *why* would anyone do such a thing?

I had hesitated only briefly before accepting the invitation. It was too good a chance to pass up. And I had to admit that there was a part of me that thrilled at the mystery, that loved the idea of bluffing my way into the social event of the season. I could feel my heart beating harder at the thought of such an adventure, and I watched in the mirror as the colour rose in my cheeks.

The opportunity to disrupt Helena's careful plans

had literally fallen at my feet; how could I possibly ignore it? I couldn't. I was going to grasp it with both hands.

My wish had come true. Perhaps Serena Fox *was* my fairy godmother. It certainly felt as though I had willed the whole thing into being.

Without any further hesitation I held the mask against my face and tied the ribbons behind my head. I looked like a stranger. Even my eyes were different, a darker blue, dancing with secrets. I smiled, and the girl in the mirror smiled back – a smile like the sharp edge of a knife.

"Coo! Iris!" Mrs Turnbull exclaimed when I made my way downstairs. "You look like a fine lady! I can't believe you're going to such a fancy party."

Knowing that I would have difficulty sneaking out of the house and back in an enormous ball gown, I had hastily constructed a story about modelling dresses at a society do, which Mrs Turnbull had thankfully accepted without question.

"I've sent Tommy to hail a cab for you," she said, her fingers half-reaching towards my skirts as though she longed to touch them but didn't quite dare.

"Thank you," I replied. "I shouldn't be back too late."

"I'll leave the door on the latch," she said. "But you know you can always shout up for Tommy. You go and have fun, it's nice to see you enjoying yourself for a change, and you look pretty as a picture."

I smiled at her, touched by the genuine pleasure in her voice. She didn't need to know that I wasn't going to this party for fun.

If the driver of the hansom cab was surprised to be picking up a woman in a mask and a spectacular ball gown from an unassuming boarding house, then he showed no sign of it. I suppose London cab drivers have seen it all. Once I had clambered into the cab and adjusted my skirts – which rather overpowered the cramped interior – he set the horse going with a snap of his whip.

The carriage rattled over cobblestones, the world outside the window a silver-streaked blur of fog broken only by the brief flicker of the gas lamps. I clasped my hands in my lap, forcing myself to breathe deeply, to remain calm and steady. I was ready for this. I had been born to it, after all.

It was half-past nine when I arrived. The rest of the guests would have enjoyed sumptuous dinner parties across town before making their way towards the party. I had made do with a bowl of Mrs Turnbull's beef stew. At least, I think it was beef.

My cab joined the long queue of carriages drawing up to the house. Already I could feel the festival air of excitement that filled the street. There were squeals and laughter, and the sound of people calling to one another from the windows of their coaches.

I asked the driver to set me down. I would continue up to the house on foot. It might be unusual, but I thought Serena Fox was unlikely to pull up in a common hansom cab. Once I got close to the house itself, I could join the eager throng, and hopefully no one would look too closely at where I had come from.

I checked that my mask was firmly in place and picked up the silk train of my dress, looping it carefully over my arm so that it wouldn't drag on the ground. It did not technically belong to me, after all.

I reached the gates that I had stood in front of only yesterday, my invitation clutched in my hand. At the top of the gate the Devonshire family crest gleamed gold, a trio of stags and the words: *Cavendo Tutus*. Safety through caution. A breath of nervous laughter escaped me. Well, that was a neat joke.

There were two men in elegant black uniforms stitched with silver thread, who were guiding coaches through. One of them blinked as I approached on foot.

"My invitation," I said, in my most blue-blooded voice. I craned my neck past them and gave a wave, as though I had just seen someone I knew inside.

The man took the invitation from me and examined it. I could see his eyes taking in the extravagance of my gown, the aristocratic tilt of my chin. I forced myself to stand straight under his scrutiny, to school my face so that it only betrayed a slight boredom at being held up.

"Very good, madam," the man rumbled in a deep voice. "Enjoy your evening."

"Thank you." I flashed him a smile, and sailed past him, joining the press of bodies making their way up the drive and through the enormous front doors. Despite the cool of the evening, the air was feverish, heat coming off the crowd in waves, as if the growing excitement was burning inside everyone.

"Bloody ridiculous herding us about like cattle," a man next to me complained. He wore a dark coat and a mask that covered the top half of his face.

"Oh, don't be so impatient, John," the woman with him chided. "They have to make sure they're not letting just anyone in, after all." I smiled.

We were ushered through into the entrance hall. I had never seen anything like it, and I had to stop myself from gawping like a provincial fool at the grandeur already on display. The walls and the ceiling were covered in gilt, candlelight flickering over the crowd.

The room was dominated by the famous Devonshire House staircase. I had heard about it, but never really believed it could exist – as if it were a creature from a myth or fairy tale.

Curving along the wall, shallow marble steps stretched upwards, smooth and shining. The handrail and all the intricate carved posts that ran the full length of the staircase were made of crystal, and the effect was dazzling. The light winked and gleamed off them, sending miniature rainbows dancing across the walls, the floors, and ladies' gowns.

A waiter in another dark suit, this time accompanied by a black domino mask, offered me a drink from a silver tray: a coupe of champagne, the palest shade of lemon and sparkling with bubbles. I took a glass gratefully, enjoying the sharp, cool taste.

The last time I'd drunk champagne was to try a sip from my father's glass. The bubbles had tickled my nose and made me sneeze.

I could hear his laughter now. "That will teach you, little cub! You're not supposed to swig the lot!"

It was a shame that seamstresses didn't get much chance to drink the stuff – I found that I liked it much better now. Strange that you could grow into a taste, as if it were a pair of shoes.

People were milling around in the entrance hall before climbing the staircase. I could guess why: the ballroom was at the top of it, and no one wanted to enter in a large group. They wanted a moment with all eyes on them. There were clothes to show off after all. It seemed that I was alone in wanting to keep a low profile.

I drained my drink in one more long swallow and placed the empty glass back on the tray. The effects were invigorating, and I took my long skirts in one hand, and placed the other on the crystal handrail.

With a final deep breath, I began the climb.

My plan was to slip in quietly, but it seemed that whatever mischief making spinners of fate were at work that evening had other ideas.

As I reached the final stair, the makeshift lace on my shoe came untied, and I almost left it behind on the staircase. I stopped on the landing and bent down to re-tie it. The sound of music drifted through from the open doors; a lively waltz played by a large orchestra.

If I hadn't stopped to tie my shoe, it would never have happened.

As it was, I entered the room alone, just as the music came to a finish, and the couples on the large dance floor swept to a halt, most of them facing the door, and therefore ... me.

CHAPTER SEVEN

The final notes of the song still resonated from the violin strings, a sweet humming that hung in the air, an echo of something beautiful, that seemed in that moment like a bugle announcing my arrival.

I thought I was prepared for this party, for what a society occasion would entail, but suddenly I found hundreds of pairs of eyes on me – eager, rapacious eyes that devoured the sight of me in my dress and my mask. Eyes that all seemed to ask one question: *who is she?*

I felt a brief, shattering moment of panic – an

overwhelming urge to turn and run back down the staircase, through the doors and down the drive, past the gates with their Latin warning, and through the city streets and shadows, all the way home.

I wasn't going to do that. Instead of running, I lifted my eyes, staring them all down. I allowed my mouth to curl into the sort of smile I had seen Helena wear – a smile that spoke of power and confidence and something else. Something seductive.

A man stepped forward. He was dressed elegantly in a dark suit, almost severe in its simplicity. The black mask that covered the top half of his face framed warm, sherry-brown eyes. His hair was blond, so fair that it looked threaded through with silver. He wore a dark red rose in his lapel, and the smile he aimed at me was a crescent moon of straight white teeth.

"Madam," he said with a bow. "You have brought the party to a standstill. Shall we get it moving again?"

His English was perfect, and yet his words were touched by a light accent, one that sounded faintly Germanic. He stood now with his hand held out to me, an invitation to waltz.

I placed my fingers in his and smiled again. "I would be delighted."

A glimmer of pleasure lighting his eyes, he bowed once more and led me on to the dance floor. The crowd parted before us.

So much for keeping to the shadows.

There was a brief, taut moment, like the feeling before a storm breaks, and then the orchestra began to play. The room seemed to exhale, and the dance began again, only this time I found myself in the centre of it.

It had been a long time since I had danced, but fortunately for me, the waltz largely consisted of being spun around the room by an able partner. All I had to do was relax into his arms.

It was no hardship. A firm hand clasped mine, the other pressed gently against the small of my back. The man was taller than me, and broad shouldered. I could feel tight bands of muscle beneath my own fingers.

We twirled around the room, and I had only a confused impression of colourful gowns like wild paint strokes daubed around me, high, ornate ceilings, and the fractured light from an enormous chandelier strung with jewels. The walls were covered in paintings framed in heavy gold, and the long windows were draped with rich crimson velvet, the same colour as the rose in my partner's lapel.

It was stiflingly warm, and there must have been at least three hundred people in here. Somewhere among them was Helena. I wanted to find her. Here, and on my own terms, I finally had the opportunity to talk to her face to face. If I wanted to keep Agatha's engagement from going forward then I needed more information … and perhaps the man with his arm around my waist could help with that too.

"You dance beautifully," he said, smiling down at me.

"Thank you, Your Highness," I replied. "I think on this occasion I owe my success to my partner."

The prince laughed and shook his head. "Tell me, what is the point of a masked ball, if you know at once who I am?"

"I'm afraid it was quite obvious," I said apologetically. "All eyes are on you, you know."

This was true. There may have been other couples

dancing around us, but it was as though the prince was illuminated, the crowds unable to keep from staring.

"I think I bear only half the responsibility for their interest."

"A very pretty compliment," I said approvingly.

He laughed again, a deep, carefree laugh, as if laughing came easily to him. "May I have the pleasure of knowing who I am sharing a dance with?" he asked.

I smiled at him. "I don't think so, Your Highness. After all, *I* may still take advantage of the mystery that a masked ball can provide."

"Very true," he sighed. "At least one of us should enjoy the benefits."

"Oh, I intend to." I grinned.

The music ended then, and there was a light smattering of applause, but the prince didn't stop. Instead he kept hold of my hand, immediately spinning me into the next dance, the orchestra leaping to keep up with him. Two dances in a row ... I felt the interest in the room quicken, like a piece of kindling catching light.

"A second waltz?" I raised my eyebrows. "It's not the done thing." Even I knew that.

The prince's grin only widened. "And I think such rules are made to be broken."

There was no ignoring the hum of gossip now, I heard it buzzing all around us, the ballroom transformed to a furious beehive, and the prince and I caught at the centre. It seemed as though the other couples on the dance floor had fallen back, making more space for us as the prince turned me faster and faster. It was exhilarating, as the music spiralled around us, building to a crescendo. We didn't talk, but he held my gaze for several long, crackling moments.

He spun me one final time, and the music ended. Then he bowed over my hand, holding it tightly in his own.

"I am reluctant to let such a charming partner escape me," he murmured.

"I do not think even you dare risk a third dance." I smiled, and then, seeing the words land as a challenge that he was all too inclined to accept, I added hastily, "Perhaps we will meet again."

"I hope so. And then I shall uncover your secret identity, mysterious lady."

The words cut too close for comfort and I made my curtsey and left, but not before directing another flirtatious smile at the prince – after all, if he was looking for me then he would be too busy to propose to Agatha. It seemed that another opportunity had fallen in my lap – this time in the form of a handsome prince. This evening truly was a fairy tale.

The ball was spread over three rooms: the enormous ballroom, a card room where many of the gentlemen and several of the ladies would gamble with one another's fortunes, and a dining room, where refreshments were served, which was where I was headed. It was hot and I was thirsty for a cool glass of lemonade; besides, going in search of a drink also gave me a sense of purpose that I desperately needed.

Despite leaving the prince behind, many eyes continued to follow me from behind their masks. My entrance, I supposed, had not been what one might call *subtle*.

I turned the last few minutes over in my mind, The prince had seemed charming – and willing to be charmed. Perhaps matters with Agatha were not as far along as Helena hoped. I thought about this as I made my way towards a long table covered in clean white linen and helped myself to a glass of lemonade. Unfortunately, it was almost as warm as the room, and I grimaced as I took a sip.

"Horrible, isn't it?" a bright voice asked from beside me. I turned to find a small woman in a purple silk mask and a dress that I recognized well. It was Nicholas Wynter's cousin, Teresa, and she was beaming up at me.

My pulse stuttered, and I was gladder than ever for the mask that I wore.

"It's a little ... warm," I agreed.

"I know, I know, but then you don't come to Devonshire House for the refreshments, do you?"

"What do you come for?" I asked.

"Well, for the pageantry," Teresa said, waving her hand around her. "To admire all the ladies' gowns." She smiled impishly. "And the gentlemen's fine suits too."

"And the gentlemen within them?" I felt an answering grin tug at my mouth.

"I am an extremely happily married lady," Teresa

73

said primly, ruining the effect with a laugh. "But it *is* nice to look."

I laughed too.

"Your gown is beautiful," Teresa said, and my laughter stopped. "Is it from Madame Solange's?"

"Yes," I said weakly, and then, though it felt bizarre to be talking about my own work, I added, "Yours is lovely as well."

"Yes," Teresa agreed, satisfied. "I had it from Madame Solange's too, and I tell you I'll be going there for *everything* from now on."

I couldn't help the twinge of professional pride at those words.

"Even my awful cousin Nick was impressed and he's *such* a stickler, impossible to please," she continued. "He's around here somewhere, I must introduce you." She pulled herself up short at that. "I suppose I should introduce myself first! Teresa St-Clair." She held out her hand and I shook it.

"Serena Fox," I replied, the name feeling strange in my mouth. If Nicholas Wynter was here that was one more person to avoid. I was certain those cold eyes would see straight through me – mask or no mask.

"I saw you dancing with the prince," Teresa said, and I winced. Seeing it she laughed again. "Yes, you caused quite the stir."

"It was not my intention, I promise."

"I should perhaps warn you that the gossips here have him as good as married off to someone else. They're expecting a proposal any moment."

"Oh really?" I smiled innocently.

It was at that moment that I spotted her.

Helena.

She was on the other side of the open door, the one that led to the ballroom, resplendent in ivory satin. She wore a matching mask, but there was no mistaking those green eyes, that almost unnatural grace.

"I'm sorry," I said to Teresa, "but I see someone I've been trying to catch up with. Will you excuse me?"

"Of course!" Teresa exclaimed. "It's so difficult to find one's friends in this den, isn't it? It was nice to meet you."

I smiled and turned away, my eyes not straying an inch from Helena as I began to edge in her direction.

I wondered how I would begin the conversation, but it turned out that I didn't have to. *She* was looking for *me*.

"Ah," Helena said, reaching out for my arm as I approached, her tone dripping with warm honey. "Our mystery guest."

Finally, after seven years, here we were, face to face. My stomach was doing somersaults, and my mouth had gone dry. It had been such a long time, and I had changed so much, but still – what if she recognized me?

"My dear, I was hoping to meet you, you're all anyone is talking about!"

She might have fooled anyone else, but she couldn't fool me. I heard the steel in those words. The attention that I had received from Prince Stefan had been unwelcome.

Good, I thought, pasting on a smile that was a mirror to her own.

"How funny," I said lightly. "I promise that I'm not the least bit interesting." I was proud of the steadiness of my voice, the way my words came out, cool and smooth. As if they were words that belonged here in this great room thronging with the aristocracy.

"Surely that is for us to decide." Helena's smile

sharpened into something more feline. "Forgive me," she said. "Have we met? You seem ... familiar."

I shrugged nonchalantly, the merest raising of a shoulder. "I don't believe so, but it's hard to know for certain with all these masks."

"So true." Helena leaned in conspiratorially. "But then I suspect that's the appeal of a masked ball, isn't it?" She laughed, and my fingers curled at my sides. It was a musical laugh, a twinkling cadenza. I remembered my father's face when she would laugh with him.

"I expect you're right," I managed.

"I don't think we're technically supposed to introduce ourselves until the unmasking at midnight," Helena continued, "but I suppose we might bend the rules, mightn't we?" She gave me a warm, confiding smile – one that I never saw as her stepdaughter. "I am Lady Scott-Holland, and my daughters Agatha and Cassandra are about the place somewhere... Ah!" She smiled. "There's Agatha over there, dancing with the prince."

"What a beautiful gown," I said, turning to look at them. "And how well she dances."

In fact, Agatha did dance well, and the dress – a

frothy pale pink confection on to which I had laboriously stitched hundreds of seed pearls – suited her perfectly. She and the prince made a handsome pair.

"Are you much acquainted with Prince Stefan?" Helena asked.

I widened my eyes. "Me? No, I have never had the pleasure of meeting the prince before this evening."

"Yet he seemed quite taken with you." Helena's smile was getting nowhere near her eyes, which were watchful. "To be singled out to dance twice in a row! I really must ask the question on everyone's lips. *Who* are you?"

"I suppose you will all find out at midnight," I replied sweetly.

"How mysterious," Helena said, her voice flat.

"Are *you* well acquainted with the prince, Lady Scott-Holland?" I asked innocently, ready to gather as much information as I could on the progress she and Agatha had made.

Helena's eyes lit and her mouth opened in response, but suddenly a familiar voice caressed my ear.

"There you are," said Nicholas Wynter. "I've been looking for you everywhere."

CHAPTER EIGHT

My eyes flashed to his, an unreadable frost blue. Mine, I hoped, did not betray the utter panic I felt.

"If you'll excuse us, Lady Scott-Holland, I need to borrow this lovely young lady." He was utterly calm, unruffled.

"Of course, of course." Helena nodded.

I had absolutely no desire to go with him, or to cut short my conversation with Helena. I had waited years for this opportunity.

"Lady Scott-Holland and I were talking," I said,

allowing a touch of ice to creep into my voice.

Unbelievably, Nicholas Wynter laughed. "No need to get on your high ropes with an old friend, is there?" he asked me. Then, sharing a conspiratorial wink with Helena, he added, "Honestly, she's always been like this. She used to order me around with great authority, even when she was in the nursery."

I stared at him, my mouth opening, but no words coming out. Out of the corner of my eye, I saw Helena absorb this detail thoughtfully.

Unfortunately, Nicholas used my momentary confusion to turn away, making it clear I was to follow, tossing a charming smile over his shoulder at Helena as he did so.

I walked beside him, rigid with fury, as he made his way through the ballroom. It would hardly help matters if I refused to go with him or made a scene.

"Feeling faint?" he said loudly, out of nowhere. "Of course, we must get you some air!" He led me out of a pair of French doors and on to an enormous stone balcony.

I looked around. There was no one else here, which

suited me just fine. It was time to tell Nicholas Wynter exactly what I thought of him.

"What on earth do you think you are doing?" I snapped.

"Finding us somewhere to talk privately, Miss Grey. What else?"

So he knew who I was.

He leaned back against the balustrade, the picture of tranquillity. He was partly in shadow now, but still disgustingly handsome. His dark hair gleamed; his eyes behind the silver mask he wore seemed an even more dazzling arctic blue than when I had seen him last. He wore a waistcoat of silver brocade underneath a black suit. As a dressmaker I had no choice but to admire the craftsmanship. It fit him like a glove.

"I have no desire to talk to you," I said. "I thought I had made that abundantly clear. In fact, I am worried that you may need medical attention. Tell me, did you suffer any head injuries as a child?"

His eyes flashed appreciatively. "I knew that I had a good feeling about you."

"I've had enough of this." I turned to go.

"Wait!" Nicholas called out, and something in his tone made me stop. "I know you said that you didn't want anything to do with me, but that was when – and please do correct me if I'm wrong about this – you were under the impression that I wished to make you my mistress. I do not."

"You … do not?" I repeated, my hand falling away from the door handle.

"No." He shook his head. "Forgive my bluntness, but I think we should get that cleared up straight away. I've never found the idea of *keeping* a woman anything other than distasteful."

"But you said…" I trailed off, trying to remember our earlier conversation.

"I said that I had a proposition for you, and I do."

My eyes narrowed. "Yes, that's right. Then I believe you told me you would buy me a canary."

"I said –" Nicholas held up a finger – "that I had *never considered* a canary, which was true."

I shook my head. "I believe my original impression of you still stands."

He pulled himself away from the edge of the balcony,

taking a lazy step towards me. "Just hear me out," he said. "Please."

It was the please that did it. It was not a word I had imagined was in his vocabulary.

"Fine." I crossed my arms. "Let's hear this *proposition*. Quickly, if you will. It is cold."

Almost before the words had left my mouth, I found myself being draped in a thick, dark jacket – still warm with the heat of his body. It felt shockingly intimate.

"Thank you," I mumbled, thrown.

He brushed the thanks aside, and stood for a moment, eying me with a speculative gaze that was disconcerting. It didn't help that without the jacket I could see how nice his arms were in his fine linen shirt. The man could certainly wear a waistcoat.

"It is an idea that I think will sound … strange to you," he began.

"As opposed to everything else you've said and done so far," I said.

"What I wish to do is to employ you."

"You need a dressmaker on your staff?"

The briefest hint of a smile touched his lips, gone

before I could even be certain it was there at all. "It is not your dressmaking abilities that I require."

"This sounds suspiciously like we're coming back to something improper."

"I suppose to most people it would seem that way," he agreed easily. "I want your help, so that I can ruin a man. A specific man, in fact. Prince Stefan of Saxe-Illyris."

I felt my mouth drop open. Whatever I had been expecting him to say, it was not that.

"I would like for you to convince the prince to propose to you, and then I would like for you to jilt him. Publicly."

"Propose ... marriage?"

"No, Miss Grey, I want you to get him to propose a game of whist," he snorted. "Of course, *marriage.*"

"Lord Wynter," I began.

"I believe you should call me Nick," he said. "If we are to be co-conspirators."

"Lord Wynter," I tried again, more firmly this time. "I have no idea what you are talking about, or frankly *how* you expect me to get a prince to propose to a seamstress..."

"Oh, that." He waved my concerns aside. "You're not going to be a seamstress, are you? You're going to be Serena Fox, the extremely wealthy heiress whose factory-owning father is in line for a title."

With dazzling clarity, the pieces fell into place in my head. "*You* sent me the dress and the invitation?" My words rang out, aghast.

"Of course. I thought you had already worked that part out."

"Why would I... Why would *you*..." I stammered, my mind grasping desperately for anything that made sense of this. "You mean to tell me that *you* are my fairy godmother?"

For the first time since we had met, Nicholas Wynter looked disconcerted. "Your *what*?"

It was not a question I could answer though, because I was too busy laughing. I think it was some form of hysteria, but the idea that I had – for even a moment – considered the man in front of me to be my fairy godmother was, frankly, hilarious. The perplexed frown he wore did not help.

"It doesn't matter," I said, finally getting a hold of

myself. "What matters is that I'm afraid that I can't help you. I have no idea why you would want to embroil anyone in such a plan, but I would never—"

I stopped.

Lord Wynter wanted to get the prince to propose to me.

If the prince proposed to me then he would not be proposing to Agatha, as it was increasingly clear *everyone* expected him to do.

And Helena's humiliation would be absolute.

I liked that idea; I liked that idea very much.

Nicholas was still talking, saying something about renumeration and the sums he would pay me for my involvement.

"...enough to set up your own shop should you wish to do so, though, of course..."

"How would it work?" I interrupted him.

His eyebrows rose. "It is perfectly simple," he said. "You will become Serena Fox, with the personal history that I have created for you. I will vouch for you as an old family friend and spread the story of your enormous wealth – no one will doubt my word."

Arrogance dripped from every sentence, but I couldn't argue with it. If anyone could control society's opinion of me, it was Nicholas Wynter.

"It was clear to me from the start that you could pass for well-born – it's in your voice and the way you stand." He paused then, but if he was waiting for me to fill him in on my family history then he would be waiting a long, long while. Seeming to realize this, he continued. "I can help to polish you up, and we can pass any mistakes off as those of a sheltered heiress whose doting father has kept her in the country."

"You think the fact that I'm an heiress will be enough to snare a prince?" I asked, incredulous.

"Prince Stefan has come to England with a single purpose," Nicholas said. "In order to avoid marrying the lady his grandmother, the queen, has chosen for him, he must arrange an advantageous match, and fast. Stefan has expensive tastes. He's here to catch a rich bride, one who can keep him in the manner to which he has become accustomed. I believe that, were he to think you wealthy, you would have no trouble succeeding with him. You are exactly his ... type." He gave something of a grimace.

"So Serena Fox doesn't exist?" I asked.

"She will do – if you agree to become her for the next two weeks."

"Two weeks?"

A lock of his hair fell forward and he pushed it back with an impatient hand. "That's how long the prince has left before his grandmother requires his presence at home. She was reluctant to allow him to come in the first place and if he doesn't return with a respectable match arranged, then he must marry her choice of bride. A cousin of his, I believe – a woman of good standing, very wealthy – and entirely under her thumb. Prince Stefan has no desire for a wife whose fortune will be under his grandmother's control."

I watched him thoughtfully. I wondered what it was that Nicholas was not saying.

"Rumour has it that he is about to propose to Lady Scott-Holland's daughter," I said carefully.

"Precisely." His eyes gleamed in the dark.

"So you want me to prevent him from finding an acceptable partner before the time runs out, by directing his interest towards me?"

"Correct. And then, when his interest is confirmed, when he has thrown over all others, I would also like you to reject him, publicly and in the most humiliating way possible."

"But ... *why*?" I asked.

His eyes shuttered. "That is not a matter for discussion," he said coldly.

I hesitated. Would I really conspire to harm an innocent man, in order to revenge myself against the woman who had taken everything from me?

Yes, yes, I would. I would steel myself against any softer feeling, I would do what I needed to do to pull Helena's perfect life apart, stitch by stitch if I had to. Preventing her family from marrying into royalty was only the beginning. When I was through with her, Helena would be ruined. I owed it to my father.

Something of my resolve must have showed in my face.

"You'll do it," Nicholas said quietly.

I nodded. "Yes." He didn't need to know the reasons why. Let him think it was for the money.

"Good." If he felt any surprise, he didn't show it.

"Then we will have to get you ready for the house party."

My stomach dropped. It felt like I was falling from a great height at a great speed, as if the ground had been snatched from under me. *The house party. Two weeks.* I already knew what was coming.

"At Holland Hall," I croaked.

"That's right."

I closed my eyes.

It seemed that I was going home.

CHAPTER NINE

"Is something the matter?" Nicholas asked.

I shook my head, recovering my voice. "Not at all."

What could I say? I could hardly tell him the truth. Could I really go back there? I wanted to, so desperately that the thought of it made my chest ache. But how could I possibly hope to avoid discovery if I spent two weeks at my *home* with Helena? Fear and excitement churned inside me. It was entirely possible that I was about to cast up the warm lemonade all over Nicholas Wynter's highly polished shoes.

Fortunately for me, he was oblivious to my inner turmoil.

"The key thing is for you to capture Stefan's attention tonight," he said. He cast a critical eye over me. "You should have no trouble." If it was meant to be a compliment it didn't sound like one. "Your entrance went off better than even I could have planned."

"You're welcome," I muttered. "So, I capture his attention tonight. Do you have any idea of how?"

He smiled then, something dangerous lighting his eyes. "Oh, yes. I'm going to flirt with you as outrageously as possible."

"That will work, will it?" I raised an eyebrow.

"It will with Stefan." There was a grim note in his voice.

I sniffed. Men were such ridiculous creatures.

"And then?" I asked.

"We make sure everyone notices you. I will dance with you – that should do the trick."

Again, that arrogance.

"And *then*?"

"And then *you* will flirt with *him*. As outrageously as possible."

I thought this over for a moment. I wasn't so sure that would work – not with a man like the prince, so sought after. Still, this was his plan, not mine. "Fine," I said, not wanting to delay now that the decision had been made. "Let's get on with it." I shrugged his jacket from my shoulders and held it out to him.

Without another word, Nicholas pulled his jacket on and we slipped back inside the ballroom.

The heat hit me like a brick wall. There seemed to be even more people in here now, dancing giddily and talking loudly to one another so that they could be heard over the orchestra, who were still playing with great enthusiasm. I felt a wave of claustrophobia. So many bodies pressed into this space, and everyone looking about them with glittering, hungry eyes.

"May I have this dance?" Nicholas asked, and he took my hand in his, bowing over it in an old-fashioned gesture.

It was the first time he had touched me. His fingers

wrapped around my own and I felt a tug of awareness in my belly.

"Of course," I replied. Eyes were sliding in our direction, just as he had said.

He swept me on to the dance floor, and then – in the moment before the music began – he gave me a look so warm it bought a flush to my cheeks.

It's only pretend, I told myself sternly.

I had a part to play as well. I dropped my eyelashes demurely before glancing back up at him, offering a smile of my own.

There was a quiet buzz of conversation, and I forced myself to keep my eyes on Nicholas, not to acknowledge the fact that the air was once more thick with the sound of gossip – and that, yet again, I was the centre of attention. It seemed that Serena Fox had made quite a splash.

The music began, and he took me into his arms.

The fine cloth of his jacket was soft beneath my fingers, but his shoulder was taut. His arm was around my waist, my face close enough to his chest that I could see the individual stitches on his waistcoat. I knew he was tall, but suddenly he seemed even bigger, filling my vision. I had to crane my neck to look up at him.

"You are very tall," I said.

Nicholas kept the smile pinned to his face. "What an astute observation. I might comment that you are very short, but it would be impolite."

Do not roll your eyes, Iris.

"I was only trying to make it look like we were having a conversation. Isn't that what people who are flirting do?"

He pulled me a bit closer to him, closer than was really decent, and lowered his head so that he could murmur softly in my ear.

"*This* is what people who are flirting do."

I glanced up at him. "Not terribly comfortable for tall people, I'd imagine."

"Being tall has its advantages."

"Such as?"

He gave me a long, burning look, and then – almost in a whisper – he said, "I'm very, *very* good" – he paused for a second – "at tennis. Long arms."

I choked on a laugh.

"Please don't laugh when it looks like I'm trying to seduce you. It will give people a poor opinion of me."

We danced in silence for a moment, Nicholas spinning me expertly around the enormous ballroom. He danced well, and I was sure that he knew it.

"How will it work?" I asked quietly. "Going to Holland Hall, I mean."

"Nothing could be more simple," he replied. "I am invited to go, along with my grandmother, who will thankfully be able to act as your chaperone. Yesterday I begged an invitation from Lady Scott-Holland for an old family friend who was visiting on short notice."

"Serena Fox," I murmured.

"Exactly so." He nodded. "Our hostess graciously extended the invitation to include my guest." He said it all with the arrogance of a man who was used to getting his way.

"What about your grandmother?" I asked. "Surely *she* knows I am not a friend of the family."

"She believes that we are old friends who met as children. My grandmother didn't accompany us on our family holidays so you have not met before. She would also not expect to be familiar with the daughter of a man of business." He smiled thinly. "I'm afraid she may think you somewhat below her touch, though in this case it will work in our favour. It would be different if we were trying to pass you off as a titled lady, of course."

"Of course," I agreed, thinking that was actually precisely what I was.

His grandmother would know Iris Scott-Holland's history. I knew from the investigators' reports that Helena had not told anyone I had run away. Instead there had been some story about an accident – no body found, but as time passed it was thought likely that poor Iris Scott-Holland must have perished. A terrible tragedy, especially so soon after Lord Scott-Holland's death.

"Wonderful," I said, forcing my mind back to the matter at hand. "So, your grandmother is a snob who is predisposed to dislike me."

Nicholas looked thoughtful. "I wouldn't be so sure. She's been trying to get me married off for some time – desperate to secure the family line. She may be happy that you've come along, even if you are a shopkeeper's daughter."

"I thought that my imaginary father was a factory owner, on the brink of receiving a knighthood?"

He smiled faintly. "To my grandmother I'm afraid that amounts to much the same thing. We need her to act as your chaperone in any case – we must observe all the proprieties if we're to pass you off as an eligible young lady."

It really did seem like he had it all worked out.

I would be going home. *Home.* As well as a chance to prevent Agatha's advantageous match, to get my revenge on Helena, another, terrifying opportunity presented itself. Being back at Holland Hall meant that I would finally be able to investigate my father's death myself.

My heart raced faster. My investigators had failed – but if I was actually there, at the scene of the crime... Surely Helena must have left evidence behind of what she did to my father. Even all these years later, some clue must remain.

The orchestra rose to a crescendo, and Nicholas spun me one final time.

The dance was over. Nicholas tucked my hand in his

arm again and guided me from the floor. He rested his other hand on top of mine.

"Do you think he noticed?" I whispered.

"Why not ask Stefan yourself?" he said, glancing over my shoulder. "So predictable."

I turned to see the prince behind me, his easy smile and cheerful manner utterly at odds with the man still holding on to my hand.

"Nick!" Stefan exclaimed in his deep, rich voice. "You devil! You've stolen a march on me with the most lovely lady in the room." He turned to me with a shallow bow. "I have been hoping we would run into each other again." His words to me were pitched lower, his tone more intimate.

"You'll have to forgive me, Stefan. The lady and I are old friends." Nicholas's voice was lazy, but I noticed that he kept hold of my arm.

Stefan frowned. "Is that so?"

Nicholas Wynter had sprung an invented history on me in front of Helena; now, I decided it was only fair that I get my own back. "Lord Wynter and I have quite the history," I said. "After all, a girl never forgets the first boy she pushes into a pond."

I turned a bland gaze on Nicholas, waiting to see how he responded to being thrown into a lie with no warning.

"Ah," he murmured, not missing a beat, "and I hadn't done a thing to deserve it. After all, you were the one who ate all my plum cake."

"And then *you* threw Miss Prudence in the pond," I retorted.

Stefan looked startled and Nicholas choked.

"Yes, Miss Prudence ... your ... *doll*." His voice quivered for a moment. "Was that her name?"

"You know perfectly well it was," I said. "But at least I had my revenge."

"You did," Nicholas agreed serenely. "Until the incident with the hedgehog ... but" – he lifted a finger as if to cut me off – "*that* is a story for another time."

Stefan's eyes moved between us like we were playing tennis.

"How fortunate that you should have such a colourful shared history," Stefan said. "But then, perhaps, Wynter, you can tell me the identity of your friend. She is being very secretive, I must say."

Nicholas shrugged. "I think that is up to the lady herself. Perhaps she prefers to wait for the unmasking at midnight."

"She does," I said. "And it is only a few minutes away anyway."

"Then may I steal you away for another dance in the meantime?" Stefan asked.

"You may not," I said smiling sweetly, "but you may take me in search of refreshment. It is really stifling in here."

Stefan's eyes lit up. "Even better," he said. "I can show off my gallantry, and you can tell me all the scandalous stories of my friend's past."

I felt Lord Wynter's arm tense briefly beneath my own, but his voice was light and steady as he said, "There are very few skeletons in my wardrobe, Stefan, you know that."

Stefan threw his head back and laughed, and then he held out his arm to me. I was beginning to feel as if I were being passed around like a parcel.

"You and Lord Wynter are old friends?" I asked, as we made our way through the crowds to the dining room.

"Very old friends." Stefan nodded. "Several years ago, when I was sent here to study for a few months, Nick – how is it you have it? – *took me under his wing.*"

Yet now he wanted me to help ruin this man's life. What on earth had happened between them?

"I'm sure the pair of you caused quite a stir when you were let loose on the town," I said.

"I could not possibly say," he demurred. "Particularly not when I am trying to impress you with my steadiness of character."

"Oh." I peeped up at him through my eyelashes. "I don't think there's anything wrong with a little bit of excitement every now and then."

"That is very good to know." He grinned. "Now." He steered me over to an empty sofa. It was small and I realized we would be forced to sit quite close to one another. I did not think that choice had been an accident. "You wait here while I fetch your drink. What would you like?"

I thought queasily of the lemonade. "A glass of champagne, if they have one."

It took him moments to secure drinks for us both, and then we were sitting cosily, talking.

Stefan asked me about my life, and I tried to use the story Nicholas had created to make myself sound as eligible as I could, as artfully as possible. I could hardly say, "*Did I mention that I am exceedingly wealthy?*" But I mentioned an overprotective, extremely indulgent father, and a large family home in Yorkshire. I made a mental note to share that detail with Lord Wynter.

I watched closely to see if Stefan was picking up on these hints, but it was hard to say. He was certainly easy to talk to, charming and funny and happy to listen.

"But, please, do tell me about yourself," I said, sipping from my champagne glass. "I'm sure being a prince is much more interesting than my life – it has been sadly sheltered so far."

"You are all the more charming for it, like a flower in spring," he said gallantly. "Although I'm afraid the life of a prince is much less glamorous than you might think. My duties are largely ceremonial now, and my grandmother – the queen – can be a little ... old-fashioned. She doesn't really like for me to be away.

I too have had a sheltered life in many ways, one without very much freedom, I suppose."

His voice was wistful, and I felt a twinge of sympathy. Despite myself I found that I liked him. I forced that feeling down. There was no room for sentiment: I had a job to do.

"I'm sorry," I said gently. "That sounds difficult." Hesitantly, I placed my hand on his, just a brief, light touch. Stefan squeezed my fingers gratefully and then released them. It was not the done thing, and I felt a flush rise to my cheeks, but I thought there was a heat in Stefan's gaze that had not been there before.

And, just like that, I knew what to do next.

"It's almost midnight," I said. "Perhaps before we unmask ourselves you could get me another drink?"

"Certainly." Stefan rose instantly to his feet.

As soon as his back was turned, I stood and walked away, losing myself in the crowd.

Somewhere I heard a clock begin to strike midnight. The noise from the crowd increased, as everyone prepared for the unmasking.

Ding.

Ding.

Ding.

I pushed my way through to the corridor and ran lightly down the crystal staircase. There was no one around – everyone was crammed into the ballroom, giddy on the drama of the big reveal.

As I sailed out of the door and into the cold night air, I heard the final chimes of the clock.

It was midnight, and I had disappeared into the shadows.

Part Two

Kent
October, 1899

CHAPTER TEN

"I still don't understand why you would do anything so ridiculous," Nicholas muttered as he helped me with the small case I had packed.

The ball had been two days ago. The following morning, he had sent me a note expressing his displeasure over my behaviour.

You're not Cinderella and I am definitely no fairy godmother – what were you thinking disappearing like that? At least that little fool had the good sense to leave a glass slipper behind.

Today, we were travelling to Holland Hall. I was glad that he had not stopped berating me since he picked me up from my front door; it was a distraction, at least. If I thought too much about where we were headed then I started to feel sick.

"I have already told you," I said patiently. "It was the right thing to do. I could tell he'd be caught up in the mystery. By vanishing I will have piqued his interest."

Nicholas murmured something under his breath that was certainly not appropriate for the ears of a delicate young lady.

Fortunately, I was not one of those.

"Did he propose to Agatha that night?" I asked sweetly.

"Well, no," he said. "But you couldn't have predicted..."

"Why don't you just let me do the job that you're paying me to do?" I replied.

Lord Wynter had turned up with great fanfare this morning, along with two enormous carriages – one to carry all our luggage and the staff, and a second to transport me and his grandmother, who we would be collecting from her home in Surrey. I was not especially looking forward to that part.

The carriages were beautiful, gleaming things, bearing the Wynter family crest on the side – a horse rearing up on two legs, and a fox in the same position, either side of a shield.

Nicholas had brought along his groom, his valet and a maid called Matilda who I assumed was there to look after me. Matilda was young – a year or two younger than me, perhaps, with wide grey eyes, red hair and a snub nose. She had not batted an eyelid upon meeting me at the door to my boarding house, only bobbed a curtsey and murmured a polite greeting.

There was also an enormous and quite fierce-looking black stallion who Lord Wynter would ride while I reclined, demure and ladylike, in the carriage. The horse's name was Felix, and I had run back into the kitchen so that I could feed him half an apple. His owner had snapped at me not to spoil him.

"He's quite a gentleman," I said, patting Felix's neck.

"He's a brute," Nicholas replied.

Felix nuzzled softly at my hair and I laughed.

"Well, usually, anyway," Nicholas grumbled.

It was far from a subtle travelling party, and despite the early hour, a crowd was gathering out in the road, peering at the extravagant coaches – and at Lord Wynter, who was as out of place as a panther roaming the streets.

Fortunately, they were not the type of crowd to spoil our plans. Nicholas had been unconcerned about collecting me from my lodgings, even when I had offered to meet him somewhere in town. I suppose he was right; after all, who was ever going to suspect Iris Grey and Serena Fox of being the same person? They came from totally different worlds.

I knew Mrs Turnbull would hear stories about my departure when she got home, but that was a problem for later. As far as she was concerned, I was off for a fortnight to visit family. The fact that I had not mentioned any family at all in the last two years had her itching to ask questions, I could tell, but I had just smiled close-lipped, and out of politeness she had accepted the information.

Madame, on the other hand, had been extremely

unhappy that I needed to take two weeks off work to "attend to some family business", and had threatened me with being sacked with such ferocity that this time I almost believed her. I had pointed out that orders were slowing down now that we were into autumn and the social season was over, and that I'd barely had so much as a day off in seven years.

"*Honestly*, Iris," she had said at last, "you would think I was one of those awful factory bosses, overworking a poor urchin, the way you go on." She had paused. "Visiting family, you say? I don't recall you mentioning any before."

I shrugged at that, and she had looked at me very hard.

"Just be careful," she said and I had nodded. She had said no more, asked no further questions.

After all, everyone had their secrets.

Now, I gathered my skirts and climbed up into the carriage. I was wearing the dress I wore to church, though I rarely attended. I had made it myself and it was nothing that would embarrass even a society lady. Yes, it was simple, without adornment, but the severe lines looked elegant, and the cobalt-coloured shot silk was very fine. The inside of the carriage was spacious, the seats upholstered in powder-blue velvet, the walls lined with a darker blue silk. It seemed that I had dressed to match.

I was startled when Nicholas climbed in beside me.

"What are you doing?" I asked. "I thought you were going to ride Felix?"

"Jensen will ride him for a while. You and I need to talk."

On that inauspicious note he pulled the carriage door closed with a snap, and banged his gold-handled stick on the roof, signalling to the coach driver that it was time to depart.

We rattled along the cobbled streets for several moments in silence. Nicholas stared broodingly out of the window. He did not seem inclined to begin this talk we needed to have and so I reached into my reticule for a book – one of two that were in there – leaning back in my seat and opening up to the page where I had left off. It was an entertaining novel, full of swooning heroines and wicked uncles and accidental poisonings. The hero bore a striking resemblance to the man across from me, who was currently sulking like a four-year-old child.

"Are you ... *reading*?" he asked finally, in the sort of tones with which one might ask, "Are you *eating human flesh*?"

"Yes." I turned a page. "You didn't seem to be in a particularly chatty mood."

He glared at me. "We have important things to discuss."

I closed my book and rested my hands calmly on the top. "Certainly."

He held my gaze for a moment and then sighed. "You're not going to let me tell you how to do things, are you?"

"It does seem unlikely," I agreed. "You should have chosen a more pliable seamstress for the job."

"It would appear so." He sighed again. "Have you had an opportunity to read the material that I sent you?"

I struggled to keep a straight face. "Ah, yes," I said. "The etiquette book."

"It is crucial that you know how to behave. If this

plan is to work then you must appear to be a well-bred young lady."

"And heaven knows I'm not one of those."

"I have no idea what you are, actually, but I hope that you read the book."

In fact, I had read the book and I had found it stuffy and ridiculous – full of advice on things like the order in which we should proceed from the drawing room into dinner based on everyone's titles, or admonishments that a lady *never* bites her bread at dinner.

"I now know that as a young woman I should talk only of *trifles* ... though it was a little unclear on what a trifle might be. Also that I should avoid making personal remarks in case I accidentally end up insulting someone's wife or sister to their face." I raised my eyebrows at Nicholas. "Surprising that you high-society types needed to have that one spelled out to you, but I daresay you're not generally the sharpest of tacks."

I pulled the book in question from my reticule. "I *was* confused by this part," I said, flicking through the pages. "It says here that you should avoid being the first to arrive or the last to leave at an evening party, but surely *someone* must be those things? Are all of the guests to be waiting one another out? Will no one ever descend for dinner for fear of being the first to do so?"

He glowered at me. "I hope you are taking this seriously."

"I am taking it very seriously. I know what to do."

And that was true, though it had nothing to do with Nicholas Wynter's silly book. How could I possibly tell him that I knew the rules of Holland Hall better than he did himself?

"I will admit your methods so far seem to have been effective," he said grudgingly. "Stefan has been pestering me ever since the ball. He wants to know who you are."

I resisted the urge to crow. "That's good, then."

"I still think it was a reckless decision to leave early." He frowned, his gaze turning to the window. "It's important that this plays out the right way."

There was a hardness to his voice now. I wondered again why Nicholas was so intent on destroying Stefan. Not that it really mattered. I had my own plans for revenge, and this whole charade was merely the means to an end.

"You have two weeks to get him to propose." Nicholas drummed his fingers against his knee. "He'll want to announce something at the ball at the end of the fortnight. It's to be quite an elaborate affair. The perfect scene for a public humiliation."

"Go on, then," I said encouragingly. "You've got it all planned out. How do you suggest that I secure a proposal in that time?"

Those chilly blue eyes settled on me for a moment. "If you would like my advice…"

"I would."

He leaned forward. "First of all, we will continue the fiction that I am interested in you myself."

"Is Prince Stefan really so competitive?"

"He is when it comes to me."

"He mentioned that you were old friends," I probed.

"I have known him for several years," was the only response. "To return to the matter at hand; I will attempt to monopolize you, but you should make sure to spend time with him, to snatch the odd moment alone. It shouldn't be difficult; these house parties are a hotbed of flirtation. There will be the usual activities that our hostess will insist upon – party games and tennis and picnics. At the last of these events that I attended, our hosts tried to engage us in putting on some sort of theatrical performance." He shuddered.

"What part did you play?" I asked gleefully, finding it hard to imagine.

He fixed me with a quelling look. "I declined to participate. They *suggested* I take the role of the lovestruck hero."

"Ah, and let me guess, the eligible daughter of the house was to play your swooning heroine?"

"Yes."

"What a silly idea. Surely they could see that you'd be the perfect villain?"

A smile tugged at his mouth. "I believe you mean that as a compliment."

"Well, the villains are just so much more interesting, aren't they?"

Something flared in his eyes then. "Oh, yes," he murmured in a low voice. "Much more interesting."

I felt the words like a touch across my skin, and shifted a little in my seat.

"Very well," I said, changing the subject. "I'll do my best. But you can't be hovering over me trying to manage things. I believe that I'll be the best person to decide how to flirt with him."

There was a moment of hesitation. "Fine," he said tautly. "But I shall expect frequent updates."

"I imagine you will." I batted my eyelashes. "Fortunately you'll be trying to find moments alone with me as well, because you find me irresistible."

"For the purposes of this plan, yes."

His voice was flat and I knew the words were meant as a warning – this was a business arrangement. He was right. Neither of us was looking for a friend.

As if reading my mind, Nicholas knocked on the roof again, and the carriage came to an instant halt.

"I'll leave you to your book," he said, unfolding himself from his seat and reaching for the handle on the door, which meant that he was suddenly extremely close to me. My brain dimly registered that he smelled delicious – of something spicy with a touch of citrus – and then he was climbing out of the carriage without another word.

I sat back in my seat. The nerves that had been kept at bay while bickering with Nicholas crashed over me like a wave that had the potential to drown me.

I was about to be introduced to his grandmother, a woman who by all accounts was already inclined to dislike me. But that fact paled into insignificance compared to what was to come afterwards.

I don't think I had really believed that it was going to happen, but now … here we were, on our way.

I was finally going back to Holland Hall.

And I had no idea what would be waiting for me.

CHAPTER ELEVEN

Lady Wynter was not exactly what I had expected.

I had imagined an elderly lady, with a sour-lemon face of disapproval. The dowager countess almost certainly disapproved of me, but the only sign was a slight tightening of the lips when we were first introduced. She was an elegant woman with silver-white hair and Nicholas Wynter's snapping blue eyes. She carried herself extremely upright and she wore a sombre dress of a purple brocade so dark that it was almost black.

She greeted Nicholas coolly, and he bowed over

her hand with an easy grace but little attempt at conversation. It was hardly what you would call a warm family reunion, and he swiftly shut her in the carriage with me, before mounting his horse again. The coward.

"So, Miss Fox." The dowager turned her shrewd gaze on me. I felt like she saw it all, taking in every inch of me, every stitch of my gown. "I understand that you and my grandson have a long acquaintance."

"Lord Wynter and I knew each other as children," I said carefully. "We met when he and his parents were on holiday, though we have not seen each other for some years."

Her eyes seemed to sharpen further. "I have rarely seen Nicholas exert himself for someone else, yet he seems to have gone to a lot of trouble to secure you an invitation to this party," she said. "It is most unlike him – I can always tell when he's up to something."

I felt flustered by her words. Was it possible that she had some inkling as to what we planned? She seemed like the sort of woman who could see right through a lie or uncover any secret.

"Interesting," she murmured. "Perhaps there is hope for the boy yet."

I tried not to make my relief too obvious. Clearly, his grandmother believed that romance might be in the air. It seemed Nicholas had been right when he suggested that her desire to marry him off may win out over her low opinion of me.

This was confirmed when she added, "The man is Earl Wynter, after all, and he has a duty to his family name. Can't have the estate passing over to his idiot cousin."

I wondered how a real potential bride would react to such a statement. I looked down and twisted my hands in my lap.

"I am certain the earl knows his duty," I said shyly. "He's a most ... responsible man."

"Hmmmph," his grandmother snorted, but when she spoke to me next it was in a marginally softer voice. "Tell me about your family."

I held back a sigh. And so it began. Time to spin this web of lies.

The story Lord Wynter and I had agreed adhered

loosely to the truth, had he but known it. I told her that my mother had passed away, spoke warmly of my father, and described life shut away from the world on a large estate, though I moved my home from Kent to Yorkshire. I confessed a passion for embroidery, but I neglected to mention that it was also my livelihood.

Lady Wynter nodded approvingly at mention of this ladylike activity and continued to quiz me about the rest of my accomplishments. Did I sing? Play the pianoforte? Paint watercolours?

As my education in these areas had stopped when I was eleven, the answer to all of them was no. I did not think that she wanted to hear about my skill with a knife or that I was fluent in boxing cant.

"A pity," the dowager countess sighed. "Still, I believe we can do *something* with you."

I bowed my head meekly, largely to hide the outrage that I knew was flashing in my eyes.

"It's going to be an interesting fortnight," Lady Wynter mused. "Helena will have been extremely put out by the fact that Stefan didn't propose to her daughter at the Devonshire House ball," she sniffed. "We all thought it was a certainty, but clever of her to organize this party as a contingency. Plenty of opportunity to fling the two of them together. She won't be happy to have another pretty girl around." I was treated to a sharp look.

"I wouldn't dream of upsetting Lady Scott-Holland's plans," I said sweetly.

"Hmmm." The dowager countess pursed her lips but said no more on the matter.

When I was sure her interrogation was complete, I picked up my book and tried to concentrate on the pages. The rest of the journey passed quietly. It seemed that I felt every stride the horses took, despite the well-sprung carriage we were in. Each one brought me closer to something simultaneously terrifying and longed for.

Night had fallen before we approached the house, and I was glad of it. I worried that if I had had the clear view of the house from atop a nearby hill then I wouldn't have been capable of concealing my anxiety from Lady Wynter. As it was, the sight of lights in some of the windows was enough to send a shudder through me.

I clenched my hands into tight fists and tried to look calm.

We carried on along the road, round twists and turns that were still as familiar to me as they had been seven years ago. There were favourite trees I had climbed, the village where I had spent my preciously saved pennies on sweets, the fences that I had jumped on my horse, sailing through the air side by side with my father.

I swallowed hard, my fingernails digging into my palms.

By the time we approached the drive I felt like I had lived several lifetimes.

There was nothing I could do to hold back the tears when we finally reached the house itself. There were simply too many memories all tangled together, flashing rapidly through my mind. All I could see were images of my parents erupting on to the driveway to welcome me, as though I had only been away for a short time. I imagined them standing here, laughing, holding me close.

I wiped the tears away quickly, and the dowager countess did not seem to notice. I was grateful for the shadows that wrapped themselves about me as I climbed down from the carriage.

Lord Wynter had appeared at the door, offering me his hand. I took it. His hand was warm and firm even through his gloves, and mine was cold, betraying the slightest tremble. To my surprise, he squeezed my fingers gently.

I lifted my chin, and my eyes found his. For a brief, breathless moment he held my gaze, and then he turned to help his grandmother.

It was enough. He may not know the real reason that I was scared, but his presence had steadied me, reminded me of what I was here to do.

I faced the house. It was lit by torches and exactly as I remembered. My heart contracted painfully at the sight. Then I saw Helena emerging from the front door and any other feeling was overwhelmed by pure, unadulterated rage.

How *dare* she? How dare she look so comfortable, like she actually belonged here?

She was moving towards the dowager countess with her hands outstretched, a welcoming smile on her lips.

The flickering of the torches danced over her midnight-black hair, and for a moment it was as if she was emerging from the flames.

"Lord Wynter, Lady Wynter," she exclaimed. "How happy I am to welcome you to our home."

Her home.

"I hope your journey was not too tiring," she continued, turning to the dowager countess. Her voice was pure music, the way she moved was like a dance. Here was a woman born to be a marchioness.

Lady Wynter's eyebrows rose. "You make me sound like an invalid, Helena. The journey was only a handful of hours. And I had Miss Fox to keep me company."

I stepped forward. Helena's eyes turned to me, and she could not mask the flash of anger that crossed her face. But then she smiled.

"Oh, it's you!"

For a second, I froze in panic.

"I recognize that lovely face even without the mask. So, Serena Fox is the mysterious guest from the ball. How fortunate we are to have you to stay, you've been the talk of the town these past two days," Helena continued gaily. "Everyone will be extremely jealous that we have you all to ourselves!"

I breathed a sigh of relief.

She didn't know me.

Her words settled. I had no idea that I had caused such a stir at the ball that people were still talking about me. I glanced over at Nicholas, but he stood there with that usual slightly bored look on his face.

"Thank you for extending the invitation to include me, Lady Scott-Holland. You have a beautiful home." The words felt sharp on my tongue. I tried to ignore the image in my mind of my father standing here on the threshold, his arms held wide open, waiting to scoop me up.

"Thank you, we are rather fond of it," Helena said lightly. "Now, let's not stand out here in the cold. I'll show you to your rooms so that you can refresh yourselves before dinner."

She led us through the front door, into the wide entrance hall, and up the carved wooden staircase. I kept my eyes down. I needed to gather myself, to steel my mind, before I took it all in.

Still, as soon as my hand touched the banister, I felt memory singing through my fingers. The wood was smooth, worn by hundreds of hands over the years – and by me sliding down it, much to my governess's dismay. She tried to get Father to tell me off, but more often than not he was waiting at the bottom to catch me.

"Here comes my little cub!" he would boom as I came soaring down the polished banister, howling like a wolf, and baring my teeth in a ferocious grin.

I was relieved when Helena led me to a wing of the house that we had rarely used. It had all been lavishly redecorated, and I barely recognized anything. It helped me to breathe a little easier.

"This will be your room, Miss Fox," she said, opening one of the doors.

The room was beautiful, blush pink papered walls, and green coverlets on a large bed. There was a cast iron fireplace with an elaborate marble surround. A vase of pale pink calla lilies, elegant on long stems stood on the dressing table – presumably cut from the hothouse. I wondered if Kielty the gardener was still here to tend to them.

"It's lovely," I said. "Thank you."

"I'll have your bags sent up right away," Helena said. "We're meeting for drinks before dinner in half an hour, but don't worry about being punctual. You've had a long journey."

If I didn't know better, I'd think she was a gracious hostess; but I *did* know better. She was trying to delay any meeting between Stefan and me for as long as possible.

I smiled, showing all my teeth.

"Thank you, Lady-Scott Holland. You think of everything."

CHAPTER TWELVE

A servant who I didn't recognise brought my cases
promptly to my room. There were a lot of them.

I knew from the notes that Nicholas had sent that
he had bought clothes for me. I didn't like the idea, but
could hardly see a way around it. I couldn't very well
turn up with my usual wardrobe and try to pass myself
off as an heiress. Still, I felt the loss of my own fortune –
and the independence it offered – keenly. It was a matter
of pride more than anything else.

Once the servant had left, I began opening the cases.

It was a distraction, and I had always found admiring good clothes to be soothing. And these *were* good clothes.

I recognized the work of The House of Guillard, Madame's fiercest rival. They had, in fact, tried to poach me several times in the last year.

As I unpacked each valise, I was reminded of Lord Wynter's excellent eye for style. I had forgotten how many times a day a lady was expected to change her clothes. There were morning gowns, walking dresses, tea gowns, dinner dresses, riding habits and ball gowns, as well as shoes, shawls, hats, gloves, corsets, stockings and chemises.

Despite the fact that I was no naive sheltered society girl, I found myself blushing over that. To have a man buying my undergarments ... well, it felt a bit too close to the role I had originally thought Nicholas was offering me.

On the other hand, it was all truly beautiful, and I had never worn anything like these outfits. The wardrobe of an eleven-year-old was much less exciting than that of a young woman of eighteen. Soon the room was buried under an explosion of colour and texture. I stood at the epicentre, taking it all in.

I ran my fingers over a beautiful dark blue velvet riding habit, trimmed with silver braid. Lots of the dresses were in various shades of blue, and I held them up to me in the mirror; they complemented the colour of my eyes to perfection. There were dresses made of silk, brocade, chiffon, jacquard; there were elegant trimmings, lace and silk ribbons and elaborate embroidery, tiny pearl buttons, and glass beads, and fringe. I could not resist touching them all, examining all the details. Even my professional eye could find no defect. They were made with extreme skill.

Hidden away in my own case was one extra addition that I hadn't told Nicholas about. I had brought the dream dress that I had been working on, and everything I would need to finish it. I planned to work on it while I was here; hopefully I would have the chance to finish it before the ball at the end of the fortnight. I had asked Madame if I could have it and offered to pay for it, but she had surprised me and given it to me as a gift.

"It's barely even a dress at the moment," she had sniffed. "You might as well have it."

She hadn't asked me what it was for.

A knock at the door snapped me out of my daydreaming. It was Matilda, the lady's maid Nicholas had employed for me. "Shall I unpack for you, miss?" she asked.

I had already started hanging things in the wardrobe, and I cursed myself for such dim-witted behaviour. I needed to act like a woman who had never lifted a finger for herself.

"Thank you, Matilda," I responded. "And if you could ring for some water, I'll tidy myself up before dinner."

"Do you know what you'd like to wear, miss?" Matilda asked. I could see her eyes widen as she took in the explosion of extremely luxurious gowns that were strewn across every surface.

"This one, I think," I said, resting my hand on a sapphire-blue silk gown, trimmed with ivory lace.

"Very good, miss." Matilda bobbed.

The water was promptly delivered, and I washed as

quickly as possible before Matilda laced me into my gown. She had also laid out a pair of fine silk stockings, an ivory shawl embroidered with blue forget-me-nots, a pair of silk slippers dyed to match my dress, and a pair of elbow-length cream gloves, each fastened with four tiny buttons.

After I had dressed, Matilda sat me in front of the mirror, and brushed out my hair before braiding it away from my face and styling it in a low chignon. It was much more elegant than I could possibly have achieved.

"Thank you!" I exclaimed, unthinkingly. "It looks wonderful!"

It was much too effusive for a fine lady, but Matilda blushed and looked pleased.

I gave myself a mental shake. I had only been back in the house for five minutes and already my grip on Iris Grey was loosening. I had to *pretend* to be Serena Fox – but I needed my own cool, calculating head on my shoulders if I was going to pull this off.

I had just stood, straightening out my skirts, when there was another knock at the door.

It was Lord Wynter.

His eyes travelled lazily over my outfit. "Thank you, Matilda," he said, his gaze still on me. "That will be all."

Matilda hesitated for a moment, glancing quickly towards me. Nicholas might have hired her, but already I sensed a tiny bit of loyalty towards me. That was nice.

"It's all right, Matilda, thank you."

Without another word the maid bobbed another curtsey and left.

Nicholas prowled – there was really no other word for it – towards the fireplace and rested his elbow against it. His face was freshly shaven, his dark hair gleaming. He wore a richly patterned pale grey velvet waistcoat covered in a dense design of blue roses underneath a suit made of dark grey superfine.

"After all your talk of acting with propriety, allow me to tell you that you *definitely* shouldn't be here," I said. "I don't need to read an etiquette manual to know that."

"Matilda won't say anything," he said, with enough certainty that I knew my new maid must be very well paid. Good for her.

"And why," I asked, "are you here at all? Have you come to check me over like a piece of furniture? Because I've been dressing fine ladies for years now."

"I think you look perfectly acceptable," was his response.

"Stop!" I raised a hand to my forehead. "You'll overwhelm me with such high praise. Can't have me falling into a swoon before dinner."

"Your mirror tells you well enough that you look beautiful," he said, with a shrug. "You hardly need me to confirm that. Though I am glad to see that the dress fits – I had to take a guess at your sizing. I presume you'll be able to make any necessary alterations yourself."

"Then you did hire me for my dressmaking skills, after all." I smiled.

He did not smile back. Again, I reminded myself that I wasn't here to be his friend.

He reached into his pockets and pulled out four velvet cases.

"I brought you these." He walked over to the dressing table and set them down before returning to the fireplace.

I made my way cautiously towards the boxes. With slightly unsteady hands I opened the first one.

I had been prepared to look unaffected by whatever I found there, but I couldn't help the gasp that fell from my lips.

"Are these—"

"Diamonds." He nodded.

I stared at them for a moment, almost afraid to touch them. There were dainty drop earrings, a short necklace that looked like it was made of stars, and a matching bracelet. My etiquette book said that young debutantes didn't typically wear diamonds. It seemed he was determined to cause a stir. I didn't know much about jewels, but I couldn't imagine that Nicholas Wynter would settle for anything less than the best.

My hands moved to the next box: a set of emeralds, the green so deep that they contained an elusive flash of blue. In the third box was a necklace made of multiple strands of delicate shell-pink pearls, and matching earrings. The fourth box was the best of all: dazzling sapphires, a luminous deep blue that danced with light.

"I can't—" I began, but Nicholas waved a hand, cutting me off.

"They'll expect it," he said. "All the other ladies will be weighed down with their best jewellery. It will seem decidedly odd if the one who's supposed to be the richest of all never wears any. They'll remark on it."

I was silent then. Objectively, I knew he was right, but it still made me feel uncomfortable. Clothes and jewels – things that I had been offered by other men, men with very different motives.

As if reading my mind, he said briskly, "They're only borrowed, so you needn't look so pained. When we're done the jewels go back to the jeweller. They are not a bribe, they are not a gift, they do not come with any demands attached to them. They are simply part of your costume."

I found his argument to be reassuring.

I nodded. "You're right."

"Always," Nicholas replied, that half-smile on his lips.

I reached for the sapphires and slipped the solitaire earrings through my ears, then I picked up the necklace and undid the clasp.

"Allow me." He pulled himself away from the fireplace and moved towards me.

He took the necklace from my hands, and I turned around with my back to him. He was close enough that I could feel the heat from his body against me. For someone so determined to appear ice cold, he certainly seemed warm-blooded.

I felt the brush of his fingers across my collarbone as he pulled the necklace into place. There was the slightest touch of his breath against the nape of my neck. The necklace was cold and heavy against my skin. I shivered.

Then he took a step back, the warmth of him receding.

"I'd better go down," he said. "Wait five minutes before you join us." He scanned me once more. "You should make quite an entrance."

I nodded in agreement, and he slipped from the room. I returned my attention to the jewellery for a moment, and then snapped the boxes shut. Nicholas was right; they were simply props for the part I needed to play.

I took a deep breath, preparing not only to meet the other guests as Serena Fox, but to wander the familiar hallways of my home.

I looked at myself in the mirror. It was time to wrap myself in the cloak of uncaring frost that I had worn every day as a young girl alone in London. The sapphires winked at my ears and at my throat, a perfect match for my eyes.

My reflection looked back, steady, unafraid. I could do this.

Taking hold of my skirts, I swept out of the door and down the stairs. I moved swiftly, as if I could simply outrun my own emotions. I felt my breath coming shallow and I tried to push all the feelings right down inside me.

Helena had explained how to reach the drawing room – not that I had needed the directions. I felt that I was walking through time, as if I was simultaneously seeing the walls around me as they were now, and the shadow of how they had been seven years earlier. It was an overwhelming and disorienting feeling, this dual perspective. Helena had redecorated quite extensively but I still saw to the heart of the house, like an archaeologist, peeling back the layers of history.

I briefly closed my eyes, trying to dispel the visions of

my father striding through the doors, a riding crop in his hand, a smile on his face. I saw his broad shoulders, his sandy hair and brown eyes, could almost feel the tickle of his beard against my cheek.

I stood for a second with my hand on the door to the drawing room, and then I opened it.

The author of my etiquette book would be gravely disappointed in me; I was the last to arrive. The other guests were gathered around the fireplace, the butler serving drinks from a silver tray.

Conversation ceased and all eyes turned towards me, some filled with curiosity, some with dislike, and at least one pair with stunned pleasure. I was sure then that Lord Wynter knew precisely what he was doing. The sapphires, a chill weight at my neck and in my ears, felt like armour. I could see each person taking my measure, and I stood, cool and straight, as if I were unaware of their attention.

"My god!" Stefan exclaimed, starting towards me. "It's you!"

At those words the butler turned, and the glass in his hand fell to the floor, shattering instantly.

CHAPTER THIRTEEN

"Tookes!" Helena snapped, getting to her feet.

"My apologies, madam," the butler replied sombrely, with a slight bow. "I will have this mess cleared up at once."

As if by magic, a maid appeared. The glass was swept up and the mess from the drink cleared in the blink of an eye.

In the time it took for this to happen I had an opportunity to look around me. My eyes landed first on Agatha. She sat near the fireplace, still leaning towards

Stefan, who now had his back to her. She looked lovely, in a pale yellow gown that I had made myself, a sleek silk construction that flattered her colouring. Her dark, shining hair was piled on top of her head in glossy curls, and she was the picture of pretty innocence – apart from the calculating look in her grey eyes as they rested on me. I supposed that the girl sitting beside her was her sister, Cassie.

"That will be all, Tookes," Helena said coldly to the butler. "You may leave the rest of the drinks on the trolley. Now that Miss Fox has arrived, we will want dinner shortly."

"Certainly, my lady." The butler glided past me and out of the door without another word.

"My apologies, everyone." Helena's icy tone melted. "I believe it may be time for Mr Tookes to retire, but it is so difficult when one becomes attached to an old family retainer, isn't it?"

"That's just like you, Helena," simpered a lady seated on the sofa beside my stepmother. She was small and pale, with beady brown eyes and mouse-coloured hair. Her gown did not fit her properly, as if she had recently lost weight, and, though it was done well, I could see that it had been reworked at least twice. "Such a kind heart."

Helena smiled – a soft, modest smile.

I fought the urge to laugh. *A kind heart*, indeed. If only they knew.

"But where are my manners?" Helena twinkled. "In all the commotion, I haven't yet introduced you all to our guest, Miss Fox. She does seem to make an entrance wherever she goes."

I smiled, and dropped into a light curtsey. There were a dozen people in the room, not including me, and for a moment I felt overwhelmed.

As though he had been held back by an invisible lead which had now been released, Stefan bounded forward, bowing deeply over my hand.

"It *is* you, isn't it?" he asked, his tone warm and eager. He had the sort of presence that set a person instantly at ease. "My partner from the ball."

"Yes." I smiled. "It's me. I'm glad to meet you again, Your Highness."

"I half-expected to find a glass slipper on the stairs,"

Stefan chuckled. "Where did you disappear off to on the stroke of midnight?"

"I felt a little unwell," I said. "It was stuffy in that room. I *did* almost lose my shoe on the stairs – but I'm sorry to have to disappoint you – they were made of silk. I always thought glass slippers sounded terribly uncomfortable."

Stefan laughed. Helena interrupted, her tone all concern. "My dear, I'm sorry to hear you were unwell. Are you generally of such a delicate nature?"

She might as well have said outright that I clearly did not have the constitution necessary to be a princess.

"Oh, no, Lady Scott-Holland," I said pleasantly. "I am usually the least sickly person, I promise you. It was just that the room was warm, and there were a great many people." I gave a disarming little shrug. "I'm afraid I'm not yet used to these large events, but I daresay it will all be quite normal, soon."

"Yes, I confess, I was surprised that we hadn't met before," Helena said. "Forgive me for asking, but you have not made your come out yet?"

I lowered my eyes and introduced a slight quiver into

my voice. "My mother's death meant that I had to forgo that event for a year. To be perfectly honest I fear that I would have been poor company at the time, even if etiquette had not dictated it."

"I am sorry to hear that," Stefan said gravely, understanding in his eyes. "The loss of a parent is a wound that cannot be healed."

"That is true," I agreed, with no need to rely on my acting skills.

Helena looked as though she had bitten into a lemon. Then her gaze became cunning.

"How fortunate that you have such a *good* friend to ease your way into society. I believe that you and Lord Wynter are well acquainted," she said, gesturing towards Nicholas, who stood a little apart from the rest of the group with a red-headed man.

Her voice was full of implications; but clearly Helena did not know Stefan as well as Lord Wynter did. The idea of a prior romantic connection between Nicholas and me seemed *more* likely to make me of interest to Stefan, not less. I noticed a small frown furrow Stefan's brow. He was not pleased.

Nicholas made his way leisurely to my side.

He stood close enough beside me that the sleeve of his jacket brushed, feather-light, across my bare arm.

"Oh, Serena and I are old friends," he said, then he placed his hand at the small of my back. "Come, let me introduce you to everyone."

He moved me away from Helena and Stefan, and I heard Helena begin to ask the prince bright questions about his grandmother.

I took the opportunity to look around the room. Helena had changed the wallpaper and the furniture and it was clear no expense had been spared. The effect was luxurious, decadent, and I noticed that the emerald-and-gold colour scheme complemented Helena's raven-wing hair and green eyes.

"This is Colonel Thacker and Lord Bell," Nicholas said, as we approached two older gentlemen. "Gentlemen, may I present Miss Fox?"

"Charmed, my dear." The colonel bowed over my hand. He was a portly man in military dress, with a bristling grey moustache, red cheeks and a benevolent gleam in his eye.

Lord Bell was almost his precise opposite, tall and spindly with an extremely uninterested expression. His eyes flickered over me, lingering for a moment on the jewels, and then he gestured to a young man who made his way towards us.

"Miss Fox, may I present my younger son, Lord Percy?"

The young man was about the same age as me, with a round face and an air of intense shyness.

"H-hello," he managed.

I gave him my most dazzling smile. "It's a pleasure to meet you," I replied.

Nicholas then steered me over to the cluster of deep green velvet seats. "Of course, you already know my grandmother," he said. "And this is Lady Bell." He gestured to the mousy woman in the worn dress, who inclined her head. "And her daughter, Lady Sophia."

Sophia was closer in appearance to her brother than either of her parents. She had a sweet face framed by light brown ringlets. Like her mother's I could see that her dress had been cleverly mended and altered on more than one occasion. She smiled tentatively, and I did the same.

My cheeks were starting to hurt. Unlike Iris Grey, Serena Fox was happy and charming. I was quite out of practice. All this smiling was a test in itself.

Suddenly, Helena was at my shoulder. "And you must allow me to introduce my daughters from my first marriage to Baron Weston. This is my eldest, Agatha, and my younger daughter, Cassandra."

I lifted my gaze to look at my stepsisters. So far it didn't seem that Helena had recognized me, though I had spent more time in the nursery with her daughters, and we were closer in age. Would they see through my disguise?

I had seen Agatha already, but this was our first proper meeting. Her beauty was marred slightly by the sullen mask that descended when she looked at me.

Cassie, I remembered as a quiet, watchful little girl; now she looked at me with a direct and curious gaze. Her eyes were brown, her hair a glossy chestnut, and her jaw had a determined set to it. She was the same age as me, and she wore an air of confidence that owed absolutely nothing to her gown, which was well made but plain, unadorned and unstylish in a drab lilac.

I scanned their faces and saw no hint of recognition. I didn't think I would have recognized *them* had we passed in the street, let alone if they were introduced under different names. I supposed that the difference between eleven and eighteen was a significant one.

"Agatha will be able to share some advice about your come out," Helena murmured confidingly. "Her own was quite the success. Several most eligible offers for her hand over the last two years, you know." She laid her hand on my arm. I felt the zing of her touch like a bee sting. "But she hasn't accepted any yet. My daughter may shoot for the moon, after all."

I heard the warning in her chatty tone and followed her gaze as it rested pointedly on Stefan for a moment. Then she returned her attention to her other daughter.

"And Cassandra is," Helena hesitated, "here as well," she finished brightly.

I had the impression that it took everything in Cassie not to roll her eyes at that, and I repressed a smile.

"Miss Weston," I said, bobbing a curtsey to Agatha. "Miss Cassandra."

"I prefer to be called Cassie," she said. Her voice was

deep and pleasant, and her eyes remained fixed keenly on mine.

"Cassie," I said, hoping that I was giving nothing away under that interrogative look. "A pleasure to meet you."

"And this is my good friend Jack Waterford," Nicholas said, resuming his introductions. He had no idea how interested I was in my stepsisters, of course.

I was surprised to hear him speaking so warmly of anyone, let alone the man who stood before me. Jack Waterford was a handsome, copper-headed man, probably only a couple of years older than me. His smile was full of humour, and his blue eyes twinkled.

"It is good to meet you, Miss Fox. Nick has talked of little else since you arrived in town." Jack nudged Nick in the side.

"It is always nice to be able to catch up with old friends, Mr Waterford," I said.

"And to make new ones, I hope," Jack replied.

Stefan had clearly had enough of being ignored – I had been careful to avoid looking over at him while all of these introductions took place – and he interrupted us. "I'm sorry, gentlemen, but I am going to have to steal Miss Fox away. You see, she owes me a dance."

"We can hardly break into dancing in the drawing room," I pointed out.

"I don't see why not," Stefan teased, "but I suppose I will settle for pleasant conversation. As long as you remember that your next dance, whenever that may be, is mine."

"I'm afraid I'm terribly forgetful sometimes," I said, fingering the fringe on my shawl.

"Ah," Stefan purred, "but I will be there to remind you."

The door opened, and the butler, Tookes, appeared.

"Dinner is served."

CHAPTER FOURTEEN

I was led into dinner by Jack – he being a mere mister, and I a mere miss – just as my etiquette book had advised. As the daughters of a baron, Agatha and Cassie may not have been titled, but they were honourables, and therefore far above the offspring of a factory owner in the pecking order. We were an odd number, but Nick solved this by offering one arm to his grandmother, and another to Lady Bell.

In the dining room, I found that I had been seated between Nick and Colonel Thacker. Stefan was as far away from me as possible. Helena was taking no chances.

"I'm sorry about the slightly odd arrangements," Helena said. "Thirteen is *such* an awkward number. But when a last-minute addition is as charming as Miss Fox, I'm sure we can all overlook it."

Ping. The first of what I was certain would be many shots fired during this meal.

"It's kind of you to include me, Lady Scott-Holland, particularly at such short notice," I said meekly. "I hope Lord Wynter didn't put too much pressure on you. He can be maddeningly high-handed at times."

Further down the table, Jack smothered a laugh. My eye caught his and he winked. Apparently, he enjoyed hearing someone tease his friend.

I knew that Helena wouldn't want to risk offending Nicholas and so there wasn't much she could say, except, "No, no, my dear, you must not think of it."

Nicholas turned towards me and murmured, "*High-handed?*" His lips were close to my ear, so close that the words were almost a caress. I fought the urge to squirm. Did this appearance of flirting need to feel *so* convincing?

"We're in polite company," I murmured back. "Otherwise I would have used different words."

"You seem to have rattled our hostess," Nick replied in the same low tone.

"And you seem to have rattled your prince." I knew without looking that Stefan's eyes were on us. I saw Nick's gaze flicker over my shoulder, and he smiled.

"Such a beautiful room, Helena," I heard Lady Bell exclaim. "And a beautiful table as well."

She wasn't wrong.

The room was decorated in a rich red paper, threaded through with gold, with a darker burgundy-and-gold border at the top. The tall windows were framed with heavy crimson velvet drapes. Like the drawing room, it felt like we were inside a jewellery box.

The table was gleaming mahogany dressed with crimson roses, the finest crystal glassware, silver cutlery polished until it shone like a mirror, and heavy silver candlesticks. Tall, ivory candles flickered, casting everything in an intimate glow.

It seemed that every room in the house had been given Helena's opulent treatment. In one way it made my job easier, not to have so many constant reminders, but I felt a pang over it, nonetheless. I preferred the rooms as they had been: slightly shabby, comfortable and cluttered. It felt as if my family had been erased.

I glanced to the side of my plate where a small card, embossed with gold, declared tonight's menu. My eyes widened as I took in the endless list of dishes: Mulligatawny soup; turbot with lobster sauce; crimped cod and oyster sauce; fried, filleted soles; fillets of beef with vegetables; mutton cutlets and tomato sauce; lobster rissoles; oyster patties; partridges with herbs; larded sweetbreads; roast hare with game sauce; chicken with watercress; salad; artichokes; stewed celery. I hadn't even come to the list of desserts yet. It was a far cry from Mrs Turnbull's cooking.

Plate after plate was laid out on the sideboard and served to us. I had a hearty appetite, but even I began taking only a few mouthfuls of each dish the further we waded in.

It took a long time.

As etiquette dictated, I split my time making conversation between Lord Wynter and the colonel on my other side. The colonel was a nice man, but extremely dull. He wanted to discuss nothing but fishing, despite my claiming little knowledge on the subject. Rather than putting him off, he decided to educate me on the differences between fishing for trout and fishing for perch. I made certain to cast shy glances across the table at Stefan at intervals, and more often than not, he was already looking at me. Nicholas was attentive, checking that my glass was filled, that I was served the best of everything, leaning a shade closer than was strictly proper.

Eventually, the chatter opened up, with people speaking across the table to one another.

"Miss Fox," Agatha cooed from her position beside Stefan, "do tell us, how did you and Lord Wynter meet? I'm sure we're all dying to know."

Like her mother, Agatha was making the mistake of thinking this would quench rather than fire Stefan's interest.

"I cannot quite remember how old I was – I believe I was around ... six or seven?" I looked to Nicholas for guidance. I had absolutely no idea what he had already told people.

"You were six," he said firmly, "and I was ten. It was over the summer, when we were staying in Sussex. Miss Fox was our neighbour – her own home was next door to the house we had taken for the summer."

"I thought you said your home was in Yorkshire, Miss Fox?" Stefan frowned.

I tried not to wince. "I did," I improvised wildly, "and it is … but we often summer in our Sussex home."

"And so it went, every summer for some years," Nicholas agreed swiftly. "You'll remember, Grandmother – which summers did Mother and Father take me?"

"I believe it was '87 to '91," the dowager countess replied crisply.

"A shame you couldn't join us," her grandson said.

"You know I do not like the seaside, Nicholas," Lady Wynter replied. She paused majestically. "I do not care for sand." The words rang out, and Lady Bell nodded enthusiastically at this wise pronouncement.

Jack sputtered into his wine glass, and the dowager countess's steely glare swung in his direction.

"Lord Wynter was awfully grand at first," I said. "He

didn't want to associate with a provincial little girl. But I won him over with my charm."

Nicholas snorted. "Your charm? Is that what you call following me around like a shadow?"

I tutted. "Ah, but then things changed, didn't they? You went through your awkward phase, and *I* was the only one to take pity on *you*."

"It's hard to imagine Lord Wynter having an awkward phase," Lady Bell tittered.

"I don't know about that," Jack put in. "I for one would *love* to hear all about it, Miss Fox." He was sitting back, his wine glass cradled in his hand and a look of great enjoyment on his face.

Lord Wynter's jaw twitched.

"He was so sweet," I said. "Ever so gangly and shy, and" – I turned to face him – "do you remember? There was that whole summer you carried that teddy bear everywhere with you, you couldn't stand to be parted." I was enjoying myself now, watching to see how he would react to being teased.

"His name was Edward," Nicholas said easily, though his eyes promised murder later on.

Jack gave a bark of laughter, and Sophia choked on her drink.

"My, my," Helena said drily. "How lovely to have such a long acquaintance."

"I've been fortunate," I said. "I don't have a wide acquaintance outside of our country circles, but – after some persuasion – my father has agreed it's time for me to make my come out in society. He was quite nervous about it, and so knowing that there is someone watching out for me has reassured him greatly. Lord Wynter has been extremely kind in arranging things for me."

"I'm sure Wynter was more than happy to help such a lovely young lady," the colonel said gallantly from beside me. The wine we'd been drinking with dinner had only added to his rosy complexion and he beamed at me like a benevolent Santa Claus.

Nicholas nodded. "When I heard from Miss Fox's father that she was coming down to London for a few weeks and didn't know a soul, I couldn't resist taking her under my wing."

I cleared my throat. "Of course, my formal come out will not be until next season."

"Which is why an occasion such as this one offered the perfect opportunity to introduce Miss Fox to society in a more *intimate* setting." Nicholas cast me a smouldering look.

Suddenly the whole situation struck me as irresistibly funny. I dropped my eyes to my plate, fighting the urge to laugh. I felt Nicholas's hand grip my knee beneath the table, warning me that I needed to keep a hold on myself. The touch was so unexpected and sudden that I felt it tingle all the way up my leg, but it did have the benefit of shocking the giggles out of me.

"It seems to me that Nick is indeed fortunate to have such a longstanding friendship with Miss Fox." Stefan smiled, holding his glass up in a little salute. "And I for one am glad that the next two weeks offer us *all* a chance to make new friends." It was impossible to miss the competitive gleam in his eye.

"I don't believe I know your father, Miss Fox," Helena cut in swiftly. "I think Lord Wynter said he was in some sort of *trade*."

She said the word "trade" as if it was something she would only touch with her fingertips. It seemed she didn't care too much about being subtle any more.

"My father owns several factories," I said, lifting my eyes to hers. "He worked hard to provide for me. He's the best person I have ever known, and I'm proud to be his daughter." I spoke more forcefully than I had intended.

There was a pause.

"I think it is admirable to be a self-made man," Sophia put in, her voice trembling at her own boldness. "To have provided for his family through his own hard work."

Another beat of silence followed this pronouncement.

"Hear, hear," Jack jumped in. "It's all well and good inheriting things you've never worked a day in your life for, but changing your own fortune through sheer effort and determination – that shows real strength of character." He smiled at Sophia, and her cheeks flushed.

The conversation turned to other things, and Nicholas leaned towards me.

"I think you're about to bend that fork in half," he said quietly.

"I'm fine," I snapped, and then I exhaled a slow breath. "I really am."

Luckily, we were interrupted by the arrival of dessert.

As soon as I glanced at the mixture of treats on offer – all sorts of tarts and puddings and trifles and every other dainty you can imagine – I found that my appetite had, thankfully, returned, and I gratefully accepted a dish of Charlotte Russe.

It was absolutely delicious, and I closed my eyes for a moment in appreciation as the Bavarian cream melted on my tongue.

I was surprised to see Nicholas digging in gleefully beside me. He had not seemed particularly interested in the rest of the meal. He noticed me watching.

"Sweet tooth," he said with a shrug.

For the remainder of the dinner, I chatted with the colonel and it was easy and undemanding. He seemed delighted that I had more questions about the various bait he chose to use. I had never imagined there could be so much variety.

After dinner came the part that I had been dreading –

where the men stayed and smoke and drank, and we ladies had to return to the drawing room.

I desperately hoped that the men wouldn't linger too long. I could feel strong waves of dislike coming from Agatha and Helena, and I knew that I was still under scrutiny from the dowager countess. Sophia and Cassie had been largely silent throughout the meal – Sophia had looked shy and Cassie bored. Lady Bell was obviously desperate to be on Helena's good side so it seemed unlikely that I would find an ally in her.

As I hesitated on the threshold, Cassie patted the seat beside her in invitation.

I accepted with a mixture of relief and anxiety, but she gave no sign at all of having recognized me as her erstwhile stepsister.

"These things are just awful, aren't they?" she said.

I hesitated. "It seems quite hard work," I agreed finally, slumping slightly in my seat and hoping that perfect posture wasn't going to be something that Lady Wynter had particularly strong feelings about. I did not like my chances.

"It's all dull, polite conversation while they stuff you

with food like you're some sort of ceremonial goose." Cassie rolled her eyes.

"I actually didn't mind being stuffed with food," I said, thinking dreamily once more of the Charlotte Russe. "But Colonel Thacker certainly has a one-track mind."

"He wasn't flirting with you, was he?"

I laughed. "Not unless you count describing every fishing spot, and possibly every fish, within two hundred miles as flirting."

"It may well be with the colonel." Cassie shrugged. "He's one of my mother's many admirers, the poor sap. She's not giving up her title for anyone."

I was surprised by Cassie's bluntness. "You and your mother aren't close?" I asked.

"My mother and I barely take any notice of one another," Cassie said. "I'm an enormous disappointment to her, and ... well, I suppose she's an enormous disappointment to me." The words were said lightly enough, but I detected bitterness beneath them.

"What makes you a disappointment?" I asked.

"Mostly that I have absolutely no interest in getting

married. But also the fact that I want to study, go to university, join a profession." Cassie was ticking her list off on her fingers. "Then there's the clothes, the bicycle … so many things she doesn't understand or care to understand."

"A bicycle!" I exclaimed. I had seen them back in London. They looked like fun.

"I can teach you if you want," Cassie offered. "I've recently bought a new one, so you can borrow my old one. I call her Betty and she's perfectly serviceable."

"Would you really?"

"Of course." Cassie nodded. "It might actually mean that I get to have some fun during this whole tiresome event." She glanced at me. "I'm glad you're here."

And just then, just for a moment, so was I.

CHAPTER FIFTEEN

It was barely ten minutes later when the men returned, and I could tell from Lord Wynter's expression that it had been more than sufficient.

He didn't approach me at all this time; I suppose he thought that the prince had been left to stew long enough. Instead, Nicholas cornered Agatha and Helena, who were clearly torn between annoyance at being monopolized, and being flattered by his rare attention. In the end I think flattery won out, though I caught Helena watching me with narrowed eyes.

"At last, we have a chance to talk!" Stefan exclaimed, taking the seat next to me. Cassie had quit the room as soon as the men returned. I couldn't imagine her mother being pleased about that. Then again, perhaps, as Cassie had said, she wouldn't even notice.

"I thought you were more interested in dancing," I teased.

Stefan shot to his feet and held out his hand to me. "As the lady wishes."

"Sit down!" I laughed, tugging at his sleeve. "You'll disgrace yourself in front of our hostess!"

He fell into the seat. He was a large man, with a build more suited to a pugilist than a prince, but he wore it well. Once more I found myself warming to him. He seemed so ... solid. It was easy to imagine resting my head against that strong shoulder and unburdening myself.

We began to talk in a comfortable way. He was quick and funny and I didn't have to feign my amusement. In the ornate mirror over the fireplace, I could see our reflection. I barely recognized myself – laughing and polished, my sapphires dazzling in the firelight. The couple in the mirror made a well-matched pair – fair-haired and beautiful, obviously wealthy, with an air born of entitlement.

It was the life I could have had, I realized with a sharp twist in my gut. I might have laughed, I might have shone, I might even have married a handsome prince.

I might not have become so alone.

A loud, rather desperate laugh recalled me. Agatha was laughing uproariously at something Nicholas had said, all the while glancing at Stefan to see if he had noticed. *A bit too transparent*, I thought.

"She is very lovely, isn't she?" I said to Stefan. "Miss Weston, I mean."

"Hmm," he said. "Yes, she is. I confess, though, tonight my attention has been elsewhere."

I widened my eyes in surprise. "But – but I thought—"

"What did you think?" he asked.

I made a show of embarrassment. "It's just – Lady Scott-Holland – I had the impression that you and her eldest daughter had … something of an arrangement?"

I looked at him with as much innocence as I could

muster. Just a naive country girl, repeating what she had heard.

Stefan frowned. "I have a great deal of admiration and respect for Miss Weston," he said hesitantly. "But there is no such arrangement."

"Perhaps I misunderstood."

"I don't know why she should say that," he murmured, almost to himself. "Things are not so advanced..." He sat back in the chair and ran his fingers through his hair, then smiled ruefully at me. "Perhaps just a misunderstanding, as you say."

I felt a pang of sympathy for him. I could only imagine the scenes that followed him wherever he went. Many mothers would go to great lengths to make their daughter a princess.

Stefan cleared his throat. "I am – not yet attached," he said, rather haltingly. He lifted his eyes to mine. "But I hope, soon, that I may be. My grandmother has her own plans for me, but I would like to find a bride with whom I can share my life, one where there is love as well as duty. I would like to be a good husband, to one day be a good father."

The look he gave me was steady and I did not have to feign any reaction to it. I felt a blush rise to my cheeks, and I dropped my own gaze to my hands.

"Will you ride with me tomorrow morning?" he asked.

I started. For some reason, I hadn't thought about riding. "I-I can't," I stuttered. "I have made plans with Miss Cassandra."

This was true, while they had been out the room, Cassie had agreed that she would give me my first cycling lesson, but it was also a relief to have an excuse ready.

It had been a long time since I was on a horse. I had grieved that as I had grieved the loss of everything else. My first memories were of riding with my father, and I simply could not imagine life before then.

But to ride again ... *here*. It was too much. Was my father's horse, Hercules, still in the stables? Was my own? I hadn't let myself think about Asteria for a long time. Father had bought her for me for my eleventh birthday, and I had loved her with all of my battered, broken heart. Leaving her behind had been the hardest decision

I had ever made. I knew that neith[...]

Helena had been enthusiastic about [...]

sold the horses once my father and I we[...]

I realized that Stefan was talking, and I [...] to pay attention.

"—but perhaps another day?" he asked.

I nodded. "Yes, perhaps."

Stefan's brow furrowed. "Miss Fox," he said earnestly. "I hope I haven't made you feel uncomfortable. If I have been too forward…"

"Oh, no!" I exclaimed, impulsively resting my hand on his arm. "No, I have enjoyed our conversation … very much."

Stefan covered my hand briefly with his own. "I'm glad."

His hand dropped and so did mine, but I felt his touch linger. I flexed my fingers as if to dispel the sensation.

After that, we didn't get much chance to speak again. Lady Bell practically pushed Lord Percy over towards me, while simultaneously engaging Stefan in conversation, earning herself a smile from Helena.

Percy was shy and stammering and I felt sorry for

…n. It seemed I was not about to escape being the victim of a matchmaking mama either. The dangers of being an heiress, I suppose.

After we had struggled through some painful small talk, I leaned forward. "Do you know this is the first one of these things I've been to?" I said. "I'm feeling quite nervous about it. It's all a bit like being under a microscope."

There was a moment of hesitation, then, with a relieved sigh, he said, "Well, you're certainly better at hiding it than I am!"

"Perhaps we can muddle through together," I replied.

The smile Percy gave me then was not a bit shy, it was wide and adorable, and made me want to take him under my wing. A boy like that wouldn't last two days in my world.

Stop it.

The words echoed through my brain. I'd barely been here five minutes and I could feel this soft, comfortable life thawing my icy shell. It would be so easy to slip back into it, I realized with a jolt, to let myself become Serena Fox – untroubled and trusting and raised to privilege.

The thought was horrifying. I had left my home, *this* home, as a child. The woman I was now was no sheltered miss. She was hard edges, she was knives drawn in alleys, she was moonlight and shadows and London fog.

She did not belong.

I needed to remember that. I could feel my spine stiffening. Stefan was not my friend. Percy was not my friend. Cassie was not my friend. I just had to *pretend* to like them, because that's what Serena would do. She was a character, nothing more. I could not allow myself to be picked apart at seams that I had stitched together so carefully.

I was pleased to escape to my room as early as possible. Matilda was there, waiting to help me out of my jewels and gown and into a soft white linen nightgown. She had tamped down the fire so that the room was just the right temperature, and pulled back my bed covers, as if my own ladylike fingers shouldn't have to do anything so strenuous. She brushed my hair until it shone. I said little and examined my face in the mirror for any sign of weakness. I didn't know precisely what that would look like, but I did look pale and tired.

And the night wasn't over yet.

I thanked her distantly, and Matilda left. I sat on the edge of the bed, sinking into the crisp white sheets. I fought the urge to moan. I had forgotten that a bed could feel like this. I knew that if I lay down then it would envelop me, a light cloud of down and cotton. But I couldn't let myself sleep. There was still one thing that I had to do.

I don't know how long I sat there in the end. Long enough to be sure that everyone was in bed, long enough to hear the house settle into a thick, unbroken silence.

Then, I pulled on a pair of slippers and a warm red dressing gown, and opened the door, inch by inch. I had asked Matilda to leave me a brass candleholder and I held the candle up to the gap I was creating, holding my breath as it penetrated the darkness.

I wasn't sure how many people were staying in this part of the house, but the hallway was empty. The third stair down creaked, I remembered, and I stepped over it now.

I didn't have to worry about getting lost. I knew exactly where I was going.

I padded down the stairs, then headed down a long corridor until I had almost reached the dining hall. I paused here, my heart beating faster, the light from my candle sending shadows leaping across the walls.

In the dark, I knew my home better.

It was an overwhelming feeling. There was a scent so familiar to me, one of silver polish and beeswax, and something floral. One that transported me to a different time as efficiently as any horse and carriage moved from place to place.

The rooms seemed full of ghosts, and I was one of them. Images of my father dancing with me standing on his feet; my mother laughing as I breathlessly recounted some adventure I'd had in the village; a game I had played, knocking down pins by rolling a ball along the long corridor – these things flickered around me like the haunting, soundless new films that the Lumière brothers made.

I stood for a moment, frozen. Nausea rose up in my throat, and my hands grew clammy. My breathing was shallow, and I tried to steady it, to make my body silent.

I closed my eyes, took deep breaths. Eventually, I regained control. I turned to the service staircase and began to descend into the basement floor. I winced at each squeak that came from under my feet, stilling and listening carefully for any sign of detection.

When I reached the bottom of the stairs I turned left.

There it was. The faintest glow emanating from beneath the kitchen door, just as I had anticipated.

I turned the door handle and walked through.

A man sat at the table, his eyes lifting to meet mine. There was a woman with him who had leaped to her feet at my entrance. They were both wrapped in shadow, their pale faces illuminated by a single candle.

"Hello, Mr Tookes," I said.

CHAPTER SIXTEEN

"Oh, my!" the woman gasped, gripping the back of her chair as if to steady herself. "I didn't believe it. I *can't* believe it. When Tookes told me, I said he must be wrong – but it *is* you. It *is* you, Lady Iris, isn't it?"

"Yes, Mrs Chambers," I said, giving my old housekeeper a cautious smile. "It's me."

The three of us stood frozen like a painting. They were much as I remembered them from seven years ago – perhaps a few more lines and grey hairs, but that was all. Mr Tookes was tall and angular, and he wore his dignity like it was a part of his uniform. Mrs Chambers was small and spare, with dark hair peppered with silver, ruthlessly scraped back into a bun, and kind eyes. She was from the west country and her soft accent concealed a brisk, no-nonsense approach to the world. Between the two of them, they ruled over the household as efficiently as any battleship.

I wanted nothing more than to throw myself into Mrs Chambers' arms. This was a woman who had patched up my scraped knees, given me extra pieces of cake and winked and told me not to tell my parents, a woman who had held me as I cried over first my mother's death, and then my father's. I wanted to unburden myself to her, pour out my woes as I had once done.

Instead, I held myself stiffly, my back straight. I wasn't Iris Scott-Holland any more. I was Iris Grey. Or Serena Fox, depending on who you asked.

Mr Tookes was on his feet as well. "Please. Won't you sit?"

I slid into the chair across from them. I had tried to prepare myself for such a moment, but now that it was here, I didn't really know what to do or how to feel.

"Can I get you anything?" Mrs Chambers asked awkwardly. "The kettle's on the stove..." She gestured towards it.

"A cup of tea, if it's no trouble," I managed.

She bustled about, fixing the tea, as Tookes and I sat in silence, and then she placed the cup in front of me.

A little milk and half a cube of sugar. Exactly as I liked it. Something about that made my eyes fill, and I swallowed hard.

Silence fell again, and tension stretched between us, like threads pulled so taut they were about to snap.

"We thought you were dead!" Mrs Chambers burst out, quick tears filling her own eyes. Her voice was shaking. "Where have you been?"

"In London," I said.

"*London!*" Mrs Chambers exclaimed. I might as well have said the moon. "All this time?"

I nodded. "What did she tell you, the day I left?"

The two of them exchanged a look. They didn't need to ask who I meant. I had heard a brief account of Helena's story from my hired investigator, but I wanted to hear it from them.

Tookes cleared his throat. "That morning you didn't appear for breakfast. It was most unlike you." A smile tugged at his lips, then vanished swiftly. "By lunch time we were frantic. Her Ladyship said not to worry – that you were probably just out playing and had lost track of time."

"Lost track of time, perhaps," Mrs Chambers put in, "but lost track of two meals in a row? Never! And so I told her."

"Eventually," Tookes said, taking up the story, "it got to early evening and Her Ladyship sent some of the servants out to look for you." He let out a deep breath. "It was Jones, the stable boy, who found Asteria down by the river."

I stilled. Asteria was my Arabian mare, small, sleek and dark as a moonless sky. Father had named her after the Greek goddess, whose name meant "of the stars". A foolish purchase for an eleven-year-old, perhaps, but she and I had moved like a single shadow.

"There was no sign of you," Tookes continued, "but you know how strong the current can be down there…"

"They searched for you," Mrs Chambers carried on,

her voice breaking. "They couldn't find you, but they did find your hat further downstream. And then, of course ... you never came back."

Their faces were bleak, pain etched across them.

So that had been Helena's story – she who would have known that I had finally been driven to run away – she had left enough clues to hint at a tragic accident. No wonder no one had searched for me. I cleared my throat. "I never took Asteria out. I ran away the night before."

There was a pause. "But that means..." Mrs Chambers raised a hand to her ashen face.

I nodded. "Helena engineered all of that. She wanted me to be thought dead."

There was a moment of stunned silence as that was absorbed.

"*Why* would your stepmother do such a thing?" Mrs Chambers' tone was bewildered.

Tookes had sat back into the shadows, and his face was hard to read.

I watched them both for a long moment, trying to decide how much to tell them. In the end I decided to risk telling the truth. I had no idea if they would believe me.

"Helena killed my father," I said calmly. "I'm sure of it. And I believe that she was going to try to rid herself of me. One way or another."

Mrs Chambers gasped again, her hands shaking so much that her teacup clattered in its saucer.

"How can you say such a thing?" she exclaimed. "Oh, Iris – you were such a young girl, your imagination..." She looked to Tookes. Without a word he shrugged.

"Are you telling me you believe this too?" Mrs Chambers said.

I only had eyes for Tookes. "Do you?" I asked urgently. "Do you believe me?"

Tookes cleared his throat. "I don't believe she killed him, no," he said gently. "Mrs Chambers is right, you were just a child and you didn't get along with your stepmother. She didn't kill anyone – that's your imagination talking. But I don't pretend she was sorry to see your father go. You know how they were, Caroline," he said to Mrs Chambers. "The two of them at each other's throats..."

"Who?" I asked, startled. "Father and Helena?"

I had hated my stepmother, but I did not remember any arguments between her and my father.

"Yes," Mrs Chambers said reluctantly. "It had got very bad by the end, very bad." She fussed with her skirts. "But then you know what he was like, your father – always worrying that something was going on that he didn't know about. He was the same with your mother, you'll remember."

I stared at her. Fragments sifted through my mind, just for a moment – raised voices, accusing tones – but then they were gone.

"No, I don't know what you mean," I said.

"Oh." Mrs Chambers bit her lip. "Well, just that your father could be a bit of a recluse. Liked to have you all at home, didn't like a lot of entertaining. He liked the horses and some hunting and that was all. I suppose that meant his wife didn't have so much opportunity for socializing, and nor did you. I always worried that you were lonely."

"Lonely?" I repeated blankly. "No, I wasn't lonely. I had my parents." The words came easily, but for a moment I wondered if they were really true. *Had* I been lonely? I put this aside to think about later and returned to the matter at hand. "So Helena was unhappy before my father died?"

Mrs Chambers looked flustered. "I suppose so. They argued, I remember that. But that doesn't mean that she would ... that she would..."

"Father couldn't have fallen," I said firmly. "Not with his skill on a horse."

A different look passed between them then. Mrs Chambers reached across the table as if she were about to take my hand. I pulled my arm back, placing my hand in my lap.

"What is it?" I asked. "What aren't you telling me?"

"Iris." Her voice was full of sympathy. "There's something you should know about your father. You wouldn't have realized at the time – you were so young, and he was your hero."

"Go on," I said tightly.

She glanced at Mr Tookes and he nodded.

"He ... well, he liked his drink," she said. "A little too much."

"Oh, for goodness' sake," I laughed, disbelieving.

"Are you trying to tell me that Father was drunk when he fell? That's nonsense. I know he liked to have a glass of wine or two at dinner, and there was brandy in the library, but that's only the same as all the other gentlemen here right now."

"I don't wish to speak ill of His Lordship, especially to you," Mrs Chambers said, her voice more steady now, "but if you've been torturing yourself over this, you should know. It was more than that, when it came to him and drink. I don't say he wasn't a fine rider, but he didn't know his limits. He had a flask that he carried with him, so that he wouldn't have to go without. No one questioned what happened that day because it was all too easy to believe. I'm sorry, dear heart."

A memory flitted through my head then – the hard feel of something in Father's breast pocket when I hugged him. The sweet smell on his breath.

I pushed it away.

"It's impossible," I said. "And you" – I whirled on Tookes – "you said Helena was glad to see the back of him."

"I think she was. But that doesn't mean she killed

him," Tookes replied. "Your father's death was an unfortunate accident. You forget, I found the man myself."

I shook my head. "No," I whispered. "It was no accident. Why else would Helena be so keen to be rid of me as well?"

Tookes rubbed his temples. "There *was* some strange business with his will," he said slowly.

"What sort of strange business?" I asked.

Tookes frowned, trying to remember. "I don't know exactly. But they were arguing about it before he died, him and Her Ladyship. I heard raised voices – something about the will, I know that much." The sympathy in his eyes made me feel worse. "Arguments, maybe, Lady Iris – but not murder."

"I still don't believe that," I said stubbornly. "Maybe my father drank more than was good for him – he was still the finest horseman in the county and he would never have fallen. I'm here to find out the truth. But I need to know that you won't, either of you, give me away. No one must know that I'm here."

"How did it come about that you *are* here? Posing

190

as someone else?" Mrs Chambers' face puckered with worry.

"I have a friend. He got me the invitation and helped with a false identity." It was the best version of the truth I could manage.

"He?" Tookes asked blandly.

"I hope you haven't got yourself in trouble," Mrs Chambers fretted. "You know we would stand by your side … if someone … I mean, if he…"

Even after all the dire revelations of this evening, their worry almost made me laugh. They wondered if Nicholas Wynter had been making advances – which was about as far from the truth as possible. His whole plan revolved around getting another man to fall in love with me.

"No, no," I said. "It's nothing like that, I promise you."

They both looked doubtful but said no more on the matter.

"So will you keep my secret?" I asked.

"You know we will," Mrs Chambers said. "Though I don't like it." Her tone made me feel five years old again.

"Your objection is noted," I replied, pulling myself up as tall as possible, trying to remind her that I was an adult now, in control of my own destiny.

A smile played on her lips. "You look like her, you know. Your mother. She'd make that face when I fussed too much."

The words went straight to some vulnerable part of me and I felt a strange, sweet ache in my chest. "Then we should just be grateful that Helena never met her," I said stiffly. "Is there anyone else here who may recognize me?"

Mrs Chambers shook her head. "Her Ladyship let most of the staff go, not long after you ... disappeared. A handful stayed on – like Kielty the gardener and some of the grooms – but they've all retired now."

"Good," I said. "I should go."

They both nodded.

I got to my feet.

"Goodnight, Lady Iris." Tookes had risen smoothly from his seat and bowed.

"Thank you, Tookes," I replied calmly. "But it's Miss Fox now."

CHAPTER SEVENTEEN

The next morning, I sought out Cassie, ready for my first cycling lesson, and to begin to put my own plans into motion. Questioning Cassie about my father's death – as delicately as possible, of course – seemed the easiest place to start.

It had been late when I returned to my bedroom after talking with Tookes and Mrs Chambers, and they had given me a lot to think about. Too much. In the end, I think I had snatched only a couple of hours' sleep.

When I did sleep, I dreamed, as I had so many times

before, of the day my father died.

He had been out all day. He often had business to attend to, tenants to see, land to look over. Before Mother died I used to go with him more often than not. He'd tell me that I was in training, that one day I would run the place myself and that it was good to learn these things as early as possible.

We'd ride all over and then I'd go home and tell Mother all about the people we met and the things I had seen. She never came with us, but she always seemed interested in any story I had to share, no matter how small.

But after Helena had arrived, Father no longer took me with him. He went out all day alone, and I stayed with Cassie and Agatha, learning the sort of lessons little girls learned, from a new governess with a short temper and a passion for the under-gardener that she didn't think I knew about.

That day Father didn't come home. That wasn't unusual – sometimes he stayed out, went to the village with some of the locals to visit the tavern there. Those nights he'd come back late and sleep until the afternoon.

I assumed he had done that and went to bed. I think about that often, that last night when I was asleep, blissfully unaware that my whole life had been turned upside down again, that things were already changed for ever.

At the breakfast table, Helena's face was pale and pinched. Tookes came in and reported that no one had seen my father since the previous afternoon. She had sighed.

"Have some of the men sent to look for him," she had said. "He's probably just out carousing." Her smile didn't reach her eyes. Agatha was arguing with Cassie over a piece of toast, and I stared out of the window.

I remember it was sunny – a fact which seemed obscene later on – a peaceful, pastel-blue sky without even a whisper of a breeze, and a fat golden sun, like a child would draw in the corner of a picture.

As soon as I heard the shouting I knew that something was badly wrong. I ran out of the house and along the drive, but Mrs Chambers caught up with me, bundling me in her arms, dragging me towards the house.

She pulled me past Helena, who had come outside

too, her hands limp at her sides as she stared up towards the men moving slowly, leading the covered wagon.

I saw it then – just for a moment, there and gone in a blink, but burned into my memory – the look that blazed to life in her green eyes: triumph.

I had woken up from the dream in a cold sweat. The rush of memories, the nearness of the past now that I was here where it had all happened, had made the dream so much more vivid than usual. The feeling of loss crashed over me like a wave and I burrowed deeper under the blankets, suddenly cold.

All of this made for an uneasy mood. It was a relief when Cassie came thundering down the stairs, and I was temporarily distracted from my own troubles by her bizarre costume.

"Oh!" I exclaimed, unable to resist circling her like some kind of hungry lion.

"Do you like it?" Cassie asked with a smile.

"I do!"

Cassie was wearing a pair of brown tweed knickerbockers and a matching jacket. Unlike her gowns, the costume fitted her beautifully and was made of very fine materials. Her jacket had a bottle-green velvet collar and shining brass buttons. A small dark hat with the same green trim was perched on her glossy hair. She looked wonderful, but then I have found that most people do when they're wearing something that makes them feel fully themselves.

"What does your mother think about it?" I asked curiously.

Cassie grimaced. "She hates it, but I think she considers it a small price to pay for me to be off amusing myself. She's never been particularly concerned about having my company – for that she's quite satisfied with Agatha." She spoke briskly, pulling on a pair of dark leather gloves. "Come." She gestured outside. "I've asked the servants to bring both bicycles around to the front of the house."

I followed Cassie outside, and there were indeed two bicycles leaning against the wall.

"I haven't the faintest idea what to do," I murmured.

Cassie laughed, and hopped nimbly on to her bicycle, riding in swirling curlicues around the driveway. "It's very simple once you get the hang of it!" she called over her shoulder before arriving back in front of me and climbing off. "Let's take them further into the grounds. You need a smooth surface and a nice soft place to land."

We both took hold of our handlebars and I followed her, pushing my bicycle alongside me.

"You anticipate me falling off a lot, do you?" I lifted my eyebrows.

"Everyone falls off at first."

"Just like riding a horse."

"I suppose so." Cassie shot me a sideways glance. "Do you care for riding?"

I shrugged. "As much as anyone does."

"We have plenty of horses in the stable," Cassie said, "if you would like to ride. Most of them were my stepfather's. He was a fine judge of horses, and Mama kept them on. I think she believes it adds to her consequence." She snorted dismissively.

Questions immediately leaped to my tongue and I forced myself not to ask them.

Which horses? Was Asteria still here?

Still, I couldn't miss an opening like that one. "Your stepfather passed away some years ago, I understand?"

Cassie nodded. "Yes. It was only around a year after he and Mama married, so I didn't know him that well. It seems wrong, when he gave us all of this." She gestured at the scene around us.

Careful, careful, I thought. "He left Holland Hall to your mother?" I asked innocently. "I thought that big estates like this went to male heirs."

"Holland Hall hasn't been entailed for several generations," Cassie replied. "My stepfather had some rather progressive ancestors, luckily for us. Lord Scott-Holland left everything to my sisters and me, with an allowance for Mama."

"Sisters?" I feigned surprise. "I thought Miss Weston was your only sibling?"

Cassie's eyes slid from mine. "My stepsister. She died in an accident a few years ago."

"I'm sorry to hear that," I said. "But I'm sure the marquess would be happy to know he had left his estate in such good hands. Your home is beautiful." I made the words light.

"It is beautiful," Cassie agreed. "And, truthfully, I don't know what would have become of us without his

199

generosity. Our own father was ... not a good man, and as I understand it he left Mama in a terrible state with two young daughters to support. She and I may not be close, but she's always fought to provide for us."

Would she kill to do so? That was the question I could never ask. My own investigators had revealed that Baron Weston had been a gambler and a womanizer, leaving his wife and children nearly destitute after his death – a lengthy illness, with no sign of foul play.

I had never really considered what Cassie and Agatha had endured. Still, surely once Helena had married again then her daughters were safe?

There was some strange business with his will. That was what Tookes had said. There must be a clue there – but what? The terms that Cassie described – that everything was split between the three of us, and that Helena had her own allowance – meant their future was secure. My father hadn't denied his stepdaughters anything. Why would Helena have any need to kill him? Still, if Helena and my father had been arguing over it...

We were quiet as we walked through the gardens, and deeper into the park that surrounded the house, stretching on beyond the horizon in every direction.

Unlike being inside the house I found myself able to enjoy being outside. It was exactly as I remembered, untouched by Helena, who I assumed had left it in the hands of the gardeners and groundskeepers. I had only happy memories of being here, and it felt more like a homecoming than anything that had come before.

The October sunshine spread like a fine gauze across the landscape, illuminating the trees – a blaze of crimson and amber – as if we were surrounded by stained glass finer than you would discover in any church.

The air was sweet and fresh, and filled with birdsong. Leaves crunched beneath the soles of my leather boots, and I felt for a moment as though the weight had been lifted from my shoulders. As we climbed one of the gentle grass slopes I looked out at the undulating landscape, at the river snaking in the distance, at the small woodland where the red deer would be dozing peacefully under the golden canopy of the trees. Or perhaps not; it was mating season after all. Perhaps soon we would hear the roar of a stag, searching for his mate.

Home. My body sang. *Mine.*

"Here," Cassie said. "This is a good spot."

We were on a footpath cutting a gentle slope down through the grass.

"The first thing to learn is how to balance. There's hardly any slope here, but it's enough to help you glide without worrying about the pedals."

She showed me how to get on the bicycle. It felt strange and awkward, and I soon understood the reasons for Cassie's outfit. Wrestling with my skirts was an enormous issue.

"This is why the idea of rational dress has been around so long," Cassie said crossly. "These skirts give women no freedom to move."

"Precisely why people like them, I suppose," I huffed, still attempting to balance the bicycle without falling off.

"Exactly!" Cassie's eyes gleamed. "They don't want women to run or jump or ride bicycles. They want to cram us in tiny corsets that bend our ribs out of shape, and they tell us that wearing trousers will stop us from having children."

As a woman whose life was dedicated to clothes, I had thought about such things before, but hearing

Cassie talk with such passion was a new experience. My job was largely to make incredible gowns for fine ladies. There wasn't much call for bicycle-riding outfits. Perhaps that would change. One should never underestimate the power of good clothes: good clothes could start a revolution.

For the next hour I wobbled down the slope again and again, falling over in a tangle of skirts more than once. By the time Cassie and I made our way back to the house I was flushed and mud-spattered, my hair falling from its pins. We left our bicycles propped where we had found them and stomped into the entrance hall.

"I'm absolutely famished." I placed a hand over my stomach with a groan. "But I suppose I'd better go and make myself presentable, before anyone sees me."

"Too late for that," drawled a voice from the bottom of the staircase.

I swung round to find Nicholas – as meticulous as always – leaning against the banister with his arms crossed. His eyes travelled over Cassie and me with a questioning gleam.

I felt a pang of guilt, as if I had been caught out. I

supposed that I should be charming Stefan over eggs and toast in the breakfast room.

"What have you two been up to?" he asked. He didn't sound annoyed or interrogative, only mildly interested.

"Cassie has been teaching me to ride a bicycle," I said defiantly. It had only been about ten minutes into the lesson that we had become "Cassie" and "Serena" to one another. Something told me that Cassie wasn't too worried about keeping up the formalities.

"I see." His eyebrows rose. "How did she do?" he asked Cassie.

"Very well, for her first lesson." Cassie grinned.

I found that I was smiling too. I couldn't help it; it had felt wonderful.

"You look as though you enjoyed yourself," Nicholas said, and his lips quirked, as though he too was trying not to smile.

"I did," I replied.

"You'll do much better when you buy a proper cycling outfit with about a dozen less yards of material." Cassie tugged at my skirt.

"Oh, I—" I began awkwardly.

"Perhaps you could order one tomorrow?" Nicholas suggested. "I understand that some of the ladies are going into town to shop for the party on Friday." He hesitated. "It's nice to see you enjoy something so much."

There was a warmth in his tone; I supposed it was all for Cassie, who might notice his interest and report back to the others.

"Perhaps," I said.

"Are you going for breakfast?" Cassie asked.

"I am." Nicholas rolled his eyes. "Even though it is practically the crack of dawn. I can't stand these country hours."

"Crack of dawn!" I exclaimed. "It must be almost midday."

"I know," he sighed. "An ungodly hour to be awake."

He stepped aside then, allowing us both to pass him and head up the stairs.

I fought the urge to turn and see if he was watching me go.

CHAPTER EIGHTEEN

I washed and dressed quickly with Matilda's help. She twisted my hair into a simple knot, and I tugged on a plain powder-blue morning gown. My cheeks were still unfashionably pink from the exercise that morning.

The breakfast room was less formal than the dining room, decorated in light lemon yellow, with a long sideboard groaning under covered dishes that were constantly refreshed by the handsome footman standing inside the door. He looked like a Greek statue dressed in livery.

"Good morning," I said, as I entered the room. Agatha and Helena were both there. I knew that the colonel had already eaten because we had seen him that morning, and that Lady Bell and the dowager countess had both decided to eat in their own rooms. Jack, Sophia, Percy, Nicholas and Stefan were all present, and only Lord Bell was unaccounted for. A chorus of greetings rose from around the table.

"Miss Fox!" Helena exclaimed from behind her coffee cup. "Are you quite well? You look positively feverish."

"Thank you, Lady Scott-Holland," I said serenely. "I am very well, only a little pink from exercise. Miss Cassandra is obviously much fitter than I am."

"Oh, she hasn't had you out on that horrid contraption of hers?" Helena wrinkled her nose. "So unladylike."

The footman pulled out a seat for me, next to Stefan, and across from Nicholas.

"I enjoyed riding the bicycle," I said, leaning slightly to the side so that the footman could pour me a cup of tea.

"Bicycle?" Percy's face perked up. "I'm a member of the Cyclist's Touring Club, myself."

"Miss Cassandra is teaching me the ropes," I said, adding sugar to my tea. "She seems very proficient."

"I wonder if she's a member as well?" Percy frowned.

"Do you allow women to be members, then?"

"Yes, for almost twenty years," Percy said proudly. "People talk a lot of nonsense, but there is no rational reason why women shouldn't cycle just as well as men, nor why it would have anything but a positive effect on their health."

I smiled. It seemed the boy had hidden depths.

"Well, I loved it despite being only a very shaky beginner," I said, enjoying his enthusiasm.

"I think it has left you glowing with health, Miss Fox," Stefan said gallantly.

I thought I heard Nicholas snort into his tea, but I ignored that, directing my brightest smile at Stefan. "Thank you, Your Highness. That is a kind description of my windswept appearance."

Stefan laughed and lowered his voice. "Not at all windswept," he said. "Only very pretty."

"Speaking of exercise," Jack said from across the table, where he was sitting beside Sophia. "Some of us are going for a ride this afternoon. Won't you join us, Miss Fox?"

"Oh!" I exclaimed, remembering Cassie's comments about the stables. "I-I'm not sure."

"Please do," Sophia said, with a tentative smile. I knew that smile; I had last seen it on Claire when she was trying to befriend me.

"You must," Percy said firmly. "It will be fun."

"Perhaps," I said, as kindly as I could manage. I was still feeling very mixed up over the thought of even visiting the stables. And I wasn't sure about all these new friendships. I didn't want it to start feeling real.

"Serena," Nicholas said, "you haven't had a thing to eat yet, and you said you were ravenous. No, no." He waved away the footman who had started forward. "Don't trouble yourself, it will be my honour to serve Miss Fox myself." He gestured me towards the waiting sideboard.

I rose to join him as he picked up a plate.

"Nowhere in my etiquette manual did it suggest I

should be waited on by an earl," I said, my voice low beneath the bright chatter that Helena coaxed the rest of the group into. "I'm not even sure that you and I are supposed to make direct eye contact in public."

"I'm just being attentive," he murmured, uncovering a plate of kippers.

"Is there another way for you to show how attentive you are?" I grimaced. "I hate kippers."

He replaced the lid and moved on. "I needed to talk to you about the riding."

"The riding?" I asked, startled.

He nodded. "I should have realized that we'd come up against this. Don't worry, though – we'll come up with an excuse."

So he assumed I had never sat on a horse. I pressed my lips together to hide a smile. "Must we?" I asked innocently.

"Of course," his voice was stern. "Potted ham?"

I was briefly confused until I followed his gaze to the sideboard. "Oh! Yes, thank you."

"The easiest scheme might be that you feign some sort of injury," he continued. "Perhaps a twisted ankle.

It is inconvenient, of course, but it should serve our purpose ... it might even be an asset. Stefan would dance attendance..."

"Don't I get any say in this?" I asked. "I don't want to affect a limp on top of everything else. I won't remember which leg it's supposed to be. I'll end up lurching around like a pirate."

"In that case" – he pierced me with a glare – "I suggest that you remain seated as much as possible."

I looked at him from beneath my lashes. He was so sure of himself. I couldn't help it, I wanted to unsteady him, to leave him off-balance. And as easily as that, my decision was made.

"Do you know," I said airily, "I never thought riding looked all that difficult."

"Let me assure you that it *is* difficult," Nicholas replied through clenched teeth.

"I mean, you just *sit* there," I carried on, as if he hadn't spoken.

"*Miss Fox*," he hissed. "You can't ride like a lady and they'll see straight through you."

"I doubt it will be as bad as all that." I grinned. Then

I raised my voice. "No, thank you, not the kedgeree, I never can face fish in the morning," and I sailed back to my seat, leaving Nicholas gaping after me.

"I'd love a soft-boiled egg and some toast, please," I asked the footman, and then I took my seat.

"My, what an appetite!" Helena exclaimed gaily.

"Mmm," I agreed, digging into the plate of food Nicholas had made for me, "but then, I'll need to gather my strength. I've decided that I *will* ride this afternoon. Thank you for the invitation, Mr Waterford."

"Excellent," said Jack. I noticed that he was looking at his friend in obvious amusement. It was clear we had had some sort of disagreement. Nicholas was stony-faced with disapproval.

"Wonderful," Stefan agreed warmly. "I'm looking forward to exploring some of this beautiful parkland."

"What I saw this morning was spectacular," I said truthfully.

"I'm sure we can find a mount for you, Miss Fox," Helena said, in a way that implied it would actually be a tremendous ordeal.

"Thank you. Miss Cassandra was telling me this

morning that you keep an extremely superior stable," I replied.

Helena couldn't help but preen a little. "It is true that our stables are the envy of the rest of the county."

"More than one county, Mama!" Agatha trilled, making eyes at Stefan, who, it seemed, was a keen horseman. I repressed the urge to laugh. Agatha was (literally) trotting out her assets for his gratification.

"My late husband," Helena said, "had an exceptional eye for horseflesh."

The laughter died within me. She was talking about my father. There had been nothing in her voice or face when she mentioned him – no sorrow or grief, no sense of victory or gladness. They were just easy words.

"So your daughter told me," I said, keeping my voice steady. "Was he a keen rider himself, then?"

There was an infinitesimal hesitation, as Helena sipped from her teacup. "I believe he preferred his horses above any person he ever met," she said.

And who could blame him? I thought bitterly, longing to leap to his defence.

"Well, if we are to ride, then I had better go and

change," Agatha said, laying her napkin on her plate. She looked pleased with herself, and I knew why. Her new riding habit was extremely flattering.

The rest of our breakfast passed peacefully enough while Helena recommended various routes we might take – it seemed it was only the younger half of the party who would be setting out.

Undeterred by my stepmother's sly comments about my appetite, I ate a very hearty breakfast and enjoyed every single bite. I may not like the improvements that Helena had made to the house, but I couldn't deny that her cook was excellent.

Matilda was waiting for me upstairs, with a full riding habit laid out across the bed. I wasn't sure precisely how she had anticipated that need but I appreciated her hard work. I knew what it cost to spend long hours working only for someone else's enjoyment. That was something I would never have truly understood if I hadn't left this place.

The riding habit was a deep azure-blue velvet, with silver military-style frogging down the front, and silver buttons on the sleeves, embossed with the image of a fox – clearly Nicholas Wynter's idea of a joke. There was a matching hat: small and neat, in the same colour, with a ribbon of a slightly darker blue, a feather, dyed to match, and a short blue veil that pulled down over the top half of my face.

Matilda pulled all my hairpins out and styled my hair again, lower this time to allow for the hat. I couldn't imagine ladies being able to get anything worth doing done with all the time they had to spend changing their hair and their clothes.

It was strange, being Serena. Like a glimpse of what could have been. There were things that I liked about her life, but also things that I didn't. It already felt like every minute of the day was accounted for, but there was little to show for it.

Still, I thought with a shiver of excitement, there were *some* compensations.

And I set out for the stables.

CHAPTER NINETEEN

I had timed it well, arriving before anyone else. It had blossomed into one of those days that felt more like late summer than autumn. Only the slight breeze saved it from being too warm in my new habit.

The stables were a series of low buildings on the west side of the house. In my father's day, they had been where the money went. He may not have added his own wing, or decked out the house in luxury, but the stables were world-class, immaculate and filled with prime horseflesh.

Now I saw that some of the shine was off. They were still obviously looked after – I couldn't imagine Helena allowing anything to fall into disrepair – but there was not the same sense of energy, the same number of grooms and stable hands busy at work.

I wandered along the long row of stalls.

Several stood empty that had once been filled. Some of the horses had obviously been sold – I wasn't sure how much Helena's allowance was. It would have cost a lot to maintain for someone who didn't have a passion for it.

I spotted Helena's grey, and Agatha's chestnut mare. There was a new horse that must belong to Cassie, and there were several of my father's horses still here. Helena must have been well-advised, because she had kept the cream of the crop, including my father's stallion, Hercules.

I approached Hercules' stall cautiously. Part of me was afraid that he wouldn't know me and that would feel somehow like a rejection from someone dear to me. His dark head bobbed up, over the gate, and he whickered.

I held out my hand and he lipped at my fingers. I

scratched his neck and tried to keep myself from crying. It was almost as if he was a piece of my father.

"I know, I know," I sang softly. "I miss him too."

There was a thump on the wall that divided the stalls, and I felt an answering one in my chest. She had heard my voice. She knew me.

"Asteria," I breathed.

There she was, beautiful as ever. Her dark coat gleaming, that imperious way she shook her head, the dangerous spark in her eyes – I remembered it all. I felt the velvet of her muzzle tickle my hair, and for a moment I stood, my face pressed to her neck, just as I had as a child.

I could hear footsteps and low humming and a moment later, a stable boy came round the corner. "Hello, miss," he said. "Is everything all right?"

I gave him a watery smile. "Of course," I managed. "I was just saying hello. There are some real beauties in your stables."

"Yes, miss," the boy said. He grinned. "Though that one there's usually wary of strangers. You must have the touch!"

"I must have," I agreed, reluctantly taking a step

back. "I'll get out of your way and wait in the yard."

I turned and hurried back towards the doors. I could hear the boy humming again to himself as I left.

I emerged, blinking, into the sunlight.

"There you are!" a voice snapped. It was Nicholas, with a face like thunder. He swept his eyes over me and frowned. "Is something the matter?"

"No," I said gruffly. "It's nothing."

He looked at me for a long moment. "I know what it is. You've seen the horses, and now you've realized what you've got yourself into."

"What? No! I—"

He carried on, regardless. "We can still tell people you're hurt. It could be even better actually," he said thoughtfully. "That way Stefan gets the full effect of you in the riding habit too. I knew it would be spectacular on you."

"You – you—" I stuttered incoherently. "I am not a piece of meat in a butcher's window!"

He raised his eyebrows. "I never said you were. In fact, I said you looked spectacular."

"You most certainly did *not*," I snarled.

"Well, anyway." Nicholas cut me off with a wave of his hand.

Ooooh, I wanted to stomp on his shiny black boots.

"Of all the supercilious, patronizing, *arrogant*..." I exploded.

"Don't forget insufferable," he put in. "I believe you said I was insufferable the first time we met."

"You *are* insufferable," I snapped. "And ... and ... that green does absolutely nothing for your complexion!"

He held up his arm and eyed the sleeve of his beautiful hunting-green riding jacket. "Really? I thought it was nice, but I suppose you're the expert."

I took a deep breath. "Then perhaps you'll listen to me. I would like for you to stop underestimating me. I—"

"Hallo!" a voice behind us called, and I saw that Percy, Jack, Sophia, and Stefan were approaching.

Stefan's face clouded briefly at seeing me in Lord Wynter's company; but then his eyes widened as he took in my figure, elegant in the riding habit. Nicholas had chosen well.

"Lovely day for it," Percy said cheerfully.

"We're just waiting for Miss Weston," Sophia observed.

"And, more importantly, the horses," Nicholas replied. "Ah, here is Jensen now."

I saw Nick's groom, leading Felix out towards us.

"And here's Miss Weston," Jack said.

"I'm sorry to have kept you all waiting," Agatha said, a smile playing on her lips.

She had stage-managed the moment to perfection. She stood in a shaft of soft sunlight that fell across her dark shining hair, illuminating her skin so that it had the look of flawless porcelain. The rich red habit skimmed her curves and brought out the hint of green in her eyes. I had no doubt that once Agatha was seen in London wearing the habit, Madame Solange would be turning away customers desperate to recreate it.

"It is a pleasure to wait for such a vision as you make this afternoon," Stefan said somewhat breathlessly.

"Oh, Your Highness!" Agatha's laugh was self-deprecating. She went over and linked arms with Sophia. "I always think a really good riding habit is something every woman should invest in – don't you, Sophia?"

It may have seemed innocent, but Agatha was her mother's daughter. Next to Agatha, Sophia looked pale and drab in her ill-fitting habit, and the flush on her cheeks said that she knew it.

"I-I suppose so," she said, smoothing her own outfit, which was threadbare.

"We are fortunate to be out for the day with so many lovely young women," Jack said, smiling at Sophia, who rallied somewhat under his kind gaze.

I found myself liking Jack more and more. He seemed easy-going, gentle and kind – and I wondered why on earth he was such good friends with Nicholas. I suppose they do say that opposites attract.

My mind turned again to Lord Wynter's recent insults, and I surreptitiously flicked my whip through a small, muddy puddle that lay between us.

A spattering of mud pebbled audibly against the side of his shiny boots, and I smiled sweetly. "Oh dear."

I had to admit that his glower was quite impressive, but seeing the dirt that now marred his perfect boots gave me a sharp snap of satisfaction. I felt my smile grow wider.

We were interrupted then by the stable hands leading out the rest of the tacked-up horses. Like Nick, Jack and Stefan had brought their own horses and grooms, but the rest of us were making use of the Holland Hall stables.

There was no sign of Asteria. Sophia had been brought a pretty bay, and I a dappled grey whom I recognized.

"Hello, old girl," I whispered, holding her long face in my hands for a moment. I fished out the sugar lump from my pocket that I had stolen from the breakfast table.

"This here is Biscuit," the stable boy said. "'Fraid she ain't much of a goer, miss."

Biscuit crunched the sugar cube in my hand and butted at me with her nose, searching my pockets for more. "Oh, I don't know," I laughed. "There may be some life in her yet."

"Let me help you," Stefan said, striding towards me. He guided me gently to the side of the horse, cradled his hands for me to step into, then threw me up into the saddle. I adjusted my skirts and looked down at him.

"Thank you, Your Highness."

Stefan stood for a moment looking up at me, his hand resting on the horse's neck. "You look very well up there, Miss Fox."

"I feel very well," I said. "Perhaps Biscuit and I shall give you a run for your money."

He laughed then, that deep, happy laugh that echoed my own feelings at the moment, and looked pointedly over at his own mount, an enormous grey, who must have been at least eighteen hands.

"I wish you luck, Miss Fox."

With that, he strode over to his horse and mounted with ease.

Nicholas rode up beside me, looking predictably splendid even with mud-spattered boots. "Well, there's no going back now," he said, eyeing me with a displeasure that may have been masking anxiety.

"I should hope not," I replied, and with a flick of my whip I was off.

For all of my bravado, I had wondered whether I might have forgotten how to ride; but the instant I took the reins I knew that I could have no sooner forgotten this than my own name. I felt anticipation taut in my limbs; the longing to lengthen the reins and fly across the ground was like a hunger gnawing at my bones. Still, I took it easy at first, riding alongside Sophia, who I noticed rode well.

"You enjoy riding, Miss Fox?" she asked.

"I do, though I admit I'm a bit out of practice." I glanced towards her. "You?"

Sophia nodded. "I used to love it."

"Used to?"

Sophia bit her lip. "I'm surprised you don't know all about it."

"If it's town gossip then I assure you I'm the last person who would hear it," I said. "There's absolutely no obligation for you to tell me either, whatever it is."

Sophia hesitated for a moment. "No," she said at last, "I'd like to tell you. It will actually be nice to talk to someone about it myself, rather than knowing it's all passing through the rumour mill."

Sophia took a deep breath. "My father made some bad investments several years ago," she said. "The property he inherited was already in debt and part of an entail, so he wasn't allowed to sell any land off. For generations the Bells have been stretched further and further."

I nodded.

"I'm afraid it's all become quite dire," she sighed. "It seems..." She trailed off awkwardly for a moment. "Well, it seems my father has got into trouble with several wagers that he made recently. Large wagers."

I felt my mouth thinning. Like Agatha and Cassie's father, Lord Bell seemed to have no care for the consequences his actions may have for the women in his family.

"I don't think my parents are foolish enough to hope I'll make a good match – other than my name, there's very little to recommend me," Sophia continued with a frown. "It's my brothers I worry for. Poor Percy ... my parents will try to marry him off to an unsuspecting heiress, I suppose, though I don't really think he's the marrying type..." She raised a gloved hand to her mouth. "Oh! I shouldn't have said that."

"Don't worry," I said. "I expect they're doing what they think is best for your family. As for me, I like your brother very much, but I am certain we wouldn't suit each other – nothing you've said has changed my opinion of either of you, one bit."

Sophia looked relieved. "Anyway, that's why there's been no riding lately. No horses."

"That's a shame," I said. "You ride well. We shall both just have to make the most of every opportunity to take out Lady Scott-Holland's horses while we're here."

"Yes!" Sophia's face crinkled into a smile with the same sweet quality as her brother's. "You're right, Miss Fox. It is pleasant to have someone to ride with."

We rode in silence for a while, but it was a strangely comfortable silence.

We made our way further into the park, twining through clusters of trees until suddenly the view opened up as it had this morning. We were closer to the river now, which shimmered off to the side of us, like a trail of iridescent-blue ribbon stitched into the landscape.

I found myself alone, taking it all in, tipping back my head to gaze at the cloudless sky stretching over me. It had been a long time since I had left the city. There did not seem to be this much sky there.

"What do you say, Miss Fox?" Stefan appeared at my side. "Will you give me a *run for my money* as you had it? Down to the big oak tree by the river?"

The truth was, I was itching to let go and run, to feel the wind on my face. I required no encouragement from Stefan, indeed I felt like a firecracker already lit.

"You're on!" I exclaimed, but the words were already being carried back to him on the breeze, as I streamed forward, coaxing Biscuit into a reluctant gallop.

I could hear Stefan laughing behind me, and I leaned closer to Biscuit's neck, whispering in her twitching ears, urging her forward.

It was no surprise to me when her pace picked up. I knew all of Biscuit's tricks, knew exactly what she was capable of.

After all, I was the one who named her. Who else but a five-year-old girl would have come up with the name Biscuit?

"Because she's so sweet, Papa!" I had said, stroking her nose.

"Just like you, my little cub!" Father had laughed.

It was like flying.

It was *better* than flying. My body relaxed into the smooth gait, until I could hardly tell where the horse ended and I began. The landscape rushed away beside me – broad watercolour strokes of green and gold.

Stefan drew up beside me, his grin a blur of white, a streak in the sky as he passed.

I didn't care. He reached the oak tree only just ahead, and he let out a loud whoop as I pulled up.

"That was wonderful!" I exclaimed.

He brought his horse up beside me and looked across, his cheeks pink, his eyes sparkling.

"*You* were wonderful," he said, leaning over and brushing a strand of hair away from my face, his fingers gentle against my skin.

Our eyes held for a long moment.

"We'd better get back to the others," I said, turning away and fussing with Biscuit's reins.

"Of course," Stefan replied.

We trotted towards the group, who were noisy in their appreciation.

"I thought you might have had him beat for a moment, Miss Fox!" Percy exclaimed excitedly. "And on that horse as well! I never saw anything like it!"

"Shush!" I scolded, patting Biscuit's neck. "She can hear you, you know."

"She's a darling, isn't she?" Sophia too was animated. "Ran her heart out for you just because you asked."

"I'd love to see what you could do on a real goer," Jack said. "Miss Weston, you'll have to tell the groom to choose a more suitable mount for Miss Fox."

"Indeed," Agatha said frigidly. "If only Miss Fox had made us aware of her skill beforehand I'm sure something could have been arranged."

Jack gave me the faintest wink then, and I thought that he saw a lot more than he let people know.

Stefan swept in, giving them a point-by-point account of the race. Agatha tried to look enchanted by his skill but was obviously seething.

Nicholas caught my eye and I dropped back with him.

We rode without speaking for a while.

"I told you to trust me," I said at last.

Silence.

Then, finally, "It seems I was right about one thing,"

he murmured, treating me to a long, unreadable look. "You certainly don't ride like a lady."

The laugh that erupted from me then was one of pure delight, and when I looked over, I thought that even he was smiling.

CHAPTER TWENTY

The rest of the day was uneventful. Percy's enthusiastic retelling of my race with Stefan went down as well as one might imagine with Helena, who proceeded to spend the entire evening making small, sharp comments as skilfully as a surgeon with a blade. It was death by a thousand cuts, as I smiled at her and she smiled at me.

In the end, I didn't have to feign a headache to retire early. I winced as Matilda pulled out every pin, and collapsed into bed. My muscles ached from the riding, and from being squeezed into such a tight corset while

I ate dish after dish at dinner. *Wouldn't it be heaven to eat dinner in my nightgown?* I thought dreamily. So much more room. Tonight, there had been brown bread ice cream, and sherry syllabub with cherries, and lemon trifle wrapped in a cage of intricate sugar-work. Despite my best efforts I had been unable to do it justice.

I lay there, my mind ticking over. I hadn't realized how time-consuming being a society lady would be – there had been no opportunity to investigate my father's death, and time was something I didn't have the luxury of. I frowned, gazing up at the ceiling, and my mind returned to what Tookes had said about the will.

I hadn't been at the reading of the will – I was too young. No one had been in a hurry to explain it to me, and so while I knew the general terms were as Cassie had said, I had no other ideas as to the specific bequests. I thought about the horses, my mother's jewellery ... surely Father wouldn't have wanted that to go to my stepsisters?

I rubbed my nose absently. I had been looking at this through the eyes of a child, but I wasn't one any more. Maybe there was more to my father's will than I knew.

And if Tookes was right, the will might well be at the centre of Helena's machinations.

I groaned. It didn't make any sense – surely Helena had a handsome allowance whether my father lived or died. Why had they been arguing about it?

Then I sat upright. Here was something tangible that I *could* do. I could try and find a copy of that will.

But how to go about it? The family solicitor was hardly going to disclose it to Serena Fox, nor could I waltz in declaring myself Iris Scott-Holland. Perhaps there was a copy somewhere. Perhaps *Father* had kept a copy.

Perhaps there was a copy in the house.

And, I thought, if Father *had* kept a copy, then I had an idea where it might be, and there was also a pretty good chance that Helena had absolutely no idea about it.

Of course, it did mean another late night.

With a tired sigh I settled in to wait.

I was almost dozing off, my romance novel in my hand, when the clock in my room chimed one o'clock. Surely that was late enough for everyone to be in bed.

As I had the night before, I drew my dressing gown around me, tying it tight, and I picked up my candle.

This time, though, it wasn't the servants' quarters I was heading for. It was the library.

I crept through the winding hallways until I reached the right door. I paused, listening, to make sure no one was around, and then I slipped inside.

"Oh, god," someone groaned as I stepped through the doorway, illuminated by the light in my hand. "It's you."

"Lord Wynter?" I asked, dismayed, moving around so that I could see the figure sprawled in an armchair in front of a fire that had burned down low. He had discarded his jacket and his hair was rumpled. He did not look at all like his usual polished self.

"Lord Wynter?" He raised an eyebrow. "I thought I told you to call me Nick."

I took a step forward. "What are you doing here?"

"I might ask you the same question."

"I couldn't sleep. I came to get a book." I gestured around the room at the walls lined with shelves, filled with thousands of books. Some of them, I knew, even had the words *Iris Scott-Holland* written inside their covers in uneven calligraphy.

I loved this room. It smelled of leather and wood and burned earth, and, despite its size, it still felt cosy. My father had an office but he had always preferred to work in here, often with me playing at his feet. I glanced around; his desk had gone, though that didn't worry me – it wasn't his desk I had come to search. Not that it mattered now... I could hardly do any sleuthing with Nick here.

"Your turn," I said. "What are you doing here?"

He held a glass in his hand, full of something that glowed like amber, lit from within in front of the fireplace. "I couldn't sleep either." He frowned into the glass. "I tried a different solution."

"Drinking and glaring into the fire?" I laughed. "You really can be a cliché, Lord Wynter."

"Not drinking," he said with a reluctant smile. "One drink. Speaking of clichés, here you are, creeping around in the dead of night in your dressing gown, holding your candle aloft in trembling hands. You might as well be in one of those books you're always reading.

Will the ghosts and spectres appear soon?"

"A spectre *is* a ghost," I said crossly. "And I'm not trembling, I'm shivering because the floor is cold and so are my feet. Besides which, there are no ghosts in this library, only sulky young men." This was true; everyone knew that the ghosts kept to the east wing of the house – the part built by the Mad Baron three hundred years earlier.

"What an unromantic imagination you have," Nick sighed, leaning back in his chair, his eyes closed. He looked weary, I thought – suddenly older, frown lines etched between his brows.

"Well," I said awkwardly. "I'll leave you to it."

"What about your book?" he asked, his eyes still closed.

"Oh, yes." I turned to the nearest shelf and plucked one at random. "Got it." I held it up, and his eyes peeled open.

"*The ABC of Bee Culture?*" He raised an eyebrow at the gilt title picked out clearly by the light from my candle.

"I have recently become very interested," I said, "in bees."

"There's a lot more to you than meets the eye," Nick said. He still hadn't moved from his chair.

"I'm sure the same could be said of anyone," I replied cautiously, making my way towards the door.

"Are we going to talk about it?" he called.

I turned back to face him. "Talk about what?" I asked, clutching my book so tightly that my fingernails pressed into the leather cover.

"What you're really doing here," Nick said calmly. "How you ride better than anyone I know."

"I-I don't know what you're talking about." I fought to keep my voice even.

He sat back in his chair again and gestured to the seat beside him. "Will you join me for a drink?" he asked.

"It's late."

"But you can't sleep."

His eyes held mine for a moment, full of challenge. I knew if I decided to leave that he would let me go. He really was *asking* me. It wasn't an order.

"Very well," I said in a clipped voice. "One drink." I made my way to the other armchair and sat, my feet curled up under me. I set the book and candlestick on the side table that stood between us, next to the silver tray that contained glasses and several bottles of old brandy.

He poured a splash of the brandy into another glass and handed it to me. Our fingers touched. The sleeves of his shirt were rolled up, his shirt collar undone, revealing a small V of flesh at the base of his neck.

The sparks in the fire jumped, as though it were about to catch light again.

A shiver ran over me, one that had nothing to do with the cold floor.

"For your cold feet," he said, as if reading my mind. He raised his glass to me.

I took a sip, only a small one, feeling the liquid flames burning down my throat, stinging my eyes.

We sat in silence. The logs in the fire popped and crackled, the sound splintering the air between us.

"What do you want to know?" I asked.

"Who taught you to ride?"

"My father did," I said. Nick left a space for me to expand on that information, but I didn't. I simply took another sip of my drink. He was right, my feet were warming up.

He looked at me thoughtfully. "Nothing to add?"

"What else is there to say?" I shrugged. "He's dead now." The words fell hard and sharp between us, like shards of something broken that could not be put back together.

"What was he like?"

I shot a glance at him, but the question didn't seem pointed. It seemed more like he knew that I wanted to talk about my father. I wanted to talk about him quite desperately, actually, especially since Tookes' and Mrs Chambers' revelations. I couldn't, though, and certainly not with Nicholas Wynter.

"He was very important to me," I said quietly. "Riding today made me think about him."

Nick absorbed that. "He taught you well," he said finally.

"Yes, he did."

"Have you got any other hidden skills that I should know about?"

I tipped my head. For a moment I considered telling him about the blade currently hidden in the pocket of my dressing gown.

Perhaps not.

"I'm a decent shot." I shrugged. Quite scandalous enough, even though these days there were ladies who took part in shooting contests. Still, I had a feeling that Nick would not be so easily shocked, and I was right.

A glimmer of a smile played across his lips. Something in that look made my stomach flip. "I'm not considered too bad myself," he said. "Perhaps a wager is in order. A competition."

"What? Now?" I asked, startled. I didn't think Helena would be too keen on firearms in the library, and on this front, I couldn't blame her. Think of the books!

Nick chuckled. "No, not now."

"Ah." It was my turn to smile. "Running scared?"

"I am learning not to underestimate you."

I liked that.

Our eyes met.

"Tell me," he murmured after a moment, his voice soft. "Why did you come here, really? I don't think it was for the money."

I hesitated. Part of me actually wanted to tell him, to

lay out the whole messy story, but I knew that I couldn't. *Fugitives don't have friends*, I reminded myself.

"All right," Nick conceded as the silence stretched out. "Let's drop the matter for now. Tell me, how are things going with Stefan?"

I straightened in my chair. "They're going well, I think." I thought about my race with Stefan, of the admiration in his face when he looked at me, and I felt an unwelcome twist of guilt.

"I believe it's going *very* well." Nick leaned forward, resting his elbows on his knees, scrubbing his face with his hands, in a way that left his hair even more dishevelled. "The party on Friday will be a good opportunity to make sure of him."

"I think it's my turn to ask you a question," I said. He stilled. "Why do you want to do this to Stefan? What happened between the two of you?"

He carefully placed his glass back on the table. The burgeoning warmth between us, the undercurrent of some sort of understanding, was gone, as if it had never been there at all.

"I told you," he said. It was as though the temperature

of the air around us had dropped. "That is not an area that is up for discussion."

I exhaled slowly. "How can you ask me to trust you with my secrets, if you won't trust me with yours?"

"I don't require your trust," he said. "Only that you do the job I am paying you for."

I got to my feet. Did he think he was the only one capable of putting up a wall?

"Very well," I said with all the dignity that I could muster as I stood there, barefoot and in a dressing gown. "I am glad that we have clarified our positions. I believe there is no more to say on the matter."

He had returned to glaring moodily into thin air. I picked up my book, and the candle which had burned itself out. It hardly mattered. I knew my way through the shadows of this house – after all, I had become one of them myself.

"Goodnight, Miss Fox." His voice was little more than a low rumble.

"Goodnight, Lord Wynter," I replied.

CHAPTER TWENTY-ONE

The day was already off to a bad start. Not only was my headache back, not only had I not been able to search for the will, *not only* had I been fuming all night after my conversation with Nick, but this morning I had to go shopping. With Agatha.

And I was going to have to smile the whole bloody time.

I was living in my own personal nightmare. I couldn't even summon a kind word for Matilda, wincing silently as she did my hair.

"Something loose today, please," I murmured. "I have a bad head."

"Of course, miss," she replied. After working in silence for a moment, she asked in a hesitant voice, "Are you going out with the prince? Just the two of you?"

"No, I'm going into town with the ladies. Why do you ask?"

Matilda's eyes dropped from mine in the mirror. "No reason, miss," she said quickly. "He's extremely handsome."

"Yes." I smiled. "He is." I supposed Stefan was quite the romantic figure below stairs.

The weather outside my window was very different from the day before – grey and flat, with pebbles of rain striking the glass. It did not seem like auspicious weather and it suited my mood.

As I descended the stairs I met the dowager countess, who was on her way back up.

"There you are," she said, giving me her habitual once-over and nodding grudgingly as if to say I was just about up to standard. "You and I need to talk."

"Of course, Lady Wynter," I said demurely. "About

245

anything in particular or will commonplaces do? This weather really is awful, isn't it?"

"That's enough of your sass, young lady." The dowager countess fixed me with a gimlet eye. "I want to discuss my wastrel of a grandson with you."

"Would you call Lord Wynter a *wastrel*?" I asked. "It's not the first word that springs to mind." *Arrogant, overbearing, stubborn*, perhaps.

"I'd call him an impertinent young rascal," Nick's grandmother replied tersely. "But then he always has been my favourite."

I laughed then. I couldn't help it.

"I'm afraid I'm expected downstairs," I said as meekly as I could manage. "We're going shopping."

She sniffed derisively. "Well, run along, then. But don't think you're wriggling off this particular hook. You and I *will* talk."

On that note she swept up the stairs, leaving me in her wake.

When I finally arrived downstairs, one of the footmen told me that the rest of the ladies were waiting in the morning room. The morning room had been one of my mother's havens. I steeled myself to enter.

When I stepped through the threshold, I was assailed by images of my mother, images that were hazy and out of focus. My father I remembered as clearly as if he were standing in front of me, but with my mother it was a different experience. Trying to build a picture of her was like trying to catch on to a cloud. I saw an embroidered handkerchief, felt the soft warmth of her hand around mine; there was the tinkling sound of silver bangles on a slender arm, the smell of ripe strawberries.

This room was bright and sunny and decorated in the colours of spring.

"Ah, Miss Fox, there you are," Helena greeted me. "I do hope you have recovered from your headache?" Her tone was pleasant, which immediately had me on my guard.

I was surprised to see Cassie in the room, alongside Agatha, Sophia and Lady Bell. She gave me a look that told me it was not by choice.

"I *have* recovered, thank you," I replied, not exactly truthfully.

"Won't you sit and have a cup of tea with us while

the coach is made ready?" Helena asked. She gestured to a seat.

"Of course." I moved to sit, when I was stopped in my tracks.

I thought I'd been erased from the house completely, but there, on the wall that I was walking past, in an unassuming silver frame, was a piece of embroidery ... embroidery that I had stitched myself.

A simple scene of the river beneath the moonlight. I remembered the day I had finished it. It was just after my father had died, and Agatha had given me a bobbin of pale silvery thread from her own embroidery basket. It was the one nice thing I ever remembered her doing for me. I had been beyond being able to talk to anyone, but Agatha and Cassie had sat next to me while I worked on it. Almost like sisters.

I felt a catch in my throat. "What a lovely piece of embroidery," I said.

Helena glanced at it. "Oh, yes," she said. "One of Agatha's pieces from when she was a little girl. Such an accomplished young lady. I tell you, Miss Fox, there's nothing she can't turn her hand to."

Agatha smiled complacently. *That* was more like the Agatha that I knew. Taking credit for someone else's work. My own smile was thin, my eyes lingering on the stitches that I had made in my darkest hours. There had been a piece of me out on display for everyone to see for all these years, despite Helena's best efforts to pretend I had never existed.

"So, you girls are off for a morning's shopping, are you?" Lady Bell said brightly. "How nice that will be."

"Well, we have to collect Cassie's gown," Agatha said. Of course, there would be no modish London-made dress for Cassie, not that I should imagine she minded that much. "And I must choose some new gloves for tomorrow night," Agatha continued. "Perhaps something for my hair as well. I'm determined to do something a little different. I'm so glad that I can get your opinion, Miss Fox." She beamed at me. "You have such excellent taste."

I almost spilled the cup of tea I had been handed. Now *Agatha* was being nice to me? She and Helena were definitely up to something.

"That's kind of you to say," I replied. "Though you certainly need no advice from me on that score."

Agatha's laugh was bell-like, but Cassie's face grew increasingly grim.

After another few minutes of painful small talk, Tookes entered to let us know that the carriage had been brought around. I noticed that he was careful not to meet my eye as he departed.

Cassie linked my arm with hers as we walked out of the room.

"Why is your sister suddenly being so nice to me?" I asked in a low voice.

"No idea," Cassie whispered back. "But don't trust a word that trips off that forked tongue."

I smothered a giggle at that. "What are you doing coming on this outing anyway?" I asked. "I thought you'd have had the good sense to get out of it."

"Do you think I didn't try? Mama insisted, and sometimes it's simply not worth the argument. Anyway"– her frown lifted – "I have some books to collect from the bookshop, so it won't be a *totally* wasted journey."

The four of us were to travel with Matilda, and

Agatha's maid, in the enormous family carriage that loomed over us on the driveway. It was new, impractically cream coloured, with the family crest – *my* family crest – painted on the doors in gold.

The inside was all rich red velvet. It was more suited to a member of the royal family than young women out for a day's shopping. It must have cost a fortune. It was becoming increasingly obvious that Helena had spent an enormous amount of money in the last seven years. Still, I knew that Father had inherited a fortune tidy enough for his daughters to call themselves heiresses. That money had grown, thanks to my grandfather's savvy investment, particularly early on in the railways.

What I didn't know were the precise details of Father's will, and how much of the money Helena had access to. I thought of last night and my failed attempts to search for my father's papers. I would just have to try again.

"Isn't this cosy?" Agatha sang, as we rattled along. "How pleasant to get away from the house, even in this miserable weather."

Sophia smiled back at her. "Yes, much better than being cooped up indoors."

I wasn't sure she actually believed that, but I could tell she was gamely trying to be a good guest.

"I think indoors is the perfect place to be in this weather," Cassie grumbled. "Anyone who says different is a fool."

Sophia sighed and I gave Cassie a sharp elbow in the side. She looked up, catching sight of Sophia's despondent face.

"But it's nice to get the chance to spend more time together," she said, clearly making an effort.

"It is," I said encouragingly. "Tell me, Lady Sophia – I know you're an accomplished rider. Have you ever thought to try the bicycle?"

"The bicycle?" Sophia frowned. "I don't think Mama would like it." She hesitated, her eyes darting nervously to Agatha, who was sitting prim and straight in the corner opposite me. She seemed to muster her courage. "But I always thought it would be exciting to try."

Cassie's eyes lit up. "It is! Miss Fox will tell you, and I have to say she made such good progress, even in just one lesson. Perhaps you could join us next time?"

Sophia flushed with pleasure. "I would like that," she said.

The conversation continued, Sophia urging Cassie on with questions not only about Cassie's experience of cycling, but also of the mechanics of it, which my stepsister was only too happy to explain.

"Well, Miss Fox." Agatha leaned towards me, speaking softly. "How nicely you handled that. Bringing them both out of their shells. You have the kindest heart."

Beneath Agatha's honeyed talk I could hear the calculating tone. So that's what the friendly act was about ... she was on the lookout for weaknesses, and I needed to remember that I should have none.

"No kinder than anyone else, I assure you."

"Always so modest," Agatha smiled, her eyes wide. "Sometimes, Miss Fox, I think you seem almost too good to be true."

CHAPTER TWENTY-TWO

I was still mulling over Agatha's choice of words while she pored over the display of gloves in the dressmakers'. Was it simply a chance phrase – or was she more astute than I had given her credit for?

I chewed my lip. I was being paranoid.

"What do you think, Miss Fox?" Agatha asked, holding up two pairs of gloves in front of a mirror.

"The lemon kid ones," I replied. "They'll go better with your gown."

"Now, how do you know that?" Agatha asked, her eyebrows lifting.

Damn. "Cassie mentioned you were wearing yellow," I said, as easily as I could manage. "I asked her – I wanted to make sure what I had was suitable. I haven't been to many balls." I was laying on the innocent country girl act as thick as possible now, and Agatha shot me a sharp look.

"I'm sure that whatever you have to wear will be perfectly suitable," she said. "You haven't put a foot wrong since you arrived."

"You're very kind to say so," I murmured.

"Cassie," Agatha turned away from me and called to her sister, "you should try on your gown." I felt my shoulders slump in relief.

Cassie yawned elaborately. "Why bother?" she said, with a tiny wink in my direction. "No one will be looking at *me*, Agatha, not with you there."

Agatha's smile of satisfaction curved in the mirror. "I suppose that *is* true," she said. Then, like a cat lazily sharpening her claws, her eyes settled on Sophia.

Sophia was perched uncomfortably on the edge of her

seat, trying and failing to look relaxed. Her face was all too easy to read. This shop in Rochester might not be as elegant as Madame Solange's, but Sophia still stood out like a sore thumb in her dingy grey dress.

"Dearest Sophia," Agatha purred. "I hope you have something suitable for tomorrow night. Perhaps we could pick up something to go with it? A new fan, some gloves, a new pair of stockings?"

"I-I don't think so," Sophia said.

"Are you sure?" Agatha asked, her voice all kindness. "I hope you won't mind me saying, but as a *friend* I think I must warn you that you're in danger of becoming something of a dowd." As she spoke, she ran her eyes appraisingly over Sophia. "I know how modest you are, but there would be no harm in a few pretty touches, I assure you. I'd hate for you to be embarrassed."

"I-I can't… That is, I'm not…" Sophia stuttered, a deep red flush washing over her face.

"Actually," I said getting to my feet, "Sophia and I were going to join Cassie at the bookshop. I believe Cassie has some things to collect?" I widened my eyes at Cassie.

"Oh – yes!" she exclaimed, pulling a watch from her pocket. "And look at the time. We'd better go before … before they close."

"Close?" Agatha's nose wrinkled. "It's barely lunch time. These country hours are so provincial."

"Will you be all right with your maid?" I asked sweetly. "Unless you'd like us to wait so that you can join us? I understand from Cassie that one can spend hours in the bookshop here."

"Ugh," Agatha sniffed. "If you want to spend all your time in a dusty old bookshop, that's fine with me. I have several new things to get, ribbons and a new shawl, and that hat in the window was rather sweet…"

With Agatha sufficiently distracted, Cassie and I hustled Sophia out of the shop, Matilda following a half-step behind.

Once out on the street I released my vice-like grip on Sophia's arm. "Spiteful cat," I said, forgetting myself for a moment.

"W-what?" Sophia asked, startled.

"Agatha," I said smiling ruefully. "I know I shouldn't say it, but … really!"

Cassie snorted. "You've got that right. Don't take it personally, Sophia. It's just a game to her. She's like my mother – enjoys watching people squirm."

My stomach turned over at that.

When my father had told me that he was going to remarry, I had tried hard to believe that gaining two sisters would be wonderful. But I was soon proved wrong.

Cassie, overwhelmed by the new house and the new situation, had been largely silent. I remember only that her watchful eyes held mistrust whenever they came to rest on me or my father.

Agatha, though, had loved to torment me. At first the incidents had been small – a pin cushion slipped on to my seat, favourite toys going missing – but soon she had discovered a new game: telling tales.

She told Helena that I'd ripped her dress, that she saw me stealing tarts in the kitchen, that I'd pulled her hair, or that I'd knocked Cassie down. It didn't matter that the stories weren't true, because Helena believed them – or pretended that she did – and she doled out my punishments with an enthusiasm that bordered on glee. She began to whisper into my father's ear about his wayward daughter, that I'd grown too wild after my mother's death, that I'd been lacking a firm hand, that I needed *discipline*.

That had been a long time ago, but still Cassie's words made me feel sick. *It's just a game to her.* That was what I had felt – that Helena and Agatha got pleasure out of hurting me. As a child it had been bewildering; as an adult it made me furious.

Now, the games may be more civilized, they may lie beneath a veneer of snide society gossip, but Agatha was still playing her same tricks on Sophia, making her feel as small as possible. Well, I wouldn't have it. It wasn't only Helena I was planning to punish, I reminded myself. Agatha was going to get a taste of her own medicine, as well.

"Let's go to the bookshop," I said, slipping my arm through Sophia's.

Sophia said nothing, but she squeezed my arm. I tried to remember that I wasn't her friend. Not really.

Rochester was the same pretty town that I remembered, and we wound our way through the cobbled streets, the castle slipping in and out of view.

I had always loved the castle. It was perfect, neat and square, with four turrets, precisely as a child would imagine it. When Father would bring me into town, I used to pretend that I was a knight, off to rescue the princess from one of its towers.

As we wandered towards the bookshop I noticed a building several doors down with a shining brass plaque mounted on the wall.

J.F. Fortescue Esq.

Solicitor

I had a sudden memory of my father taking me through that front door. Of a room with a hard chair where I waited, bored, while Father conducted business. There was a smell of tobacco and leather, the rustle of paper, and several harried-looking young men rushing about with papers in their hands.

I glanced back at the door as we walked past it. My father's solicitor. All the information I needed about his will was right there, and if I were Iris Scott-Holland I could just walk in and ask for it. I gnawed on my lip. There had to be another way.

When we pushed through the door to the bookshop a jaunty bell rang out. The inside of the shop was warm and quiet. There were long, tall shelves, creating a warren of books that seemed to stretch on for miles. In places where they had run out of space, the books were stacked up to the height of a person. It seemed Cassie had been speaking literally; you could really lose yourself in here.

In silent agreement the three of us split up, each wandering off to explore. I found myself searching for the romance novels. They were the only things keeping me awake long enough for my night-time snooping, after all.

The shop had a welcome stillness about it. That sometimes happened in rooms full of books. Strange, when each book, each page, each line was filled with a clamour of words and voices, that being in a room full of them should be so peaceful.

I ran my finger along the spines, searching for promising titles. *The Game and the Candle* – that sounded like it had potential.

I was too busy looking at the books to realize there

was someone else in the aisle with me until I banged into him, quite hard.

"Oh, excuse me—" I began.

"My fault—" he said at the same time. And then we looked at one another.

It was Nick, of course.

"Are you following me?" I hissed, all of my frustration from the night before reaching an instant boiling point inside me.

He looked startled. "Of course not," he replied, though I wasn't sure if the words came a shade too quickly.

"You knew we were coming shopping today." It is difficult to make your voice sharp and accusing when you are whispering, but I managed it all right.

"To the dressmakers'," he pointed out.

I eyed him suspiciously.

"I didn't follow you," he said steadily.

I crossed my arms.

"Good grief, woman," he snapped. "What do you want? A blood oath?"

"It would be a start."

The corner of his mouth quivered. "If you *must* know," he said, "I came to get you a present."

"What?" I was totally wrong-footed by that. Especially when he held out a parcel wrapped in brown paper. "You've already given me too much," I said quickly.

"That was for Serena Fox," he replied. "This one is for Iris Grey."

He was still holding out the parcel and so I took it from him.

"Thank you," I mumbled, with a distinct lack of grace.

Nick shrugged, and for a moment he looked awkward. It was not something I had observed before. "About last night..." he began.

I waved my hand. "You were right," I said. "I'm your employee, you owe me no explanation for your actions."

"I—" He raked a hand through his hair. "That is... It's not—" Finally, he let out a sound that was suspiciously like a growl.

"Well put," I murmured.

He glared at me, took a deep breath. "What I came here to do is important," he said finally. "I can't afford to make a mistake. However," he said lifting a finger, "I didn't mean to be so abrupt last night. I hope that we can continue to work together … as colleagues."

"Colleagues?" I repeated.

He nodded tersely.

I frowned down at the parcel that I was holding. "Very well," I agreed, holding out my hand. "Colleagues."

I thought that a look of relief flitted across his face and then he took my hand in his own, shaking it firmly. I tried not to pay attention to the tingles shooting up and down my fingers where he held them. It didn't feel like something that a colleague would dwell upon.

"Hello." Cassie's voice came from behind me. I saw Nick's usual look of sleepy amusement fall across his face, like a curtain at the end of a performance.

"Cassie!" I said, turning. "I ran into Lord Wynter."

"I can see that," Cassie said, clearly trying to hide a smile. "How convenient."

I felt the colour rise to my cheeks. She thought we had arranged some sort of secret meeting.

It was then that I realized I was still holding Nick's hand.

My blush deepened and I dropped it. Nick's eyes gleamed and I could tell he was enjoying my discomfort.

"Ladies." He nodded. "I believe that is my cue to leave."

Cassie and I watched him go.

"So…" She raised her eyebrows. "*Is* there something going on with the two of you? The others all said so – they said they had never seen Lord Wynter so taken with someone – but I wasn't sure if it was just gossip."

"I – no – I…" It was my turn to stutter. I had no idea what to say. Would it help or hinder the plan if Cassie thought she had interrupted something?

"Don't worry about me," she said airily. "I don't gossip with anyone."

I settled for silence, which seemed to answer Cassie's question anyway.

"Will you like being married, do you think?" Cassie asked.

My first instinct was to turn and run away rather

than answer the question, but I forced myself to remember that as far as Cassie was concerned, I was Serena Fox and getting married was pretty much my reason for being.

"I hope, when the time comes," I said, "that I will be very happy being married."

After all, despite Father's disastrous second marriage (a marriage that ends in murder can hardly be said to be a success, can it?), his relationship with my mother had been a different story. They'd been happy … hadn't they?

I cast my mind back for memories of the two of them together, and could land on nothing tangible. It seemed in my mind as if they were two totally separate entities. Still, I supposed that made sense. I had been so young.

"I would never marry someone," I said, the thought only becoming clear to me as I said it, "if I couldn't trust them with my happiness."

Cassie only made a low humming sound in the back of her throat.

"You said you had no interest in being married?" I asked.

"That's right." Cassie nodded.

"Perhaps you haven't met the right person yet?" I said carefully.

Cassie grinned. "It's not that," she replied with confidence. "I just don't have those type of feelings for people. I never have done."

"What do you mean?"

"When people talk about romance, attraction, that sort of thing, or when I read about it in a book, I find I can't quite understand it – I struggle to imagine those feelings." She shrugged. "It used to worry me, but now I don't mind. Thanks to my stepfather, I have an inheritance that affords me a lot of freedom, and when I turn twenty-one my mother can't stop me from using the money. I shall be an exceedingly happy woman, travelling and studying to my heart's content. I suppose I *might* marry one day – if anything changes – but the choice is mine, and I know I'm fortunate in that respect. There are plenty of women like me who won't get such a say in their own lives."

I looked at her for a long moment. Cassie had described her life in such clear terms, with poise and certainty. We both knew that it was largely my father's money that gave her that privilege – it was hardly a typical situation for a young woman – but still, I admired her self-assurance.

"Your plans sound wonderful to me," I said. "Where would you like to study? In London?"

Cassie nodded. "To begin with." The gleam in her eye and the tilt of her chin let me know that these were just the start of her plans.

"Well, that explains the enormous stack of books." I gestured to the pile she was holding.

"I know," Cassie sighed. "And these aren't even the ones I'm supposed to be collecting today. We're going to need some help getting them back to the carriage. Perhaps we should have held on to Lord Wynter."

In the end, it took Cassie, Sophia, Matilda and me, as well as the shop assistant, to carry all of Cassie's well-wrapped parcels to the carriage, where we handed them off to the footman and the groom.

"Agatha must be done by now," Cassie said. "Let's go and collect her and have a cup of tea."

"An excellent idea," I said, as the two started walking

over in the direction of the dressmakers'. "I'll be right behind you."

It took me only seconds to tear into the parcel I had been clutching since we left the bookshop. A book – of course. I turned it over in my hands so that I could read the title.

Bees and Beekeeping, Vol.1

I huffed a little laugh as I opened the cover. Inside in a scrawling hand was an inscription.

For your recent interest ... in bees.
N

CHAPTER TWENTY-THREE

It was rather later in the afternoon than we had anticipated by the time we arrived home. Cassie had guided us to the local tearoom where they made a particularly good pudding-pie, a custard tart filled with nutmeg and sherry-soaked raisins, and we had spent a happy hour there, drinking tea and talking. The only cloud on the horizon had been Agatha, and she was really more of an oncoming thunderstorm.

At first, she had largely ignored us, looking around for people she knew; then she had grown bored and decided to give us a lengthy description of everything she had purchased that day, down to the last pin. This too was not so bad, because I simply let her voice wash over me and focused on the delicious pie in front of me – it deserved my full attention.

My concentration drifted back in, just in time to hear her say to Sophia in a low, musical voice, "Of course, *I* should be mortified to be seen in it, but you're so much more resilient! To think how little you care for keeping up with fashion, or what others say about you ... well, I think it's brave, I really do!"

Sophia had no choice but to thank Agatha for her kind words while Agatha smiled like a shark, showing her teeth. I could feel my own teeth grinding, but I forced myself to say nothing, crumbling the remaining pastry in my hands to dust.

I was silent all the way home, simmering with anger – and not only over the tragic waste of a good pastry. Sophia, who had been so bright and full of fun when the three of us were alone, was now once more reduced to a pale shadow, nodding vacantly at everything Agatha said. That was when I had the idea.

Once we got back to the house, I caught her arm.

"Lady Sophia, may I speak to you in your room?"

Sophia looked startled, but agreed at once, showing me up the stairs and down the corridor until we reached the suite of rooms that the Bells had been given. We had called it the green suite, for obvious reasons, but I could only assume that Helena had changed the name, as it was now fitted out in a hundred different shades of pink, from blush to tiny splashes of fuchsia. It felt a bit like being inside a flamingo.

We went into the bedroom assigned to Sophia off one side of their small private sitting room. I noticed that her possessions looked rather shabby and threadbare when contrasted with all the opulence around them.

"Is something wrong, Miss Fox?" she asked nervously.

"Not at all, Lady Sophia," I replied. "I only wondered if I might take a look at your gown for tomorrow evening."

Sophia instantly blushed up to the roots of her hair. "W-why?"

"Because my maid is a miracle worker with a needle," I said briskly.

Sophia laughed. "Your maid?" She shook her head. "Miss Fox, to be blunt with you, I'm afraid it wouldn't matter if your maid was Charles Worth himself, there's nothing to be done!"

Her tone was slightly hysterical, and I knew that all of Agatha's carefully planted seeds were blooming now. Even though Sophia and I were the same age, I felt about a hundred years old.

"There is *always* something to be done. Show me."

Responding as I had hoped to my nanny-ish tones, Sophia reluctantly made her way to the armoire and removed the gown.

"You see," she sighed. "It's hopeless. Everyone will laugh at me."

"Nonsense," I said, stepping forward and taking the folds of the dress between my fingers. "The silk is good quality, and the shade suits your colouring." I held the dress up against her, relieved to see that the yellow silk brocade lent a bit of colour to her cheeks. "The fit, I will admit, borders on criminal, and it's about eight years out of date." I pinched the sleeves and sighed. I was extremely glad that the fashion for bigger and bigger puff sleeves had finally died a death – these were so voluminous, they must have drowned Sophia. One of her mother's old gowns, made over for her, I thought. "But there are certainly things that could be done."

"Do you really think so?" Sophia asked, a tiny thread of hope in her voice.

"I really do. Now, ring the bell and we'll get Matilda in here with a tape measure."

By the time I was done with Sophia, the air had cleared, and the sun seemed, finally, to be rallying.

I found that I wanted to be alone. It was strange, to be here with so many people, when I was used to being left alone with my work at Madame Solange's. I had colleagues, of course, but we certainly didn't socialize. I was used to being by myself – it was a choice I had made. I was finding it all a bit claustrophobic in the house, and instead of attending the card games that I knew were taking place in the drawing room, I decided to sneak out for a walk in the gardens.

I pulled my shawl around my shoulders and ventured out in the direction of the rose garden. It had always been a feature of Holland Hall's gardens, famous for the clever planting that meant that different roses were out all the time, blooming right into the winter. The rose garden was a gorgeous, showy splash of colour, and the heavy, sweet scent it gave off, carried down pathways to meet you. *Follow your nose*, was often the best instruction for helping people to find it.

It had also been one of my mother's favourite parts of the grounds. She wasn't one for hearty walks over parkland, but I remembered her sitting on the bench in the sunshine in the rose garden, as fragile and lovely as any of the flowers.

The gardens were beautiful in summer, but I liked them now too. I liked the quiet sleepiness, the elegant way that the plants folded themselves away for winter. I liked the surprising, defiant pops of colour from flowers that seemed to know just when the spotlight would be available – the hot-pink nerines, the flame of an orange chrysanthemum, the sunny lilac of a cluster of Michaelmas daisies.

I moved down the stone paths, past topiary ruthlessly groomed, like a grand lady, with not a hair out of place. The rose garden was hidden behind a long brick wall with an archway cut into it. Already, that heady perfume was coiling towards me, and I breathed in deeply. For a moment I saw dappled sunlight filtered through green leaves, an arm around my waist, tickling me as I laughed so hard, I could barely breathe, the smell of strawberry cake and the feel of cool pale silk under my sticky fingers.

Since I had returned to Holland Hall, I felt like a mystic receiving unwelcome premonitions at every turn. The memories were like ghosts on the other side of a gossamer-thin divide, reaching out to speak to me, and I had no control over them or when they might appear.

I wandered through the archway and was struck by two things: how beautiful the garden remained; and that Prince Stefan had clearly been looking for escape too.

He sat on the bench, his elbows resting on his knees, his hands clasped loosely in front of him, staring ahead. At the sound of my footsteps, he looked up.

"I'm sorry," I said, already taking a step backwards. "I didn't mean to disturb you."

Instantly, he was on his feet, holding out a hand as if to stop me.

"Please don't go," he said. "I was only enjoying a moment in this beautiful garden. But now, I think, with the addition of Miss Fox, it is lovelier still."

"How good you are at these pretty compliments, Your Highness." I smiled. "Tell me, do they come to you spontaneously, or do you think them up months in advance and keep them ready in a little notebook?"

He grinned. "A prince must always be prepared."

I laughed then and closed the distance between us.

"Please, won't you sit?" He gestured towards the bench, and I took a seat beside him.

"This is probably extremely improper," I pointed out. "Being alone like this."

"Ah, but I won't tell if you don't," Stefan said.

"It will be our secret."

We sat quietly side by side, appreciating the view that the garden presented. I found his warm, solid presence beside me peaceful, and I enjoyed the fact that he felt no need to make small talk. The feeble warmth from the sun wrapped itself around us as the walled garden kept the chill breeze away.

After another moment, Stefan spoke. "I think –

forgive me, Miss Fox, if I am wrong – but I think, like me, you are perhaps finding the amount of company overwhelming."

I glanced at him, surprised. I had been given to understand that the prince was an extremely sociable sort of man, one who enjoyed the press and clamour of society life.

"Yes," I admitted. "I am. I suppose I am used to a quiet life. I'm having a lovely time," I hastened to add. "It is only sometimes the lack of solitude that can be..." I trailed off.

Stefan nodded in understanding. "I feel this too," he said. "When I am in England it is like one long party."

"That doesn't sound so bad."

"Most of the time it is not. But no one wants to go to a party that does not end."

"I suppose not."

"When I am at home, in Saxe-Illyris, my life is a much more solitary one. I walk a lot, and I ride, and" – here his mouth lifted up in an adorably shy half-smile – "I write."

"You write?" I asked.

He reached into his pocket, and pulled out a small notebook, handing it to me. Flicking through the pages I saw lines written in a language I didn't understand. The handwriting was neat and uniform.

"What is this?" I asked. "I was only joking when I asked if you prepared all your compliments in advance, but now I'm not so sure."

Stefan puffed out his cheeks, exhaling a sound like a nervous laugh. "It is poetry, Miss Fox, or my poor attempt at it, at least."

"You're a poet!" I exclaimed. I don't know why I was so surprised; I suppose it didn't go with my image of the man.

He shrugged. "I try to be."

"Will you read me one of your poems?" I asked.

"Oh, no!" Stefan took the book from me. "I read it to no one, not even you." His eyes softened. "But, perhaps, one day."

It was as if I had landed right in the middle of one of my romance novels. If I was a proper heroine then this would be the moment that I would surely melt into his arms and we would profess our undying love for one another. I even felt myself swaying ever so slightly towards him, as though it was inevitable that it should end this way. Our hands were side by side on the bench, our fingers lightly touching.

Only then, the truth hit me. We were not in a romance novel, and I was not in love with Stefan. I pulled away.

"We'd better get back to the house before anyone misses us," I said.

"Of course." I let him guide me away from the romantic setting, from the enchanted garden where prince and princess meet.

Because, of course, I wasn't the heroine in his story.

I was the villain.

CHAPTER TWENTY-FOUR

That night I could make no attempt to search the library. The "small reception" that Helena was giving the next day turned out to be much larger that I had thought, with at least a few hundred guests – which meant the servants would be up most of the night preparing. I suppose one didn't entertain royalty in the neighbourhood very often.

I knew it would be far too risky to go snooping around in the dark. Instead, I stayed in my room and worked on Sophia's gown.

Matilda had not missed a beat when I introduced her to Sophia as an incredibly skilled seamstress, and together we had taken Sophia's measurements. Despite what I had said, the gown was in bad shape, and I had to unpick most of it. It was hard work – particularly without the assistance of a sewing machine – but by the time my candle had guttered down I was pleased with the outcome. That would take some of the sting out of Agatha's remarks, I hoped. Sophia deserved to feel beautiful.

I had spent the last two nights chasing shadows into the early hours of the morning and that night I fell asleep almost as soon as my head touched the pillow. Unfortunately, dreams raced after one another through my head: Agatha's cruel smile as she tugged at Sophia's new gown, tearing it to ragged strips. Stefan holding out a book of poetry to me. I could read the words now and they were all about me. He held me in his arms. And then we were dancing, but it wasn't Stefan at all, it was Nick, Nick with those ice-cold eyes, and I was drowning in them, and – somewhere far away – Helena was laughing and laughing.

I woke with a start.

Matilda was there, drawing back the curtains, and she had set up a tray beside the bed. Hot chocolate from a silver pot.

"Thank goodness for you, Matilda," I croaked. I had asked her to wake me early, and she had taken me at my word.

"Did you really do this, miss?" I lifted my head from the pillow to see Matilda standing in front of Sophia's gown.

"No," I sighed, sinking back. "You did."

There was a pause. "That's right kind of you, miss," Matilda said finally. "Lady Sophia is a nice lady from what I've seen, and she deserves to have something beautiful to wear tonight."

"It was nothing," I said, embarrassed.

"I don't think it will be nothing for Lady Sophia," Matilda replied, her eyes still on the gown. She had that same look that Mrs Turnbull had worn when she saw me in my ball gown, the same outstretched fingers, not quite daring to touch.

"I can make one for you, Matilda, if you want," I

said. "A dress, I mean. If you'd like. When this is all over."

The words came out before I had thought about them, and I frowned. What was I doing, offering to make dresses for people? Madame Solange was going to have me chained to my workbench as it was. All this high living was making me soft.

Matilda smiled. "I'd love that, miss. When this is all over."

Although she was only repeating my own words back to me, they still sent a shiver down my spine.

When this is all over.

Time was running out. I had been here for almost a week now and while Nick's plan might be coming together nicely, I was no further along in my investigation. Despite what Tookes and Mrs Chambers had said, I still felt certain that my father's death was no accident.

I had to find that will. It was my only lead.

I threw back the bedcovers. If the staff had bumped into me or seen me rooting around in the library in the middle of the night, it might have caused a scandal. But no one was going to bat an eyelid if I was in there in the morning, looking for a book. That was why I'd asked Matilda to wake me at this ungodly hour.

"Right," I battled a yawn. "Help me throw something on, and fetch me two bedsheets. I mustn't waste any time."

If Matilda was confused by this request, she didn't show it. Instead, she helped me to get dressed in record time, in a particularly pretty smocked lilac gown, and I left the room not five minutes later without a hair out of place.

On winged feet I made my way downstairs. It was not even seven o'clock. I was willing to bet that most of the house party guests were sound asleep. The colonel and Cassie were the only ones who tended to rise early, and it was extremely unlikely they'd be downstairs yet.

I passed several members of staff, but kept my gaze haughty, my steps firm, as though I had every right to be going where I was going – which I suppose I did; after all, I was a guest, and guests were perfectly welcome to use the library. I'll admit that the fact I was *clutching a pair of bed sheets* probably *was* unusual, but none of them turned a hair, not even the maid who was actually in the library pulling the last of the heavy curtains aside.

"Oh!" she exclaimed. "Sorry, miss. We're a bit behind because of the party, but I'm all finished now."

"Thank you," I said with my most gracious smile and a slight incline of my head. "That will be all." I was perhaps laying it on a bit thick – I sounded like a member of the royal family – but the girl looked suitably awed and scurried off at once.

I shut the door firmly behind her, dragging a chair in front of it for good measure. Then I stood in the middle of the room for a moment, listening hard for anyone who may be like to come in. Now that the room had been opened up for the day, it was unlikely. It would just take a bit of nerve, that was all, and I straightened my shoulders, reminding myself that I had plenty of that.

When my father had been alive, his desk had stood in a large recess created by the tall bow window near the mantelpiece. There were, I knew, at least two secret places where he may have hidden important papers.

First I headed straight for the mantelpiece. It was an enormous carved affair, covered in a design of climbing vines and very ripe fruit and stalks of wheat – the kind of thing that usually had some hidden message about prosperity and fertility and long healthy family lines. As far as I knew the fireplace had stood there for the past two hundred years, though it could have been older – the oldest part of the house was over three hundred years old.

I felt my way down the right-hand side of the fireplace, peering closely at the carvings until I spotted it. There, hidden in the vines, was a tiny pair of crossed keys. I ran my thumb over them, and pressed. A small square button – only visible now that I had put pressure on it – sunk into the wood, and there was a tiny clicking sound, followed by an almost inaudible groan, as a panel swung open in the side of the fireplace surround.

The groan was enough to tell me that no one had opened it for several years, and my heart stilled as I pulled the panel open to reveal a hollow, about the size of a book. There was something in there ... a piece of paper, folded roughly in four. I pulled it out with trembling fingers, and smoothed it.

The words were written in a child's round hand.

Papa,
When you get home tuday shall we take a carot
for Biscuit? I wud like to brush her tale.
Ssssh! It is a secrit!
Love from
Iris

I didn't remember writing it, but Father and I used to sometimes leave messages for one another in this spot when I was little. Whether he had seen this one and put it back, or never read it, I wasn't sure, but the simple words made an old ache twist in my chest. It was a message from a golden time, a time when my father and I had been always together, a time before Mother had died and Helena had descended on us. It was a message from a different Iris, one who knew nothing about fear or pain or anger. I folded the note back up and slipped it into my pocket. It reminded me what I was fighting for.

However, it was not what I was looking for, and so I shut the panel and glared grimly at the fireplace. There was another place to investigate, but Father would only hide something there if it was of the utmost importance.

Which I suppose meant it was the perfect place to look.

Should I risk it? No one was around. They wouldn't be for hours. This was as good a chance as I was likely to get.

With a sigh, I kicked off my shoes and slipped off my dress. Then I picked up the bed sheets from the chair where I had left them, and wrapped the first one around my body, as though I were preparing myself to be entombed in an Egyptian pyramid. I shuffled over to the fireplace and stepped into the grate (thankfully quite clean, due to the early presence of the maid). I held the second sheet over my head, covering my arms and face as much as possible, and bent under and up into the chimney itself, slowly unfolding until I was standing completely upright.

I needed to be quick.

I could only imagine the look on Nick's face if he had to clarify to Helena why his family friend had been found standing in a chimney in her underwear, shrouded in bed linen.

Actually, it would almost be worth it.

I reached my fingers out into the dense blackness

until I touched brick. It was much closer to my face than I had imagined. I kept trailing my fingers over the bricks, left to right, counting as I went until I found a brick that stood out ever so slightly from the rest of the wall. I pressed this, feeling it give under my fingers, then I counted two bricks down and one to the left and I pressed this one too. This brick popped out and I scrabbled to get a hold on the edges, slowly and carefully pulling it towards me and out of the chimney wall.

Now it was time for the bit I really hated. My breathing came sharp and fast, loud in my own ears. I slid my hand into the gap created by the missing brick and groped around. In the pitch darkness I had no idea what my fingers might encounter, but finally I felt them brush against something.

I took hold of the object and pulled it out. I had no idea what it was, but it had to be important for my father to go to the trouble of hiding it like this. My hands were shaking as I put the brick back into place, and climbed awkwardly out of the chimney, blinking at the light streaming into the room.

In my hand was a bundle wrapped in cloth –

presumably to protect it from the soot. I laid it carefully in the grate beside me. Helena kept a pristine house so the chimney wasn't as bad as it might have been, but the sheets I was wearing were fairly covered in streaks of soot, as were my hands and feet. I peeled off my stockings before stepping out of the grate, and carefully removed the sheets. I cleaned my hands as best I could on the other side of the sheets before dropping them into the fireplace, then I slipped into my dress and slid my bare feet back into my shoes.

The whole thing had taken perhaps less than three minutes, but I was breathing as if I had just run a race. I picked up the bundle and looked at it for a moment.

My fingers itched to open it, but I knew that I shouldn't, not here. I'd already pushed my luck by searching for them uninterrupted. It was time to go.

Just then, I heard a rattle, a bang as the door to the library hit the chair that I had dragged in front of it.

"What on earth?" I heard Cassie's voice as she struggled to push the door open. The chair wasn't heavy, and she was already widening the gap.

I stood, frozen.

I glanced down at my dress. There was not a smudge on it. I clasped the bundle behind me, hiding my dirty hands. I would just have to try and brazen it out.

Cassie finally got the door open and strode in.

"Serena!" she exclaimed. "What are you doing here? Did you move the chair in front of the door?"

"I must have done," I said apologetically. "I'm afraid I was climbing around looking at the books."

Had it been one of the others I might have stood a chance. But Cassie's eyes were far too sharp, her brain was far too quick.

"What's that on your face?" she asked. Her gaze darted to the fireplace where the dirty bed sheets had been thrown.

"What do you have behind your back?" she asked slowly.

"It's nothing," I replied.

She stared at me for a long moment then in silence. Finally, her eyes widened.

"It really *is* you, isn't it?" she said slowly. "You are Iris."

CHAPTER TWENTY-FIVE

A dull roar filled my ears. I tried to smile.

"I don't know what you're talking about, Cassie," I said, as lightly as possible. "I should leave you to your morning."

I took a step forward, but Cassie blocked my path.

"I thought it was you," she murmured, her eyes travelling over every inch of my face. "When you walked in the room and Tookes dropped that glass. I almost did the same thing. It's the eyes..."

"Cassie," I said more firmly, "I don't know if this

is some sort of joke, but if it is, then I'm not sure I understand it, and I'd like to go to my room."

I made to move past her.

"You told me about it, you know," she said quietly. "The hiding place in the chimney. It was not long after we arrived, you were trying to help me feel excited about my new home, and you told me there was a secret compartment inside the chimney. You just never told me exactly where."

I closed my eyes. She was right; I had done that, I remembered it now.

"Sophia says you ride like you were born in the saddle." Cassie took another step towards me. "I bet you swim like a fish too. I always said that there was no chance Iris Scott-Holland would ever drown in that river."

"Just like there was no chance your stepfather would ever fall from his horse?" I challenged, the words falling from my lips before I could claw them back.

Cassie's eyes flared.

"I have to go," I said, the words brusque, my whole body rigid.

"Don't," Cassie said, but this time I pushed past her, the bundle from the chimney still in my hands, heading as calmly as I could manage for my room. My heart was hammering wildly as I climbed the stairs. There was no sound to indicate that Cassie was following me. When I reached the door to my bedroom, I could barely turn the handle, my hands were shaking so much.

There was cold water in a pitcher by the nightstand and I cleaned my face and hands, washing away the soot, and relishing the coolness on my skin which felt hot and clammy.

What was I going to do?

Cassie knew. She *knew*. Would she tell anyone? Of course she would! She was probably telling her mother right now. What would Helena do when she found out? My blood chilled.

She was so close to being rid of me for ever and laying claim to my fortune. In only a couple of weeks she'd have me declared dead. What lengths would she go to in order to keep me out of the way?

It wouldn't be wise to stick around and find out. I remembered her face the day my father died, the spark in her eyes. That look of triumph.

I paced the room. My mind felt at once frozen, unable to make any kind of decision as to how to act next, and frantic, an endless series of questions and recriminations piling up on top of one another, a noisy clamour in my head.

My eyes settled on the wrapped object that I had salvaged from the chimney and I stilled. Here, at least, was something I could do. In fact, I had better open it at once, before Helena came bursting in.

I wrenched the wrapping away with rather less care than I might otherwise have done.

Inside was a small bundle of letters, tied with a ribbon.

I didn't recognize the writing on the front. I flicked gingerly through the envelopes. They were all from the same person. I opened the first one. It was written on headed paper in a swirling hand. I scanned it rapidly, spotting a familiar name.

My Lord –

With regards to the alterations
you propose, we can see no issue with
amending the document as you desire.
If you could attend an appointment
at our offices in Rochester at your
earliest convenience, we would be
happy to see you.

Yours faithfully,

J.F. Fortescue

At first glance the letter was uninteresting, its contents ambiguous. But there must have been a reason for my father to hide it so thoroughly. I frowned, reading the words over for something I might have missed. Then I noticed it: the date.

The letter was dated a week before my father's death.

Tookes had heard my father arguing about his will with Helena before he was killed. J.F. Fortescue was my father's solicitor, I knew that much already. Surely that meant that *the document* in question was his will?

At that moment there was a knock on my door. It would be Helena. I cursed under my breath and picked up the letters, pushing them under the bed. I didn't know what I was going to do. For a moment my brain flashed wildly to an image of Nick, and then I pushed it away. Whatever I had to face, I had to do it alone. I felt in my pocket for my knife, the weight of it reassuring in my hand.

I pulled my shoulders back and took a deep breath before putting my hand on the door handle. I waited until my fingers were steady, and then I pulled it open.

Standing on the other side of the door was Cassie. She was alone, and she was holding a box in her hands. Her face was pale, and she looked nervous.

"May I come in?" she asked.

For a moment I was too surprised to answer. "Of course," I finally said stiffly, stepping aside.

I closed the door behind her, and we stood, again, looking at one another.

"I haven't told anyone," Cassie said, the words coming out in a rush. "And I won't, I swear."

I released a slow breath. She seemed sincere, but how could I possibly trust her? I folded my arms across my chest, careful not to let my guard down.

"It wasn't right." Her voice was small but clear. "What they did, the way they treated you, after your father…" She cleared her throat. "I spent seven years hoping that you would walk back through the door, and now you have. I don't know why you're pretending to be someone else, but I'm sure that you must have your reasons. I am not going to interfere with them."

My eyebrows shot up, and she nodded. "I mean it. From what I can gather Lord Wynter must also be involved in this somehow. He brought you here, and he's also been lying about your past." Her brow crumpled. "You were always kind to me. You're my family too. The last thing I want to do is to bring you more unhappiness if you have managed to build something for yourself away from … all of this."

I felt my shoulders relax slightly, though I remained silent.

Cassie shuffled awkwardly on her feet. "I saved this for you," she said, holding out the box. "It's not much but I kept it. In case you ever came back."

It was a test, of sorts. If I took the box from her then I was as good as admitting that I was who she said I was. Iris Grey trusted no one. *A fugitive has no friends.*

But could I really be a fugitive, now that I was back here, in my home?

Was there really no one that I trusted?

The silence stretched out between us. I could hear my heartbeat in my ears. Cassie gazed at me, unwavering.

I took the box.

As Cassie walked by to leave the room, she reached forward and brushed her hand against my arm. It was the lightest touch, but I felt it all the way to my bones.

You're my family too.

As soon as she was out of the door, I felt my knees begin to give way, and I collapsed on to the bed, the heavy box in my hands crashing against my chest.

I set it gently on the bed beside me and opened it up.

There was treasure inside. Perhaps not what anyone

else would call treasure, but certainly treasure to me.

On top of the box was a fine silver shawl. I remembered my mother wearing it, and I picked it up, the cool material slipping through my fingers like water. I buried my face in it. After all these years I knew that there was nothing left of her scent, but, still, I was convinced that the smell of wild strawberries lingered.

I put the shawl to one side. There were trinkets that I recognized from my mother's bedroom: a silver hairbrush, a glass vase that always held roses from the garden, a china figurine of a grey horse dancing on its back legs. Wrapped in tissue paper I found a silver hair pin, shaped like a crescent moon and studded with small diamonds. I remembered seeing it in my mother's hair, and I wondered how Cassie had smuggled it away. There was also a piece of paper, thin and yellowed with age. I picked it up carefully and opened it. Pressed inside the sheet of paper was a beautiful iris on a green stem, its long slender petals curved in purple arches across the page, each one looking as though someone had painted a smooth line of yellow down the middle with a fine-tipped brush. Next to the pressed flower, fragile as tissue paper, my mother had written the words,

Iris Penelope Scott-Holland,
17th December, 1880.

Cassie had saved these things, these pieces of my own history, wrapped them carefully, and kept them hidden all this time, just in case I came back.

It was like a door cracking open, revealing a sliver of light.

There were things from my own room in the box as well. A cloth doll, wearing a beautiful blue dress that my mother had made herself, a hardback book of adventure stories, and, most importantly, the embroidered wall hangings that my mother had stitched. They had been rolled up tight and tied with blue silk ribbon.

I unfurled them, the sight at once startling and familiar. There were two of them: one, from the story of Rapunzel, depicted a high brick tower, standing in a garden of thorns. Rapunzel's long, golden hair tumbled from the window at the top, a glorious tangle of threads in a hundred different shades of yellow, amber, gold and copper – even the odd silver thread was stitched through. Rapunzel's face was turned away from the window so you could only see part of her profile.

As a child I had been fascinated by the beauty of the scene, of the river of tumbling hair, but now I saw sadness in the averted face. I realized there was no sign of the handsome rescuer in the garden of thorns.

The other image was stranger still. Little Red Riding Hood, her cloak a splash of brilliant scarlet against a forest made of shadows. Even as I inspected every stitch, I couldn't understand how my mother had achieved such an effect. It was as if she had fashioned smoke out of silk. To one side of the shadowy forest a pair of amber eyes glowed, the faintest outline of a wolf, radiating danger.

I shivered, and tried to ignore the feeling that took hold of me as I looked into those gleaming, predatory eyes.

It felt like a warning.

CHAPTER TWENTY-SIX

That night, the night of the party, I felt the nerves jangling in my belly like coins in a purse.

I hadn't seen Cassie since she'd given me the box, which was now hidden behind the gowns in my armoire. Some instinct told me to trust her, but my instinct was battling with years of lessons learned the hard way. Trust was not something that that came naturally to me.

Still, I had no choice but to trust her, for now. She knew who I was, and she could reveal my identity to her mother whenever she wanted to.

The atmosphere in the house felt tense in the run-up to the party. Helena oversaw preparations with an eagle eye; clearly she still believed Agatha had a chance at securing an engagement with the prince, and she was going to pull out all the stops to make it happen.

She hadn't reckoned with me.

Or with Matilda, who had decided I was getting the full "fine lady treatment" tonight.

I wasn't exactly sure what Nick had told her about me, but the way Matilda spoke to me and treated me made it clear that she didn't think of me as a highborn lady. That's not to say that she treated me badly – quite the opposite. There was a warmth to our relationship that I knew would not be usual between a lady and her maid, and even though I knew I should discourage it, I was glad of it. At least I could be certain of one ally in the house.

This evening I'd had a hot bath and been rubbed in oil that smelled like roses, I'd been wrapped in fluffy towels and left to sit in front of the fire as my hair dried. I'd been primped and polished, spritzed and dusted with fine powder. Matilda had applied a touch of rouge to my lips and my cheeks, and spent a long time curling my hair before pinning it up in a low chignon at the nape of my neck, loose curls falling softly to frame my face.

I stepped into the ball gown that Nick had ordered. It was a blue velvet, so dark that in some lights it looked black. It was cut in a wide V-neck at the front, leaving the top of my shoulders bare. The dress was largely unadorned, but its sleeves were its main feature; short, exaggerated puff sleeves gathered into the shape of a bow, with a small silver tulle ruffle just visible underneath. The skirts were flat and narrow at the front, but pleated at the back with a short train to add a little drama.

With the diamonds that Nick had borrowed for me the effect was – I had to admit – quite breathtaking.

"There," Matilda said, stepping back and admiring her handiwork with professional pride. "That'll put a spoke in Miss Weston's wheel."

"Matilda!" I exclaimed.

"Well." Matilda shrugged, unrepentant. "That maid of hers has been running on and on and on about how her mistress is going to be the most beautiful girl at the party, turning every head, and how they've already been talking about her wedding to the prince and the flowers and the dress and everything, as if they hadn't laid eyes on you, miss, when you knock all the others out of the water!"

I laughed. "Thank you, Matilda," I said.

"You *are* going to dance with the prince, aren't you?" she asked suddenly.

"I should think so. He'll likely dance with all the young ladies who are staying at the house party."

"Do you think—" Matilda broke off, ruffled, then took a breath and started again. "Do you think he'll ask you to marry him? The prince, I mean?"

I was startled. "I have no idea," I replied. I was reasonably sure that Nick would not have confided his plans to her. "Why do you ask?"

Matilda twisted her hands. "There's some talk about it below stairs. I just wondered tonight ... if you were going to be alone with him..." She trailed off.

"Oh, I don't expect any such thing," I said.

The expression that flickered across Matilda's face was hard to read. It might have been disappointment. I suppose it is quite a coup for a lady's maid if her mistress is to marry a prince.

"Will you dance with Lord Wynter as well?" Matilda asked tentatively, changing the subject.

"Perhaps," I said. I glanced over to my nightstand, where I had put the beekeeping book that he had given me. I don't know why. Every so often I opened it again to read the inscription. I simply couldn't work the man out.

Downstairs I could hear the strains of music as the orchestra warmed up. There would be no grand entrance tonight, I – like the rest of the house party – would be there from the beginning.

There was a knock at the door, and Matilda sprang across the room to open it.

The dowager countess swept in. She looked extremely grand in a plum-coloured gown, trimmed with airy cream lace.

She didn't try to hide the top to toe inspection that she gave me; it probably took a full minute, and her face remained expressionless throughout.

"Well," she said resignedly at the end, "I'll say this for young Nicholas, he certainly has style."

"Thank you, Lady Wynter. I *think* that was a compliment?" I said, pulling on the long gloves which had been dyed to match my gown.

"There's no need for smart comments, young lady," the dowager countess tutted. "I get quite enough of that from my grandson. I can see the two of you are going to be a terrible trial as a couple."

I said nothing to that, only smiled politely.

She made a harrumphing sound then, looking for all the world like a disgruntled camel.

"Now," she began, as I followed her out of the door and down towards the party, "as your chaperone I shall be keeping a watchful eye on you." She stopped suddenly, so that I almost ran into the back of her, and turned, fixing me with a beady stare. "There will be no shenanigans on my watch."

"Shenanigans?" I repeated weakly.

"I will not allow you to be compromised, Miss Fox. Not while you're my responsibility." There was that hard stare again. "I know what these parties can be like. I was young once, you know."

"And did you often fall into compromising situations,

Lady Wynter?" I asked, my eyes wide and innocent.

"Impertinent chit," she replied, turning away, but not before I caught the glimpse of something that may have been a smile. "Don't think I've forgotten that chat you and I need to have about your intentions towards my grandson."

"*My* intentions?" I murmured, but she was already striding ahead.

The ground floor of the house had been decorated lavishly with candles and flowers. Twining greenery and dancing candlelight filled every room. Helena had opened up the saloon, the largest room in the house, for use as a ballroom, and it was certainly of a grand enough size. It had been remodelled over a century ago in the rococo style, the ceiling covered in clouds and cherubs, with pale duck-egg-blue walls and a liberal amount of gilt and marble thrown in. It was like an enormous, overdecorated wedding cake. Father had hated it, but I rather liked it – it was certainly dramatic, and when I was a child, imagining being a lady at a fine ball, it had seemed the perfect setting to me. Just like in a fairy tale.

As the guests had not yet arrived, Lady Wynter and I

had an opportunity to take it all in without the crowds.

"I must say," the dowager countess murmured, "Helena knows how to put together a party. The old marquess – her husband – never had much interest in entertaining. He was a bit of a recluse."

"I didn't know that," I said, though Mrs Chambers had mentioned something similar. *Had* my father been a recluse? It was never how I thought of him. He just liked being at home, the three of us.

"Oh, yes," the dowager countess went on. "Of course, when Helena married him there was talk. She always was a social butterfly and he wanted to shut her away, just like the first marchioness. Invalid-ish, they said the first Lady Scott-Holland was, but *I* heard Lord Scott-Holland as good as locked her in the house. A shame – I remember her as a debutante. Pretty girl, gentle, wouldn't say boo to a goose. Still, Helena had no choice really – not with the straits Weston had left her in."

I was silent, trying to absorb all this information that was being delivered so casually. My mother – not an invalid, but a prisoner in her own home. My father, not an affable, loving husband, but her jailer. No – that couldn't be right, it must be some wild society gossip, taken out of context.

"Though with Helena of course there's no saying, she might have taken Scott-Holland anyway," the dowager countess continued airily. "She certainly fancied the title. Nicholas's wife will be a countess, of course…" She paused meaningfully here and fixed me with a knowing look.

"A countess, yes," I said mechanically.

"Still, Helena did well out of it in the end. Holland Hall is a fine old house, and I must say that she does seem to be looking after it. Her husband was never much interested in the place. Apart from the stables, that is."

"Was he a sporting man?" I asked, suddenly desperate to hear something of my father's accomplishments.

"Yes," she said slowly. "Though not so much by the end. He took to drinking, had a nasty accident while out riding – that's how he died, you know. It was all a terrible mess. Helena was fortunate that the property was not entailed, or it would have gone to some cousin thrice removed, I believe, and this is what I keep saying to Nicholas." Her eyes flicked to me. "One *must* secure the chain of succession."

"Of course," I said hollowly. "Succession."

The dowager countess kept talking, but I was far away. Was my father's drinking really such common knowledge that a distant acquaintance like Lady Wynter could speak of it so casually? Had I really been so oblivious?

Everything I knew and believed in was shifting under my feet and I longed for solid ground.

"Ah, ladies, there you are!" Helena came sashaying across the ballroom to meet us, her hands outstretched, the happiness on her face making her look younger. Her gown was a beautiful dusty pink, and she wore it with strings of enormous pearls at her neck and wrists. "Isn't it wonderful to feel the house come alive like this? Don't you just love a party?" For once her smile seemed wide and unaffected.

I thought then that I didn't remember there being a lot of parties at the house when I was a child. There was only ever the odd hunting party, a weekend of gaming and shooting when guests would come from the city. There weren't balls like this one, full of women in gorgeous gowns. I had never realized that my father didn't like having visitors.

"We're gathering in the drawing room for a toast before the guests arrive," Helena continued, urging us through the room.

"It all looks beautiful, Lady Scott-Holland," I said, as we passed by the small, raised stage where the orchestra were setting up. Even this was edged in strings of creamy white roses and greenery.

"Yes," Helena agreed serenely. She knew she had done a good job, knew her hard work meant that Holland Hall shone its brightest.

In the drawing room, the rest of the guests were gathered. I noticed that Stefan's eyes lit up appreciatively when I walked into the room. Nick's eyes did something different. Nick's eyes brushed over me, a light touch that skittered across my skin, leaving a trail of goosebumps. Finally, those eyes met mine, inscrutable as ever. He raised the glass in his hand in a silent salute. I supposed that meant that I had passed muster.

"Now that we are all here," Helena began, and then she stopped, doing a slightly heavy-handed double take. "Oh, no, we're not all here. Where on earth is Agatha?"

"Here I am, Mama." Agatha's sweet voice came from behind us, and we turned as one to see her framed in the doorway.

It was quite the entrance, and I had to admit that Helena and Agatha had staged it beautifully.

Agatha was wearing a pale yellow silk gown, topped with an overlay of beautifully embroidered tulle, a cloud covered in gold threads that caught the light as she moved. Her hair was piled on top of her head, and the yellow of her dress showed off her jewels to their best advantage, a stunning set of perfect pink diamonds.

Only they weren't her jewels at all. I felt myself clutching the stem of my glass so hard it might have shattered. I caught Cassie's eye, and the look she gave me was sympathetic.

They weren't Agatha's jewels. They were my mother's.

"Oh dear," said a voice from over Agatha's shoulder. "I'm so sorry I'm late."

As one we all turned, and there standing shyly in the

doorway was Sophia. No one had even noticed that she was missing. But they noticed her now.

Matilda had slipped off earlier at my request to give Sophia some extra attention and she had done a wonderful job. Sophia's light brown curls had been braided away from her face and piled up on top of her head. The saffron-coloured silk jacquard of her old dress was lovely and now, cut simply, but fitting her to perfection, the pattern of roses in a slightly darker, metallic thread glinting in the light, it looked like a completely new gown. With its scooped neckline and short sleeves, the bodice did up at the front with a row of silk-covered buttons. The skirt was full and long and trimmed with a lace ruffle. Sophia's cheeks were pink and her large grey eyes sparkled with excitement.

"Sophia!" her mother exclaimed in a tone that fell somewhere between awe and horror.

"You look wonderful!" Cassie said, stepping forward to admire her dress. I smiled; that was pure kindness, as Cassie couldn't care less about a ball gown.

"Dashed pretty girl," the colonel said a bit too loudly to Stefan. "Been hiding her light under a bushel, eh?"

Sophia's blush deepened and I grinned at her and winked.

"That gown is really very nice, my dear," the dowager countess said, in softer tones than I had heard her use before. "It reminds me of a favourite of mine when I was your age. I must say the colour suits you marvellously."

"Lady Sophia." Jack stepped forward. "You must let me join your legion of admirers and beg the opportunity to escort you through to the ballroom."

Sophia gratefully accepted the arm he offered, and he bent his head towards hers to say something in a lower voice that I didn't catch. Whatever it was made Sophia's cheeks pink.

Agatha stood trembling, white and furious. Her thoughts were written all over her face. To be upstaged … by Sophia, of all people. It seemed hardly possible.

"Well, I don't think there is anything special about that gown," she snapped. "I don't see why everyone's making such a fuss, simply because she doesn't look a *complete* frump like usual."

There was a shocked silence.

"Agatha, dear." Helena cast her daughter an anguished look.

Agatha looked about ready to start stamping her feet.

"I think we should head through to the ballroom," Jack said in neutral tones, his eyes firmly fixed on Sophia. "I'm sure I hear people arriving, and I want to be sure that I secure the first dance with you, Lady Sophia."

"Gal's going to have a full dance card tonight," the colonel agreed in his heartiest voice.

"She certainly will," the dowager countess said frigidly. "It's always a pleasure to see such a prettily behaved young lady light up a ballroom."

Sophia bit her lip, all her excitement turned to worry. Jack took matters into his own hands, tugging her gently away and whispering something in her ear that made her laugh.

Agatha opened her mouth, an angry flush on her cheeks.

"Miss Weston, may I escort you through?" Stefan said, casting me the briefest rueful glance before stepping forward to try and charm her out of her temper.

Appeased, Agatha smiled at him serenely and put

her hand on his arm. Helena fluttered alongside them. I wasn't sure if Agatha even realized she'd just shown off her worst side.

Nick appeared at my elbow. "Shall we?" He offered me his arm and I took it. "That was your doing, I suppose?" he asked, gesturing after Sophia.

I was fairly sure that I wasn't supposed to be showing off my dressmaking skills while playing the lady, so I remained silent.

Nick sighed wearily, but his voice was a mixture of resignation and amusement as he asked, "*Now* who's the fairy godmother?"

CHAPTER TWENTY-SEVEN

The party was in full swing, and though the night was far from over, it seemed everyone was already agreed that it was a roaring success – at least for most of us.

I barely had time to catch my breath, dancing every dance with plenty of charming and some not-so-charming partners. It was hard not to feel triumphant that two of those dances, including the very first one, had been with Stefan, who had reminded me with grin that I owed him a dance, and that it had to be delivered as soon as possible.

Propriety had not allowed more, but I felt his eyes follow me around the room, and he was at my side as often as his duties as guest of honour would allow. I knew that Stefan would do nothing that might be impolite to his hostess; he was – I was beginning to see – a man who took his responsibilities seriously, but I found that I was glad every time he appeared, whispering in my ear, making me laugh.

His attention marked me out as well. I felt the eyes on me again, on the pair of us when we were together. I was turning away partners who pretended to be deeply wounded, and I was introduced to dozens of people who could not have been more interested in learning every detail about the beautiful heiress Serena Fox.

Only Agatha seemed to be having a bad time, and it would take a far better person than I not to rejoice in it. Seeing her wearing my mother's jewels had been a red flag to a bull, and I hadn't hesitated to make my delight in Stefan's company as obvious as possible. Watching her dancing boot-faced with poor Percy, and glower as Sophia's dance card filled up, had been satisfying, but it was nowhere near enough. I wanted to rip my mother's jewels from her ears and throat. It made me feel quite wild, and I channelled my anger into smiling brighter, dazzling harder, as hard as any diamond.

I hadn't danced with Nick yet. He hadn't asked. In fact, I had barely seen him at all, though I found myself looking for him several times.

A swirl of yellow silk whirled past me, and I caught Sophia's bright smile as she was waltzed around the room again by Jack Waterford. He wasn't the only one to notice how well she looked tonight. The dress suited her; but, more than that, I could tell that she felt beautiful in it. It was nice to have helped, even without the bonus of antagonizing Agatha. I liked Sophia, and I knew what it was like to be Agatha's plaything. I was glad to see her having a good time.

I excused myself from the next dance, pleading thirst. Several men rushed off to fetch me a drink at once, and I used their disappearance to snatch a moment alone, slipping through the drawing room and out of the doors that led into the garden.

The night was cool, and I welcomed the sharpness of it, like tiny pins, waking my body and clearing my head of the drowsy heat that came from being so surrounded by people. The sky was clear and the moon, almost full, seemed near enough that you could pluck it from the sky and roll it between your fingers – a smooth white pearl.

And there were stars. I had grown so used to London fog and overcast skies that I had almost forgotten – or perhaps had tried hard not to remember – the night skies of my home, filled with so many flashes of silver, cascading and cartwheeling riotously overhead, stretching up and out in a dizzying display that seemed to go on for ever.

I stood, looking up at them now, my arms wrapped tightly around myself. Then I heard soft footsteps, felt a jacket being dropped around my shoulders, warm and smelling of spice and citrus. I slipped my hands through the sleeves, feeling the silk lining skim over the sensitive skin on my bare arms.

"Needed a rest from being the belle of the ball?" Nick asked, coming to stand beside me.

"Where have you been?" I replied, forcing myself not to look at him or react to his presence.

"Around."

"How mysterious." I kept my tone dry, matching his.

"Not really." He shrugged. "I have been avoiding several mothers who want me to know that their daughters are the most accomplished young women for miles around, I have danced with the daughter of a friend, and twice with a pretty widow, and I have received a lengthy lecture from my grandmother on the importance of marrying as soon as possible, when I foolishly allowed her to corner me with a plate of cherry tarts."

I laughed at that. "I'd have thought after successfully avoiding all the matchmakers, you'd have done a better job at hiding from the dowager countess."

"There were *cherry tarts*," he said, wounded. "My grandmother doesn't fight fair."

I felt the shiver of awareness that I always felt when he was beside me. Or perhaps it was the night air. That's what I told myself anyway.

"Are you enjoying it?" he asked. "The party, I mean."

"I'm not here to enjoy it," I said. The image of Agatha decked out in my mother's jewels flickered across my mind and I felt my jaw clench.

He was silent then, but I could still feel his eyes on me. I had no idea what he was thinking about.

"As I recall," he said finally, "two nights ago you challenged me to a shooting competition."

They were the last words I expected, and I turned to him in surprise. "As *I* recall, it was you who challenged me."

"Was it?" Nick mused. "I wonder what possessed me?"

"Ego, I should think."

"Well?" Nick looked at me expectantly. "Shall we?"

"Shall we what?" I asked, confused.

"Shall we see who's the better shot?"

I stared at him. "What, now?"

"Why not?" He smiled, a small, secret smile that was full of mischief. It did something to my insides, seeing him smile like that.

"Because it's the middle of the night," I replied. "Perhaps *you* can see in the dark – I wouldn't be at all surprised to learn you were some sort of creature of the night – but I'm afraid you'd have the advantage over me."

"*Creature of the night?* I quite like that." His voice

curled around me. "But the ability to see in the dark won't be necessary. Come with me."

With that he sauntered off into the grounds, and, of course, I followed him. He guided me through the footpaths that wound around the gardens, towards the large lawn where we usually played games, further from the house.

Finally, we emerged on to the lawn, and my breath caught.

The fine, silver light of the almost full moon cast a glow over the scene, aided by flaming torches arranged all around the lawn, along with hundreds of flickering candles in glass jars. There were even candles in paper lanterns hanging from the trees. The sheer number of them was overwhelming.

It was magical, a sudden blaze of light in the darkness, as if we were standing on our own star, as if we ourselves were a part of the night sky, floating through that velvet blackness.

At the far end of the lawn was a shooting target, the kind they used for contests – smaller and smaller circles leading to a bullseye, and where we were standing, a small table with a highly polished wooden box on top of it. Nick opened the box without fanfare and, nestled in the red velvet lining inside, were a pair of extremely fine silver duelling pistols.

He turned to look at me then. I felt the smile, spreading across my face unchecked, wide and unstoppable.

Oh, this was going to be fun.

I moved to his side, lifting one of the guns and checking it over.

"You know," I said conversationally, "your grandmother said she'd be keeping an eye on me, making sure I didn't slip off into the night with any young men."

"Any young men aside from me," Nick corrected me smoothly. "I have no doubt that my grandmother trusts my sense of honour implicitly."

"I think it's *my* honour she's worried about," I snorted. "She wants to know what my intentions are."

"*Your* intentions?"

"I suppose she thinks the choice lies with me."

"That choice would always lie with you," he agreed easily.

I turned to face him. "And what would she think if she knew we were having a shooting competition on the back lawn?" I asked.

Nick tipped his head. "I'm sure she'd understand that it's a matter of family pride. A man cannot simply turn down a challenge like this one. I owe something to my name."

"I'll remind you once again that *you* challenged me," I put in here, biting back a smile.

"Now, that doesn't sound terribly gentlemanly."

"It certainly doesn't."

"How fortunate, then, that I am – how did you put it so charmingly? – an *ungentlemanly oaf*?"

"And you see how right I was?" I concentrated on preparing my gun properly, but I couldn't resist stealing a glance at him.

That small, stubborn smile curled on his lips, the one he tried to hold back, the one that never quite blossomed into the full thing. He finished inspecting his gun and stood with it hanging loosely down by his side.

"So?" he said. "Who goes first?"

"I believe you should have the honour, my Lord. As the challenger in this case."

A spark leaped in his eyes, and he strode towards the point marked on the ground where we would shoot from. I tried not to notice how handsome he was, I really did. I tried not to notice the muscles in his shoulders and his back, as he lifted his arm to check his aim, the way they bunched slightly under the white linen shirt and black waistcoat. I tried not to notice the way his dark hair curled against his collar, or his strong, capable hands, or the easy grace of his movements.

Then I didn't have to try because suddenly his posture changed, and I was focused on the competition. I could see by his stance that he knew what he was doing, could see by the way he held a gun that he had done so before, many times.

In fact, he did not make a show of it; he simply lined up the shot and took it. I knew that it would be good, and it was. Together we made our way towards the target for a closer look, Nick as cool and unhurried as ever.

It was a perfect shot – or at least it was as near to perfect as one was ever likely to get, right in the middle of the target.

I let out a low whistle. "Very good, my Lord. Not just a pretty face, after all."

"Why, thank you, Miss Grey. I believe it's about time you began to realize that." He looked closer at the target. "I think a hair to the left would have been better, but not a bad effort, no." He turned back to look at me. "Are you still feeling confident about your chances?"

"A hair to the left, you say," I repeated thoughtfully, bending to examine the target myself. "I think you're probably right about that."

When I straightened up, I found that we were standing extremely close together. His face was turned towards me, and my eyes were level with his jaw. For a moment I was so tempted to reach up and run my fingers over it that my hand began to move towards him of its own accord.

I froze, looking up at him, and his eyes fixed on mine. His eyes were ink dark, glittering. I was close enough to hear a hitch in his breathing. We stood like that for a long moment. My whole body felt like it was buzzing, as if touching me would set off sparks.

But Nick didn't touch me. He just looked at me. At

my eyes, at my mouth, back to my eyes again. I think I was holding my breath. I didn't understand what was happening or what I wanted to happen.

Perhaps he found that thought in my eyes. Or perhaps he was having the same feelings. Either way, he stepped back, and all the air rushed back into the space between us.

I could breathe again.

"So," Nick said, his voice slightly hoarse. "I'll ask again, do you still think you can emerge the victor?"

"I believe I have a fighting chance, my Lord," I replied, glad to hear that my own voice sounded steady. "I also believe that when you first mentioned this competition you said it would be a wager."

"Did I?"

"You did." I nodded.

"Very well," he said, and I felt certain I must have imagined what had happened only moments ago. "A wager it will be. What shall we play for?"

We reached the table again, and I picked up my own pistol. "A shilling?" I suggested.

Nick tutted. "A shilling? We can do better than that. What is it that you really want?"

His voice deepened, and just like that, whatever had been there between us moments ago flooded back, setting my pulse galloping. Never mind that we were standing apart this time. My mouth dried, and the crackling feeling filled the air around me. His eyes narrowed and he took an involuntary step forward.

"A forfeit," I squeaked, trying desperately to break whatever spell we were under.

A frown flickered across his face and he halted. "A forfeit?"

"Yes." I nodded vigorously. "It's what my father and I used to play for. A forfeit. It can come at any time."

Usually, when Father had cashed his in, it had been to get me to eat my vegetables. If I had gained forfeits from him, they typically came in the form of sweets.

"Fine," Nick said. "A forfeit." I could tell from the look on his face that he wasn't too worried about losing anyway.

He was probably right. I took my stance on the spot. I was a good shot, but to beat him, I would have to hit the target dead centre, a hair's breadth to the left of his own effort.

I lined up the shot.

"It's not too late to call it off, you know," Nick called, smugness lacing his voice.

I breathed in, and then released a long, slow breath. Then I squeezed the trigger.

I turned to Nick, the sound of the gunshot still ringing in my ears. Our eyes met, and for a moment I thought he would take me in his arms.

"It seems that I owe you a forfeit," he murmured instead.

I didn't even need to look at the target.

I was my father's daughter, after all.

And my father never missed.

Part Three

Kent
October, 1899

CHAPTER TWENTY-EIGHT

It was late by the time the household began to stir the next morning. I was sure I would have missed breakfast, but actually found myself to be one of the earlier risers.

The party had carried on well into the early hours of the morning, and I knew that more than a few people would be feeling fragile. I, on the other hand, felt curiously invigorated. The shooting contest with Nick the night before had taken my mind off my troubles. I'd had fun. *Fun.* For the first time in a long time, uncomplicated fun.

When we returned to the party my spirits had been soaring and I had had no problem dancing and laughing the rest of the night away. I even felt optimistic about my own investigation. If I could trust Cassie, and I thought I could, then she could help me. I had thought of a way to get my hands on a copy of my father's will.

I arrived at the breakfast room in a cheerful frame of mind. Only Stefan was there and he was stooped over, helping one of the maids to pick up some broken crockery.

"Ah! Good morning, Miss Fox," he said, straightening up. "I'm afraid we have had a bit of an accident."

The maid blushed pink and cast her eyes down at the ground. Could there be many princes who would bother to help a nervous maid to clean up?

"Please," he said, stepping over and placing his hand on the small of my back. "Let me pull out a chair for you and I will fix you a plate of breakfast myself while…" He trailed off, looking questioningly at the maid.

"Lottie," she managed. "Sir. I mean, Your Highness, sir!"

"Thank you." Stefan smiled at her. "I will fix your

breakfast while Lottie here finishes clearing up. And if Lady Scott-Holland should ask, we will tell her that it was I who dropped the milk jug." He gave Lottie a tiny wink, and she bobbed a curtsey and hurried out of the room, no doubt to share the news of His Highness's attention with the rest of the staff.

"That was kind of you," I said.

"Oh." Stefan waved his hand dismissively. He began pouring my coffee. "I think people probably believe me to be as stuffy as your own royal family. In fact, we are a small kingdom and I have known all the staff at my grandmother's palace since I was a boy. We are much less formal than you English. I find it strange that you would see a person who worked for you every day and make no effort to know them – not even their name!"

"I feel exactly the same way," I said, taking my seat.

"We're always so much in agreement." Stefan wandered over to the sideboard. "It's a very harmonious way of living, isn't it?"

The implication hung in the air – ours would be a harmonious match. The scene playing out now could easily have been one between husband and wife.

"As I recall, you are fond of the potted ham, Miss Fox?" Stefan asked, and I tried not to laugh.

"Thank you, Your Highness," I said instead. "I am indeed."

"I really do think that, when we are alone at least, you should call me Stefan," he said, placing the plate of food in front of me with a flourish. "All this *Your Highness* business is such a mouthful. I think – at least, I hope – that we are friends now, Miss Fox?"

"Of course we are," I said.

"Of course we are, *Stefan*," Stefan corrected me.

"Of course we are, Stefan." I smiled. "Then I suppose in private, you must call me Serena."

"Serena." Stefan rolled the name around in his mouth like a fine wine he was tasting for the first time. "A beautiful name, for a beautiful young woman. From the Latin, I believe, for tranquillity."

"I believe so," I agreed, feeling anything but tranquil.

Stefan sat down opposite me and we began our breakfast.

"Did you enjoy the ball last night?" Stefan asked.

"Very much."

"And this time you did not turn into a pumpkin at midnight," he teased.

"Cinderella doesn't turn into a pumpkin," I replied, smiling at him. "Her carriage does."

"Ah, yes," Stefan twinkled. "You are quite right, and I am glad to hear it. Turning into a pumpkin would be most inconvenient."

"Pumpkins don't get to eat potted ham," I agreed, spearing some with my fork.

Stefan laughed. "You are an absurd creature."

"So are you!"

"What a pair we make."

He was so easy to talk to and he made me laugh. I felt comfortable with him. I tried not to let the guilt tie my insides into knots.

We had both finished eating and were nursing our cups of tea when we were joined by another guest.

To my astonishment, it was Nick. He was dressed as elegantly as ever, but there was a crease between his eyes. He looked as though he hadn't slept.

"My god!" Stefan exclaimed. "My friend, I had not thought to see you until well into the afternoon.

Is this not positively daybreak for you?"

Nick shrugged. "Last night's festivities were quite bracing," he said. "I found that I woke earlier than usual this morning."

He had barely glanced at me and I felt a strange sense of disappointment. I didn't know what had happened between us last night, but *something* surely had? I remembered again the look on his face when he realized I had made the shot – the gleeful recognition; that somehow, something about us was the same. That, in spite of the layers of deception between us, Nicholas Wynter truly *saw* me, as no one else had. And I saw him. Despite his posturing, despite the mask of indifference he wore. I saw him.

Or, at least, that was what I had thought last night. Now, though, I was less sure.

"Ah," Stefan said, gesturing towards the door. "Here is Lottie. Perhaps a cup of coffee for my friend Lord Wynter, to help him ease into the day."

Nick turned to see the maid standing in the doorway, and a look of intense displeasure fell across his face. I could hardly blame poor Lottie for standing pale and trembling under such a gaze. The girl looked as though she were about to burst into tears.

"You should not be waiting on us at breakfast," he said coldly. "Where is the footman? Please go and inform the butler at once."

I scowled at him. Lottie sketched the briefest curtsey and turned in a swirl of skirts to leave the room as quickly as possible.

"That was a harsh, Nick," Stefan said. "The household is probably at sixes and sevens after last night's party. What need have we for a footman?"

Nick's gaze returned to the prince. "It is the way things are done," he said finally.

Nick turned his attention to the rack of toast on the table, and Stefan caught my eye, giving me an amused look.

"I see someone overindulged last night," Stefan said, pushing back his chair and getting to his feet. "You always were like a bear with a sore head in the morning. I must leave Miss Fox to tease you out of your bad mood, however; I have an appointment with my groom." He turned to me, executing a bow. "Miss Fox, I hope I shall have the pleasure of your company later, perhaps for a walk in the gardens?"

"Of course," I agreed.

When I was sure Stefan was gone, I turned on Nick. "What on earth is the matter with you?"

Nick bit into his toast, leaning back in his seat. He chewed thoughtfully and then answered, "I don't think there's anything particularly the matter, though I *could* do with a cup of coffee."

The feeling of disappointment grew. The Nick I had glimpsed last night was gone again, well and truly shut away behind his society facade.

I sat up straight and sipped my tea, trying not to care.

"Tell me how things are proceeding with Stefan," Nick said.

"He has started dropping hints about how well we suit as a couple," I replied. "He is attentive. You heard him suggest a walk today..."

Nick frowned down at the table. "People were remarking about how he singled you out last night," he agreed, his voice flat.

"I thought you'd be pleased."

"I am," he said, "but it's not enough. We need him to propose. There is less than a week left."

"What exactly would you have me do?" I asked, standing up and tossing my napkin on to the table. "You want me to throw myself at him? That won't catch your prince. He's looking for a love match ... or at least the possibility of one. He's sensitive, romantic."

Nick gave a humourless bark of laughter. "Is he? No, I don't want you to throw yourself at him. I'm afraid that the next push will have to come from me."

I waited but he didn't explain, simply continued to glare at the top of the table, clearly lost in thought.

The door opened and the footman entered.

"I'll leave you to your breakfast, then," I said.

"Mmm," Nick murmured. He glanced at the footman. "Coffee, please. Strong as you can."

There seemed to be nothing more to say and so I left, deflated. In the doorway I turned to look back at Nick, but he was still slumped in his chair, turning over whatever schemes were running through his mind.

It didn't matter, I reminded myself. I had far more

important things to attend to this morning, and so I went in search of Cassie.

I found her in her room.

"You want to do *what*?" Cassie exclaimed when I had explained my plan.

"I want to go to see my father's solicitor and break into his files," I said as calmly as possible. "I need to understand the terms of the will."

I was sitting in the armchair in Cassie's room while she paced in front of the fireplace.

"But why?" Cassie asked, bewildered.

"I want to know where I stand," I said. "Before I reveal myself." It was as close to the truth as I felt I could give her. However much she wanted to help me, I could not tell her I suspected her own mother of murder, that I was looking for a clue as to her motive.

Cassie sank into the chair across from me and chewed on her lip. "It makes sense," she said. "I'm afraid I have as little idea as you do about the finer details of the will. My mother is already counting your third of the inheritance as her own, I know that much. In a couple of weeks' time, she'll be able to have you declared dead and then I think things will become a lot more complicated. No one here has seen you for seven years – even proving that you are who you are could take some time. She'll probably fight you for it." She looked at me, worry in her eyes. "Iris, you don't have to come back at all if you don't want to. I'd share my portion of the inheritance with you – I'd do it happily. I know it's not as much as you should get, but it's better than being under my mother's control for over two years."

"It's not just about the money, Cassie," I said. "It's about my home, my name … my father's name."

"Of course," she murmured. "It's all wrong, isn't it? Us living here, while you…" She trailed off.

My stepsister had been more shocked by my story of running away and living in London than I had expected. Although she had never quite believed in my untimely, watery death, she hadn't realized that Helena had fabricated the whole thing. I had also withheld the truth about Nick and his plans for Stefan – that wasn't my secret to share. I had simply told Cassie that he was a friend who had agreed to help me. How long that lie would hold I wasn't sure, but I was thinking on my feet.

"Cassie," I said firmly, "none of this is your fault. We were children when everything happened. What could you have done? I'm back now, and I need to work out what to do next. I need your help."

She seemed to absorb this, and her spine straightened a little. Some of her usual determination came back into her face, and a glimmer of humour showed in her eyes. "And the best way I can help you is by breaking into a solicitor's office with you?"

"Exactly." I smiled.

Cassie let out a long breath. "All right, then," she said. "Where do we start?"

CHAPTER TWENTY-NINE

In the end, it was easy enough. Cassie had the carriage called around and she and I headed into Rochester for the afternoon on the pretext of getting me fitted for a cycling outfit.

"If it were anyone else, my mother would have been outraged," Cassie grinned as we rumbled along the road. "Because it was you, she practically kissed my feet and pushed me out of the door. She's extremely concerned you're going to steal the prince away from Agatha. She's already told everyone she knows that Agatha's going to be a princess by the time the year is out. Before you came along everyone thought it was a done deal."

I laughed, though of course Cassie was striking closer to the truth than she knew. It was exhausting, keeping track of all the lies and half-truths I was telling. I felt like the spider at the centre of a web of tangled threads.

"Actually," Cassie perked up, "wouldn't that be the perfect solution? You could marry the prince, Iris, then my mother would probably be delighted to acknowledge you and claim a princess for a stepdaughter. And you wouldn't have to live with her at all! But how to account for you using a false name..." She tapped her chin with her finger. "I have it!" she exclaimed. "Amnesia!"

"Amnesia!" I snorted.

"Yes. You fell in the river, bumped your head, were found by a family who could have no children of their own, who took you in though you had no memory of where you came from. Your adoptive parents sadly died. Then, quite by chance you came here, and the memories flooded back." Cassie sat back in her seat, triumphant.

"Cassie," I spluttered, "it sounds like something out of a Penny Dreadful!"

Cassie got the giggles too. "That's why everyone would love it. Then at the end you marry a prince and live happily ever after! You'd be the absolute toast of the town; they'd write songs about you and sing them in the street."

"Let's call that our reserve plan," I managed.

"Fine." Cassie stuck out her lower lip in a mock sulk. "*I* think it would work a treat."

Impulsively I reached over and squeezed her hand. She squeezed mine back.

"It's true, what you said," Cassie began awkwardly. "We *were* just children, seven years ago. Still, I want you to know that I always regretted not speaking up for you when Mama and Agatha were being cruel. Especially after your father died."

"It's in the past now," I said quickly. Although that wasn't really true. It was easy to forgive Cassie – a child who never did me any harm – but the anger that I felt towards Helena and Agatha was as fresh today as it had been seven years ago.

It wasn't long before we arrived in Rochester and, as instructed, the coachman pulled up in front of the offices of J.F. Fortescue.

The solicitor's office was as I remembered it, and Cassie gave our names to the clerk nearest the door, requesting an interview with Mr Fortescue. We sat in tense silence in the same hard-backed chairs where I had once waited for my father, until a man appeared.

He was short and round, with tufts of white hair, and rosy cheeks. A pair of brass spectacles sat on the end of his nose, and all in all he had the appearance of a benevolent character from a Dickens novel – apart from the heavy frown he wore.

"Miss Cassandra Weston?" he asked, and Cassie rose confidently, offering her hand.

"Yes, that is I!" she exclaimed heartily, pumping his hand in a firm handshake. I tried not to wince. It seemed Cassie was going Shakespearean. "I know that you and I haven't met before, but as my family's solicitor I thought I had better seek your assistance. Miss Fox and I have an important matter to discuss with you."

Mr Fortescue's eyes flickered to me, and then

softened. I had worn an incredibly frothy and feminine pale pink gown trimmed with lace. I knew how I looked – sweet, vulnerable, innocent ... and expensive. Every stitch on me screamed money.

"Please, come through to my office, won't you?" he said, gesturing towards the open door.

The office was a good size, and well looked after. The huge mahogany desk was meticulously neat, and polished to a high shine. Walls of bookshelves were organized alphabetically, and several tall filing cabinets stood, clearly labelled.

Excellent. Mr Fortescue's careful nature should hopefully work in our favour.

"My client is here today to talk to you about a matter that is rather sensitive," Cassie began, perching herself in one of the chairs across from Mr Fortescue's. I sat down in the one beside her, and Mr Fortescue looked at us from over his desk.

"Your client?" His eyebrows shot up.

"An informal arrangement," Cassie acknowledged. "I am studying the law, but – as I'm sure you are all too aware – a number of extremely outdated policies mean I am not currently able to practise. It is my hope that this changes soon."

Mr Fortescue's mouth thinned in disapproval. It was easy to see that he did not share Cassie's hopes on that score. Which was what we had counted on.

"As I was saying," Cassie continued, "my client finds herself in a delicate situation upon which I am not equipped to advise her. Knowing what fine work you have done for my mother and my stepfather's estate, I, of course, recommended she come to you."

The lawyer smiled. "In a little over your head, are you, my dear?" he said indulgently, and you could see any suspicion he might have felt melting away in the face of an opportunity to put an uppity woman in her place. "Well, the law is a complicated business. I would be delighted to advise you, Miss Fox."

I twisted my hands in my lap and peeped up at him shyly. "It is about my forthcoming marriage," I said, voice trembling. "I expect soon to announce my engagement to a … rather prestigious suitor, from overseas."

I let Fortescue's brain chew on that for a moment. Prince Stefan's visit to the area was no secret and I could see him putting the facts together with almost comedic transparency.

"I am something of an heiress," I continued. "My father is an elderly man in poor health, and he has always relied on his solicitor to arrange our affairs – but it appears they have been sorely mismanaged. A country solicitor, you understand, soon to retire, not used to managing a large fortune. I'm afraid my father's business interests have rather outgrown him. My father suggests I speak to someone about it – so that things might be in order before my marriage."

"Of course," Mr Fortescue assured me with great sympathy.

"And then, when Miss Cassandra mentioned how pleased her mother had always been with your work…" I trailed off.

The little lawyer puffed up proudly. "Dear Lady Scott-Holland," he said turning to Cassie, "your mother is not only one of our most valued clients, but – if I may say so – a remarkable woman, yes, a *truly* remarkable woman." The fanatical gleam in Mr Fortescue's eye revealed we had found another of Helena's devotees.

"She certainly is," Cassie agreed.

Mr Fortescue turned back to me. "If it is not too indelicate to ask, Miss Fox, may I ascertain the scale of the fortune you are being asked to manage?"

"Oh, that I couldn't say," I said helplessly. "I know so little of these things. I believe my own inheritance is somewhere in the region of thirty thousand pounds, though of course there is money in the exchange and the shares in my father's business as well."

Mr Fortescue let out a sound like strangled cat, before clearing his throat. "I see," he said unsteadily. "That is ... quite the empire your father has built."

"You see now why I have come to you. I find myself unsure where to place my trust with such an important and sensitive matter. As a young woman almost alone in the world" – I pinched my hand, allowing the gloss of unshed tears to pool in my eyes – "I am left feeling quite ... helpless."

Fortescue was looking at me with the expression of one who had seen a vision of his own incredibly rosy future.

"Forgive me," I said, letting the tears fall. "It is all

so overwhelming." And I drooped slightly in my seat.

"Oh, no!" Cassie leaped to her feet and rushed to my side. "Serena! Serena, dear!" She turned to Mr Fortescue. "Miss Fox is of such a sensitive nature and her nerves are frequently overwhelmed. I believe she's gone into a swoon." I let out the sort of woozy sigh I imagined an habitual swooner would make.

"Naturally, naturally, a young woman of great sensibility!" Mr Fortescue jabbered, jumping to his feet. "How may I be of assistance?"

"A glass of water?" Cassie asked. "And perhaps some smelling salts if you can locate them?"

"I shall do my utmost," Fortescue said. "My secretary will arrange things."

"Perhaps, if you don't mind," Cassie said hesitantly, "a moment's privacy? I may loosen her collar to help her breathe."

Through a cracked eyelid I saw Fortescue turn a deep, mottled red. "Certainly," he managed, backing out of the room. "Please, make yourself at home, I shall return shortly."

As soon as he was safely out of the door I leaped to

my feet. Cassie had fallen into a fit of the giggles and was shaking silently, her fist stuffed in her mouth.

"There's no time!" I hissed, moving quickly over to the filing cabinets. "Keep a look out!"

"I'm sorry," Cassie spluttered, "but really … his face when I mentioned loosening your collar! I can't believe he fell for it."

I flicked a quick smile at her. "I have found that some men's low opinions of women can be used to great advantage if properly exploited."

"Wonderful," Cassie breathed.

I was busy riffling through the files. It wasn't difficult to locate them; Mr Fortescue kept things neat as a pin.

"Here!" I exclaimed quietly, flicking through the documents. My father's file was a large one and I was trying to locate the will.

"I think he's coming back!" Cassie whispered.

There was no time to hesitate and I whipped out the entire file, lifting my skirts and thrusting it up under my bodice. It was quite bulky and I bent over, drawing my shawl around me.

When Mr Fortescue opened the door I was leaning heavily on Cassie's arm.

"Forgive me," I said. "I am indisposed. Perhaps we can continue our conversation another day?"

"Of course!" Mr Fortescue agreed with alacrity. "I am at your service. Any time, Miss Fox."

I gave him a weak smile, which brought a tender light to his eye. It was obvious that I had done myself no disservice – here was a man who liked his women fragile. We made our way as quickly as possible to the door.

"Did you get it?" Cassie asked breathlessly as we bundled into the carriage.

"Yes, yes, I got it." Cassie fell back in her seat and laughed, while I wriggled uncomfortably, retrieving the file from where I had hidden it, stuffed underneath my dress.

"I just took the whole thing," I said. "Thank goodness for wide skirts."

What I held was a thick packet of documents, and as I began sifting through them on the seat of the carriage, I saw that it included everything from letters with tenants, and negotiations on the sale of farmland, to bills for jewellery that must have belonged to my mother.

"Here it is!" I exclaimed, pulling out the will, which was surprisingly short, written in a looping hand that I recognized from his letters as belonging to Mr Fortescue. It was also less pristine than I had imagined such an important document to be, the pages rumpled and stained in places. I scanned it, looking for clues, running my finger down the pages past all the long-winded legal talk.

To my daughters, I leave the entirety of the estate and all of my assets outside of the bequests mentioned here, to be held in trust until - here I turned the page - they each reach the age of one and twenty. Until such time, the bequests are to be held in trust by my wife, Lady Helena Scott-Holland. To Lady Scott-Holland, I make a separate bequest of seven hundred pounds annually, until the date of her death, or upon her remarriage.

"Seven hundred pounds?" Cassie frowned. "That is a very small sum for Mama."

"Yes, it is," I said slowly. "She certainly hasn't been living on that." Not with all the renovations on the house, and the clothes, and the new carriage and every other luxury going.

"You're right," Cassie agreed grimly. "She's been spending the estate's money."

"I suppose she thinks with it coming to you and your sister it's as good as hers anyway."

Cassie nodded in agreement. "Her spending has increased in recent years. She must have been sure you weren't going to come home to claim your part."

"But this tells me nothing!" I exclaimed. "Nothing we didn't already know, at least. I cannot access my inheritance until I'm twenty-one, Helena holds the purse strings. There's no language in here about anything personal set aside for me – my mother's jewellery, the contents of the house, my horse. I can't believe that there wasn't anything Father wanted to leave just to me!"

I flicked through the remaining pages, but they simply listed small sums to be discharged to various friends, relatives and servants in gratitude for their service. I was not mentioned at all. Each page was signed by my father, and I knew that had Helena interfered with the will she would not have left herself so small a sum – it was practically an insult.

"I suppose he thought he could trust Mama to look after you," Cassie pointed out.

"His mistake," I muttered, suddenly furious at the man who had abandoned me without any protection.

I was putting the papers back into the packet, when I spotted one that I had missed. It was an envelope, written in my father's hand.

I opened it and unfolded the letter inside. I noticed that my father's handwriting was shaky, and ink spattered, and that the letter was dated shortly before his death.

Dear Sir –

I should like to amend the petition to the court to include further details of my wife's failures as a spouse. She

is a damnable woman, and I am
determined to go ahead with these
proceedings despite your advice. I
never should have married her! Divorce
may be messy, but it's a damn sight
better than being forced to live with
this harpy. I will show the world what
she is. You say you have found no evidence
that she has been unfaithful and that
therefore I have no grounds for
divorce, but I tell you the woman is as
devious as they come! I am convinced
of her treachery. If you cannot locate
her lover then I shall _find_ one
myself. There are plenty of men of
my acquaintance who I'm sure could be
persuaded to come forward. Nothing
will sway me from this course. I will
await your response.

I gasped. "What is it?" Cassie asked, noticing my shock.
"Is it something to do with the will?"

"No," I whispered. "It's much worse." I handed her the letter. "The letter from the solicitor I found up the chimney wasn't about Father's will at all; it was a reply to this. My father wanted to get a divorce."

Cassie's own horrified gaze met mine, and I wondered if she was thinking the same thing that I was.

There was no way that Helena would have survived a divorce. The proceedings were a spectacle, having to be held in open court and reported on in all the papers. To divorce Helena, my father would have to have proven adultery and named her lover in court. That was the law.

Did Father really believe Helena had been unfaithful? Or was that merely to have been a fiction, to ensure the divorce proceedings went ahead? When he said he could persuade someone to come forward, was he hinting that he could buy them off? My stomach lurched at the thought.

Whether the judge granted the petition or not, Helena would have been ruined.

I had been looking for a motive, a reason why Helena needed my father dead in order to provide for her own family, and now I had certainly found one. It explained the argument that Tookes had heard too – she would have been cut out of the will altogether, along with her daughters.

"Cassie," I said quietly.

Her face was pale. "I know what you're going to say," she said, "but I knew nothing about this, nothing!"

"What am I going to say?" I asked, a thread of steel in my voice.

"You think – you think that my mother had something to do with your father's death." She forced the words out.

"Yes," I said. "I always have done, though I had no proof."

"He fell from his horse!" cried Cassie.

"My father?" I lifted my voice. "*My* father? Fell from his horse?"

Cassie flinched. "I know he was a great rider, but the ground was uneven. There was a rabbit hole."

I gave a short bark of laughter. "Next you'll be telling me he was a drunk, like the others, with his silver flask. But I know it was her. And now I know why."

Cassie made a sudden noise and swayed in her seat. I thought for a moment she was going to faint, and I quickly got up to sit beside her, resting my arm around her shoulder to steady her.

"Cassie?" I said. "Oh, Cassie, I'm sorry. I shouldn't have said it that way, she's your mother. It's only that I'm so mixed up and angry I can hardly think straight. Are you all right?"

"It's not that," she murmured. She closed her eyes briefly, grimacing. "Well, not *only* that. When you said about the drinking – and the silver flask – I remembered something, something from that morning, and I can't … I don't want to…"

"What was it?" I asked, a feeling of urgency humming through me. "What did you remember?"

"It was the morning that he died. I saw—" Cassie turned to me, her eyes enormous. "I saw my mother putting something in a silver flask."

CHAPTER THIRTY

That evening I claimed to have a headache and stayed in my room. I couldn't possibly sit at a table, make polite conversation, and smile at the woman I now knew had poisoned my father.

It all made perfect sense. That was why my father had fallen from his horse; because Helena had slipped something in his drink.

My head was spinning as I turned all the pieces over in my mind. There was the letter from the solicitor, but that alone wasn't proof of what Helena had done.

How *could* I possibly prove such a thing? Cassie was just a child when she saw what she did. She could hardly be said to be a reliable witness.

The hours crawled by, slow as treacle, as I stared unseeingly into the fireplace. Finally, at midnight, there was a knock at my door and Cassie let herself in. We had agreed that we would meet at twelve so that we could go and talk to Tookes and Mrs Chambers together, without being disturbed. Cassie had sent them a note asking them to wait up for us.

We made our way to the housekeeper's room in silence.

"Come in, girls, come in," Mrs Chambers clucked when we arrived, settling us into chairs and placing warm teacups into our cold hands. She fussed around us like a mother hen.

Tookes stood at attention, his face immobile but his eyes alert.

"You both look dreadful," Mrs Chambers said, once we were sitting comfortably. "What on earth has happened?"

For a moment there was no sound except the crackling of the fire.

"Cassie and I went to see Father's solicitor today," I said finally, "and we found out that Father had been about to petition the courts for a divorce from Helena when he died."

Mrs Chambers sucked in a horrified breath, and even Tookes flinched.

"You cannot be serious!" Mrs Chambers exclaimed. "They had their differences, but divorce! No, I cannot believe it."

"It's true, Mrs C," Cassie said quietly. "Iris has the letter."

I produced the letter from my pocket and Tookes stepped forward to take it from me.

"With this revelation in mind," I continued carefully, "I feel there is now a very clear motive for Helena to wish my father ill."

"Iris!" Mrs Chambers flashed a glance at Cassie. "We already discussed this. Your imagination..."

"There's evidence now," I said, looking at Cassie. "A witness."

"On the morning of the accident," Cassie began, her voice quiet but firm, "I saw my mother putting something in a silver drinking flask."

"My father's flask," I finished. "Helena poisoned him."

There was silence, and Mrs Chambers and Tookes exchanged looks. Mrs Chambers' eyes filled with tears, and she shook her head at Tookes, as though they were having a silent conversation. Then Tookes crouched down beside my chair and took my hand. It was a very un-Tookes-like gesture.

"Lady Iris," he said, "when you spoke to us about this last time, we neither of us wanted to do anything to harm the memory you had of your father. The two of you were so close – like peas in the pod, people used to call you. And so, I'm afraid we weren't exactly truthful about what happened that day." He paused and frowned. "Not that we lied, but we perhaps softened the truth. Now I see it has led you into thinking something much worse and for that I am sorry."

"Tookes," I snapped, my nerves frayed, "I have no idea what you're talking about."

Again, the two servants shared a look, and Tookes drew himself up. "Very well," he continued steadily. "It *is* true that Miss Cassie saw Her Ladyship filling His Lordship's flask, but this she did every day at his request."

Cassie's grip on the arms of her chair relaxed slightly.

"Why?" I asked, bemused.

"Your father was drinking far too much, and that's the truth. He drank brandy all day, every day, more and more. Her Ladyship challenged him about it and so he insisted his wife be the one to keep his flask filled. They argued about it often. I think it pleased him to force her to undertake the chore." Here Tookes handed the letter back to me. "I hate to say it, but I don't believe he was perfectly in his right mind at the end. You can see here from his handwriting that he was under the influence when he wrote it – it's not in his usual style at all. He had become more and more paranoid, more determined to cut the family off from the outside world. His behaviour had grown quite … erratic."

I looked at the shaky letters, the ink stains. Tookes was right. I shook my head, refusing to take it all in. My father, a drunk – I could just about believe it. Certainly enough people had told me. But not in his right mind? It *couldn't* be true. Could it?

I thought about the things I had learned over the last week. The way my father kept to himself, our lack of visitors, the fights between him and Helena. The fact he had been willing to drag his wife through a public divorce case, possibly to lie and ruin her to achieve it. My mother, shut away in her room. Hiding places up the chimney, secret compartments…

"But still," I said weakly, desperately, "Helena *could* have adulterated his drink that day, put something in it?"

Here, something like embarrassment crossed Tookes' face. "That she couldn't, miss. As you know, it was I and old Kielty who found your father that day. What with the shock and all, I'm afraid we both had need of a swig or two from that flask, and neither one of us suffered any ill effects."

"Mr Tookes!" Mrs Chambers puffed herself up, seemingly more horrified by this information than by any of the rest. In other circumstances it would have been funny.

"So, my mother had nothing to do with it?" Cassie asked.

Both servants shook their heads.

"Believe us," Mrs Chambers said firmly. "It was a tragic accident."

"And, I fear, an inevitable one," Tookes added gravely.

I sat back in my chair, all the breath leaving my body in one exhalation. So that was it; the whole mystery uncovered. There was nothing amiss with the will. Helena had no hand in what happened. It was all an accident, one brought about by truths about my father that I had never known. Everything I had thought, everything I had done up to this point had been based on my own wrong assumptions.

"Iris?" Cassie crouched down in front of me. "Are you well?"

"I have no idea." The words came out somewhere between tears and laughter. "But I suppose I will be."

CHAPTER THIRTY-ONE

I wasn't sure what to think or feel about the revelations that had taken place. I also wasn't sure what to do next.

Perhaps it would be best to let Iris Scott-Holland die. Being Iris Grey was not so bad, after all, and the things that had meant so much to me – the house, and my father's memory – suddenly seemed, well … *complicated*.

I spent the next morning smiling and flirting mechanically with Stefan. His solid, undemanding presence was a relief and, as if sensing my turmoil, he made every effort to tease me into good humour.

That afternoon, thanks to the unseasonably warm weather, we took tea outside. A table had been dragged out to the lawn, where all signs of my shooting contest with Nick were long gone.

Helena was wearing a spring green dress and a straw hat. She looked young and happy. I watched her, laughing and talking with her guests, playing the hostess to perfection.

The truth of what had happened between her and my father was a surprise. Part of me was even able to summon some sympathy for her. Then I remembered every vicious flash of those green eyes, every time she had locked me alone in my room, denied me supper, kept me from riding – whatever punishment she thought best fit my imagined crimes. I had been a child, and yet she had barely troubled to conceal her animosity towards me, had – in fact – made every effort to let me know how she disliked me, had chipped away at me with spiteful comments, had told me I brought it all on myself with my behaviour.

When Father had died she had not bothered to hide her opinion that I was an annoyance that she would rather be rid of. I had lost my parents, and she was determined to take my home. Looking at her now, bright and cheerful, enjoying every luxury that Holland Hall had to offer, I found it difficult to relinquish my deep mistrust of her.

"I have a wonderful idea," she said. "As the weather is so fine, why don't the young folk go down to the river for the afternoon? We have four rowboats that you could take out."

"Oh, what a treat!" Sophia exclaimed.

"The river?" Lady Bell asked quaveringly. "Is that really safe? Surely that's where … where…"

Her husband cleared his throat and frowned ominously at his wife. She flushed and fell silent.

I had seen little of Lord Bell, but what I had seen I didn't like. I found it hard to believe that he and Lady Bell had produced such sweet, amiable children as Sophia and Percy. The man was largely absent, clearly deeply uninterested in the house party, and when he did speak it was usually to quell his wife's chatter.

"I don't think we need to dredge up that ancient history," Agatha pouted. "The river's perfectly safe,

Lady Bell, I promise you. What happened to Iris was her own fault. We won't be going anywhere near those strong currents."

Cassie's teacup clattered in her saucer, and I kept my eyes down.

"Iris?" The name came sharply from Nick's lips. *No fool, Nicholas Wynter.*

I forced myself to sip disinterestedly at my tea.

"My husband's daughter," Helena said quietly, shooting Agatha a look. "She drowned almost seven years ago. A terrible accident. It was a tragedy that came so soon after we lost Lord Scott-Holland."

The table fell into an awkward silence.

Helena smiled bravely. "But let's not dwell on such things when we are all here together on this beautiful day. Agatha is quite right that the river is perfectly safe, if a boating adventure sounds like something you would enjoy?"

"I think it sounds great fun!" Percy put in heartily. The rest of us murmured our agreement.

"Let's see," Helena said innocently, counting off on her fingers. "Two to a boat – Lady Sophia and

Mr Waterford, Lord Percy and Cassie, Lord Wynter and Miss Fox, and that leaves ... Agatha and Prince Stefan. Perfect."

"A good job that Miss Fox was here to balance the numbers after all," Cassie murmured, nudging me with her elbow.

I smiled at her now, though that smile was edged with trepidation. I was about to be trapped in a small boat with Nick, and, short of flinging myself into the river, there was to be no escape. I didn't like the way he had glanced up at the mention of Iris Scott-Holland.

The eight of us walked down to the river, where four neat rowboats were tied up, waiting for us.

"Oh," Agatha cried, her eyes sparkling. "How lovely!"

She was right; it was beautiful. The river wound its lazy way through lush green fields, cutting under weeping willows, their long chains of leaves just turning a burnished gold. I heard a high chirping sound and then the flash of vivid blue as a kingfisher flitted across the water's surface, there and gone before I could even remark upon it. The sun was high in the cloudless sky, beating down with all the intensity of a summer day.

The men, accordingly, and to the delight of many of the women, were in their shirtsleeves – jackets and ties discarded thanks to the informality of the occasion.

As Helena had said, laughing indulgently, "We're all friends here."

I wasn't so sure about that.

"Shall we?" Nick said, without any noticeable degree of enthusiasm. He held out his hand to help me into the boat as the other gentlemen were doing, but I chose to scramble in, unaided. I took the seat facing backwards.

Nick climbed in and took the seat across from me, his expression bland. The boat was small, and Nick was so tall that our knees touched. I tried to ignore it.

Stefan had been the first into the boats, laughing as he assisted Agatha, who sat like a perfect china doll, a lacy parasol unfurled over her head to protect her from the sun. The prince had set a brisk pace from the off, skimming their boat across the surface of the water like a pond skater. He made a boyish whooping sound, and I noticed Agatha's smile looked a little frozen, that one of her hands was clinging tightly to the side of the boat.

Percy set off in pursuit, egged on by Cassie; and Sophia and Jack seemed quite happy to keep to themselves. I watched their faces as they spoke and wondered whether there could at least be one romantic success story to come out of Helena's house party – even if it wasn't the one she hoped for.

Nick was in no hurry at all. Using one oar he pushed us away from the bank and took a couple of clean strokes to send us into the middle of the water. Here he let the boat bob gently, carried by the slow current.

Nick leaned back on his elbows as we floated along, his head tipped back, his eyes half-closed. I remained silent, trailing my fingers in the water, a sharp sting of cold in the shimmering heat.

Finally, he sat forward. "Are you feeling better?" he asked.

I started, thrown by the question.

"Last night," he clarified. "You didn't come down for dinner. I was … concerned."

"Yes, thank you," I said, surprised. "I'm feeling much better now. It was only a headache."

There was a pause.

"Did you know," Nick said conversationally, "that in society I am considered something of mystery? I don't cultivate the appearance on purpose, though it does have its benefits, I suppose. I am simply a more private person than the typical society rattle. I don't wear my emotions on my sleeve."

I sat forward too, matching his posture. It seemed we were to talk about something important after all. "I knew that was your reputation," I said. "It can be difficult to know what you are thinking."

"And still, compared to you, I feel as if I am an open book."

"What do you mean?" I asked sharply.

"I mean that I cannot fathom you, I can't work you out. I thought I was being so clever, hiring someone to help me with a plan that I've been waiting years to put into action, and yet I feel as though I am a chess piece myself, being played in a far larger game." He held up his hand to cut me off when I would have interrupted. "And I find I have no objection to it, really." He actually looked angry then. "That's the most damnable thing of all. When I'm so close to doing what I have planned to do,

I actually *want* you to win whatever game you're playing. But I don't want to be an unwitting participant any more." He looked at me, and his expression was quite serious. "I'm asking you to tell me what is going on."

Panic rose in my chest. It was too much. There had been too many revelations and changes over the last few days. It was impossible to think of confiding it all in another person. Even Cassie only knew half the story and that was because she had recognized me. I hadn't chosen to involve her.

Looking at Nick now, with his shirtsleeves rolled up, the breeze blowing a loose lock of hair across his forehead, his eyes steady on mine, a part of me wanted to tell him. A part of me wanted to tell him *very badly*. But another part of me, the older, wiser part of me, wanted to lock everything away. Knew that the only person I could rely upon was myself.

"What if I asked you the same question?" I said. "What if I asked you what was going on. Why are you so intent on destroying Stefan?"

For a moment I thought he was going to say nothing, but then he sighed. "That is a long story."

x

382

"Because if you ask me," I carried on, reckless in my fear, burning my bridges behind me, "Stefan is a perfectly charming man."

Nick's spine stiffened. "Charming?" he repeated.

"Yes. He's been nothing but sweet and gentlemanly to me. Just look at the maid yesterday morning, he was there trying to help her clean up, he took the time to learn her name, and you – you ordered her away as if she were nothing."

Something flickered in Nick's eyes. "You have no idea what you're talking about. Stefan is not the person you think he is."

"He sits in gardens and writes poetry." I rolled my eyes. "What a monster."

"He *what*?" The look of surprise on Nick's face was almost comical.

"He's a poet. He writes poetry," I said, smoothing my skirts. "I don't know why you should find that shocking."

"I find it *shocking* because Stefan can barely be persuaded to read a book unless it's a particularly racy one about lusty wenches. The idea of him popping up in a garden and passing himself off as the next Lord Byron is absolutely laughable."

"Well, it's true," I said. "He showed me his notebook."

"He showed you his poetry," Nick said slowly. "Poetry that he had written. And you read it?"

"Not exactly," I admitted.

"Ah, now we come to it. You *didn't* read it?"

"I couldn't read it," I pointed out crossly. "It wasn't written in English."

At this Nick threw his head back and laughed long and loud, as I simmered angrily on my seat.

"Oh," he said finally, actually wiping tears away from his eyes. "You see what I mean about not being able to work you out. I thought you were street tough, but you're falling for Stefan's lines like any other silly innocent."

"I am not—" I began, "I mean I do not—" I took a deep breath, attempting to calm the flame of temper, flaring up inside me. "Don't you dare patronize me. I know how to look after myself."

"I'm sure you do, but I'm also sure that Stefan's

notebook, were it translated, would contain only notes on the next race at Buxton, and the odds on who was favourite to win."

"He's sensitive," I insisted.

"Sensitive as a boot," Nick grumbled.

"The two of you are as bad as each other with all this petty one-upmanship," I snapped. I'd had enough of this. Enough of the lies. It seemed my whole life was built on them. If Nick wanted to ruin Stefan's life then I wanted to know why. "Well, you wanted me in the middle of it, so here I am." With that I got to my feet, sending the boat rocking wildly.

"Sit down!" Nick hissed.

"Why?' I asked. "So that you can scold me some more? Tell me that I don't understand, when you could simply explain it to me?"

I hadn't noticed the others rowing back towards us, but Nick obviously had because he opened his mouth to call a warning. It was too late.

Stefan, with his back to us, and still rowing as vigorously as before, sent a wave of water cascading towards us. I just had time to see Agatha's tiny smirk of triumph before the boat tipped and I was tumbling towards the water. Nick reached out to me, a strong hand wrapped around my wrist, but it was no use.

I fell dramatically into the water and, worse still, I pulled Nick in with me.

CHAPTER THIRTY-TWO

The water hit me like a cold slap. I felt Nick's arm come about my waist. Even in the water I could feel it warm through my thin dress like a brand against my skin, and I smacked it away.

"I can swim, I can swim," I spluttered. "As long as you stop hauling me about."

Nick let go of me with what I thought might have been a watery laugh, and the two of us were left treading water for a moment.

"Of course you can," he said. "You make a terrible swooning heroine."

"I thought we agreed that the villains were much more interesting," I managed, and then Stefan had manoeuvred his boat in next to us and his arm was there, reaching for me.

"No, no," I said, waving him away. "I'll swim to the bank. No use hauling me in the bottom of the boat like a poor gasping fish. I'll only get Agatha's beautiful dress dirty."

Stefan's eyes glimmered with humour, and something that looked like admiration. It was nice that something good had come out of this disaster, I supposed.

I followed Nick as he swam towards the bank. Swimming in an afternoon gown was not easy, but I managed, and when I reached the side of the river, Nick was there to offer me a hand. We pushed our way up on to the bank, adding a good smearing of dirt to our soaked clothes.

The others in the boats laughed and cheered, seeing us safe on dry land, and Nick stood to take a bow, the water running off him in rivulets, while I waved jauntily and tried to catch my breath.

"We'll come across the bridge," I called, pointing upstream, "if one of you can tow the boat."

Stefan blew me a laughing kiss, and set about rescuing our boat, while Agatha glowered at me from beneath her parasol.

"Your lovely gown, Miss Fox," she called sweetly. "What a shame it's ruined."

I looked down at myself. She was quite right. The pretty pale pink was now a dirty grey, and I doubted any of Matilda's magic would be able to rescue it. It also weighed a ton.

"These are not meant for swimming in," I grumbled, hauling at my skirts while the others rowed away.

"I'm only glad I wasn't wearing my jacket," Nick said, pushing his wet hair back away from his face. "I wouldn't have been able to face my valet."

We trudged along the bank towards the stone bridge. My shoes were squelching, and I could feel my hair coming down from its pins, snaking around my head. I was certain that I looked a picture, but only if that picture was Caravaggio's *Medusa*.

I snuck a glance at Nick and caught him doing the same

at me. My cheeks burned and I turned to face forward.

We walked the rest of the way back in silence.

When we arrived back at the house, wrapped in the blankets that Nick had picked up on our way past the stables, we were met at the door by Lady Bell, and Nick's grandmother, who had been told all about our boating disaster.

"Oh dear," Lady Bell wittered. "I knew the river was a bad idea. I do hope you haven't caught a chill. Those things can be simply deadly, the way they sneak up on you."

"I think Miss Fox has a stronger constitution than that," the dowager countess said, casting me a disapproving look. No doubt future countesses did not fall in rivers and if they did they certainly didn't contract life-threatening chills. "But you had better go straight up and have a hot bath and change out of those clothes."

I longed to say that I had already determined upon that surprising course of action myself, thank you very much, but I bit my tongue.

From the smirk that Nick flashed over his shoulder at me as he headed upstairs, I could tell that he, at least, knew precisely what I was thinking.

"What a good idea, Lady Wynter. If you'll excuse me." Gathering the horse blanket about me with all the dignity I could muster, I trudged up the stairs, hurrying to catch up with Nick.

"Our conversation is not over," I said in a low voice when we reached the landing. I put my hand on his arm, tugging him round to face me. "I want to know the truth about Stefan. It's time you trusted me."

"Trust you?" Nick's voice was quiet but simmering with something dangerous. We were standing perilously close to one another. "I don't even know who you are."

"Of course you know who I am," I replied quickly, trying to deflect the accusation in his tone. "I'm Iris Grey, talented seamstress."

"You're a tornado in a pretty dress is what you are!" he snapped, and then he turned and stomped off, leaving me behind.

I felt strangely flattered.

Matilda clucked in horror when she saw me, and it took two hot baths before I felt actually clean.

The baths gave me time to think. I decided to take

a moment here, in the quiet of my room, to go through the bundle of letters I had found in the chimney and the file from the solicitor's office more carefully. It was time I found out more about my father. It was becoming increasingly clear that I had known very little about him, and amid all the other revelations, that was the one that hurt the most.

I lifted out the box and spread my mother's embroidery on the bed. I stared for a long time at Rapunzel in her tower, at the amber eyes of the big bad wolf.

"Little cub," my father had called me. He said that we were wolves. Fierce guardians of our land, wild and free.

But wolves were predators too. Had there really been this whole other side to him? One that I never knew?

I read through the letters between my father and his solicitor. They painted a fairly clear picture now that I had both sides of the correspondence. It seemed that it hadn't taken long for the shine to wear off after he married Helena. Unlike my mother, she had not been content to be kept at home, shut away. That, at least, made sense – there was nothing docile about Helena. I imagine she had made her own desires fairly clear.

Mr Fortescue had adopted a reasonable tone in his letters, trying gently to dissuade Father from following what he felt was an unnecessarily extreme path – he had clearly been horrified by the idea of divorce. He repeatedly assured my father that Lady Scott-Holland was a good and virtuous woman.

Father's answers were more blunt.

Blasted woman won't stop hounding me about throwing a house party, inviting a group of guests to stay and make free with my hospitality. I'm certain it's because she has a lover she wants to sneak in right under my nose. But I'll not have it. I tell you there's nothing that will get past me, nothing! I want you to hire an investigator, find out who the man is. I'll drag her through the courts if she thinks to make me a cuckold!

His handwriting grew increasingly spiky and erratic. I tried to remember how he had been during this time, but I couldn't. I hadn't seen much of him, I realized. I had blamed Helena for his long absences – but perhaps it had been down to something else entirely. His own paranoia, his drinking.

I turned again to the will. I could only assume that had he not died and had he divorced Helena, Helena and her daughters would have been cut out entirely.

Then again, the small amount he had left to Helena – enough only for her to live a kind of shabby genteel life, nothing like she had now – was almost an insult in itself. I wondered how Helena had felt when the will was read to her. It was fortunate that he had made such provisions for her daughters that she could remain comfortable herself. A messy divorce would have changed all of that.

I was leafing through the pages of the will again, looking for anything unusual. There was something odd about the first page that I couldn't quite put my finger on. It was as if the words were lined up differently to the rest, or as if there was more white space on the page. I noticed on the edge of one of the sheets of parchment a thin red line. On closer examination I saw that there were similar marks on several of the pages; the staining I had noticed on my initial view. It looked almost like blood. I peered closer at the pages, fanning them out on the bed.

I sighed. Not blood. Wine. Just further proof that my father was the drunk everyone said he was. There was a neat ring on the edges of the pages, where he had obviously set his glass down on top of them as they were spread over his desk.

Only the ring was not complete. I frowned, tilting the pages. I leafed through the clean pages, looking for any more that contained the red marks. There were none.

I picked up the pages that were marked and read through them. They included the pages about me and my stepsisters. Then I laid them out again, a tingling feeling rushing through my limbs.

There was a page missing.

The circle didn't quite line up, as if someone had removed a page.

I read the final words before the missing page.

To my daughters, I leave the entirety of the estate and all of my assets outside of the bequests mentioned here, to be held in trust until

The top of the next page continued, *they each reach the age of one and twenty. Until such time, the bequests are to be held in trust by my wife, Lady Helena Scott-Holland.*

The sentence made perfect sense. And yet, when I looked again at the circle made by the glass it was clear that something was not right.

A feeling of certainty spread through my bones. There *was* something wrong with the will. There had been all along. I just needed to find out what it was. But how?

CHAPTER THIRTY-THREE

By the time I had put everything away it was almost
dinner. I let Matilda choose an evening gown for me –
an indigo dress, draped in tulle, and embroidered with
a design of silver flowers.

I made my way downstairs a little earlier than usual,
and I was walking past the door to the billiard room
when I heard my own name – or rather Serena's name –
being mentioned.

"... eye on Miss Fox, have you?" I heard the colonel's
braying voice ask.

I hesitated, wondering who he was talking to.

"Certainly, Miss Fox is a very lovely young woman," Stefan replied, and there were the sounds of billiard balls being hit across the table. "Though I rather thought *you* might have your eye on her, Nick."

"You know me, Stefan," Nick replied noncommittally.

"That I do, my friend, and I think I have never seen you so taken with a young woman," Stefan chuckled.

"After all, dear boy," the colonel blustered, "everyone must settle down some time. About time the pair of you were looking for a wife."

"Preferably one for each of us," I heard Nick murmur. "And so I think the prince's luck may be out."

"Oh, do you now?" Stefan asked. "Well, I say you should not be so hasty. I think Miss Fox will quite enjoy the idea of becoming a princess."

"She's very beautiful," the colonel put in.

"That she is, Colonel, that she is!" Stefan exclaimed. "What say you, Nick? Isn't Miss Fox as pretty a piece as you've ever laid eyes on?"

There was a pause.

"I think," Nick said dangerously, "that her looks

are the least interesting thing about her."

I felt my heart quicken at the words. I pressed my cool hands to my cheeks.

"Rich as Croesus too, I'm told," the colonel put in.

"Oh, yes," Stefan laughed again. "What did you say, Nick – one of the largest fortunes in England? But you have no use for that Earl Wynter, spare a thought for those who do."

"Well, I think she's a nice little thing," the colonel said stoutly.

"She's not a nice little thing," Nick snapped then. Clearly our last conversation had left him rather uncharitably disposed towards me. I suppose I couldn't blame him, but it was strange to hear a man, usually so poised, sound so ruffled. *"Nice little thing?* Ha! She's an infuriating baggage."

I stepped away then, before I could be caught, but not before I heard Stefan crow, "My god, I think Lord Wynter's in love at last!"

I tried desperately to ignore the throb of my pulse, so loud I was sure it would draw them from the room after me. It was just a game, I reminded myself. Just part of the plan. There was no more sure-fire way to drive Stefan into my waiting arms than for Nick to pretend to be in love with me. He had said it himself; that the next push had to come from him. This must be what he had meant.

Still, I had trouble meeting Nick's eyes when the group finally assembled for our usual pre-dinner drinks. Fortunately, Cassie and Sophia had descended on me as soon as they arrived, teasing me about my fall in the river.

"We shouldn't laugh," Sophia said, though her eyes were doing precisely that. "It looked as though it was a shock, and the water was so cold."

"Oh, yes, we should laugh," Cassie interjected. "Because it was so funny, with you going head over heels and Lord Wynter trying to play the gallant hero, and what did you do but pull him straight in after you. The look on his face! I'll never forget it! So outraged."

All three of us dissolved into giggles, and I felt a warmth spreading through me like sunlight. So this was what it was like to have friends. I'd never really had any, even as a child. I had been happy to spend time with my father and had been kept at home without the company of other children until Cassie and Agatha came along. It hadn't seemed strange to me before, but now I realized that it was part of a story I was only just beginning to piece together.

We made our way through to dinner, and there was plenty of talk about my and Nick's accident, as well as an extremely delicious treacle tart, served with thick clotted cream. From here we proceeded back to the drawing room for cards and conversation, and to listen to Agatha play the piano and sing for us.

I had to admit that she sounded like an angel, even if she did make ridiculous cow eyes at Stefan the whole time.

The rest of the evening passed without incident – until, that was, Stefan gently took me aside.

It was late and everyone was beginning to withdraw to bed.

"Before you leave, Miss Fox," Stefan murmured, his voice low and serious, "I wondered if you might consent to meet me shortly in the gardens."

"I'm not sure I should," I said cautiously, my heartbeat quickening.

He gave me a sweet smile. "I wouldn't ask," he said, "only there is something of a very personal nature that I must ask you."

I flushed. It seemed that Nick had indeed played his ace.

"I see." I glanced down at my hands. "In that case I should be happy to meet you. In the rose garden?"

"The very place I was going to suggest myself. In ten minutes?"

"Very well."

Stefan left, and I glanced over at Nick to find his eyes already on me. I nodded, ever so slightly.

A fleeting look rippled across his face then, though whether it was pleasure or pain I couldn't say.

Ten minutes later, I too had excused myself to bed and crept outside towards the rose garden.

There were no lights this time, only shadows, and the garden was lit by the moon and the stars alone.

"Serena," Stefan whispered, as I approached.

"Yes, Stefan, it's me," I said, and I didn't have to act nervous at all.

"I won't keep you out here long," he murmured, his

face in shadow, his hand reaching out to clasp my own. "I think perhaps you know why I asked you to meet me."

"I'm not entirely sure," I said, my eyes fixed on my shoes.

He placed a gentle finger on my chin, tipping my face up so that I was looking into his eyes.

"I asked you to meet me here, because I would like you to be my wife," he said steadily. "I know we have not known each other long, but I am certain we would make each other happy."

I gave him credit for not pretending he was head over ears in love with me. I bit my lip. This was the moment. This was the moment when I decided whether I was sticking to Nick's plan or not.

"May I ask," I said hesitantly, "why you wish to marry? Why now? Why me?"

He exhaled slowly. "It is a fair question," he said, taking my cold hand in his. "Why now? The honest answer is because my grandmother wishes me to marry soon. If I don't return home with a suitable bride then she has one picked out for me. A distant cousin." He sighed. "I understand my duty and why my grandmother

wants this, but I myself … I suppose I am a romantic."
He flashed me a rueful grin. "I would like to marry a
girl of my own choosing. One with whom I can imagine
a life filled with love and genuine affection. That, I
suppose, brings me to the answer to your other question.
Why you? Because I can see that future for us, Serena."

It was a good answer. And one that made no mention
of the fortune I supposedly possessed, the one that I had
heard him joking about earlier.

I was about to betray a man. I had to decide, in that
moment, who to trust. I thought about Nick, about what
I knew of him. There was a reason he had asked me to
do this. I felt the heavy tug of my instinct and I decided
to listen to it.

"Yes, I'll marry you, Stefan," I said finally. "It would
be my honour."

"No," he said. "It will be mine."

He leaned forward and placed his lips against mine.
It was a chaste kiss, warm and pleasant. His smile
afterwards was triumphant.

"Now we must get you back inside and out of the
cold," Stefan said, tucking my hand through his arm

with a newfound sense of possession that I couldn't quite like. "I will write to your father. Will he have any objection, do you think?"

"None whatsoever," I replied honestly. "But let me write to him. He'll be delighted."

"Then we can announce our engagement at the ball on Friday?"

"I would like nothing better."

"Excellent," Stefan murmured, delivering me safely to the door. "Five days feels like an eternity … but I fear an announcement now would make things a trifle awkward with our hostess. Until then, it will be just between ourselves."

"You're right, of course."

I bid him goodnight, and he kissed me again. Then, instead of heading for my room, I waited until I knew he had gone and made my way to the library.

Nick was waiting for me there, just as I knew he would be.

"Well?" he said, standing by the fire, tension in every line.

I nodded. "It's done."

For a moment the look on his face was quite dreadful, and then he collapsed into the chair behind him with a bump.

I moved cautiously towards him. "I thought this was what you wanted," I said. "I thought you'd be happy."

"It is," he said, his hand scrubbing tiredly over his face. "It was. I honestly don't know any more."

He gestured to the seat where I had sat across from him before. He reached again for the brandy, pouring two glasses with a steady hand.

He downed his own drink in one swift movement, but I didn't touch mine. Despite the fire, I felt cold.

"Do you *want* to tell me about it?" I asked, because this, suddenly, felt like the right question.

"Yes." The word hissed from behind his teeth. "Yes, Iris, I do."

It was the first time he had used my real name. "Then tell me."

He stared into the fire for another moment.

"When I was growing up, there really was a little girl who lived next door," he said slowly. "Her name was Lila, and she was a year younger than me. Until the age that I was sent to school we were always together. She lived in the village. Her mother had been a lady but she married below her station, for love, of course, and so they weren't a part of society life."

He poured himself another drink.

"I was sent away to school and I didn't see her for several years. Then, when I was sixteen, I went home for the holidays and there she was. The most beautiful girl I had ever seen."

"You fell in love with her?" I asked gently.

"I was sixteen," he said. "But, yes, I thought I was in love with her. It was not reciprocated. Lila saw me as a brother figure, I think. I accepted that, of course. I was quite happy for our great love affair to be one-sided. I believe at the time I probably thought there was something poetic about unrequited love – as though it were a rite of passage. I only wanted her to be happy.

"We remained very close." His face softened. "I was shy as a boy and didn't have that many friends at school, but Lila made me laugh, she listened to me, we shared our secrets, our dreams with one another. We wrote to each other almost daily for the next year.

407

That's when she told me that her widowed aunt – her mother's sister – had decided as she had no children of her own that she would give Lila a London come out. Lila was ecstatic."

He stared into his drink for a moment.

"I had grown up a bit and started to run with a rowdier set. That's how I met Stefan. He came to my school to study for a term, and instantly we were the best of friends, but we pulled a stupid prank and got sent down – a sort of suspension, you see," he explained, and I nodded. "We had nothing to do but kick our heels. We headed for London to cause as much havoc there as possible, and then … Lila."

"She was there?"

He nodded. "Just arrived for her first season, so excited and about to be the pick of the bunch too, with her looks. It didn't matter that she had no fortune, no real name. She would have made a respectable match of it."

"*Would* have made?" I asked, a hollow feeling in my stomach.

Nick grimaced. "I made the mistake of introducing

her to Stefan. Made the even bigger mistake of telling Stefan what she meant to me. And then, of course, he had to have her."

"But he didn't marry her," I said.

"No, Iris." Nick looked at me. "He didn't marry her. He ruined her."

"He ... what?" I gasped.

"I know," Nick agreed casually. "I was rather surprised myself. I never suspected he would take it so far. It turned out that Prince Stefan *wanted* Lila, but he *needed* a fortune. It was not the first time – apparently his grandmother was unhappy with him and had sent him to England in a state of temporary exile because of a number of *indiscretions* back at home. He convinced Lila to run away with him, made her think he was going to marry her, and then left her without a word. Of course, Lila had already made the mistake of confiding in people. She thought she was going to be married – to a prince, no less! She had no idea how society worked. The way they tore her down."

"What happened?" I whispered.

"She left in disgrace," Nick sighed. "Her family sent

her away to live with a relative in France. We wrote to each other, still do sometimes. I even offered to marry her myself, but she turned me down. Always doing the honourable thing." He snorted into his drink. "But there was no season for Lila, no being the belle of the ball, no husband, no children. Not yet anyway. She's still shut away like a criminal. She had her whole life to look forward to, and Stefan took it from her, then went back home like nothing had happened. I'd wager that he hasn't ever thought about her again."

"And so you wanted to destroy him," I said.

"I wanted *his* choice taken from him. If we hadn't intervened he'd have married Agatha Weston, made himself comfortable on her fortune, far from his grandmother's control – it's only the fact that she holds the purse strings that keeps him in any kind of check. With Agatha's money he'd become even worse – he'd get his own way *again*, face no consequences.

"Now he thinks he's engaged to an heiress. Serena Fox. He thinks he's got one over on his grandmother, found himself a rich wife whose fortune he will control. I wanted to take that from him publicly, to embarrass him,

410

and then to send him home in disgrace, where he must be the one to bend under someone else's expectations. I wanted to punish him for what he did to my friend."

"Of course you did!" I exclaimed. I jumped to my feet, anger vibrating through me like I was a tuning fork. The very idea that Stefan could act in such a way and walk away without consequences, while an innocent woman's entire life was completely derailed made me furious.

"Why didn't you tell me? I could have helped you! I could have done more. I *will* do more. We have to make it as awful as possible. Humiliate him in front of everyone."

There was a light in Nick's eyes now. "Bloodthirsty, aren't you?"

"Yes, I am. And I tell you, Nick, the worst of it is that no matter what we do, he won't ever be ruined like Lila was ruined." I was pacing now.

"I know," Nick sighed.

"But I'll do it," I said. "I'll make sure he's forced to run back to his grandmother, to do her bidding."

"It's a dangerous game to play, though," Nick said.

"Stefan … I don't know why, but he seems to feel a need to best me."

"It's because he's jealous of you, of course," I said impatiently.

"Jealous?" Nick frowned.

"Yes, stupid," I replied, trying to keep up with the thoughts racing through my head. Nick's frown was replaced by a chuckle, though I barely registered it. "So, what are you worried about?" I asked.

"What am I worried about?" Nick repeated, raking his hand through his hair. "My god, Iris, how can you ask? I'm half out of my mind over it. I'm worried about history repeating itself!"

CHAPTER THIRTY-FOUR

To say that I passed a restless night would be an understatement of tremendous proportions. I couldn't sleep at all.

Of *course* I couldn't sleep. How could anyone sleep after all of that? How could I have been so wrong about Stefan? How could I have missed the signs?

With a groan I remembered the incident with the maid, Lottie. Had Stefan found her alone; had he done something to make her drop the milk jug? Was that what her blushing and stammering had really been about?

Was that why Nick had sent her from the room? Had it been relief, not fear, that caused her to turn tail and run? And Matilda – now that I thought about it, she had seemed worried about him proposing to me. Did she know something too?

The questions chased one another in an endless loop around my mind.

I thought of Nick's face when he had spoken about his friend, the way she had been mistreated, his powerlessness to stop it, his guilt at introducing her to the man who would destroy her. It had all been there for me to see, no mask to hide behind at all.

I turned over again, thumping my pillow. *I'm worried about history repeating itself.* Did that mean he cared for me too? As a friend? As more than that?

He had told me everything, the whole truth, and I still hadn't trusted him with my story. Not that he had asked me to. He'd shared his secret without demands attached to it. It was just another thing that made me like him more.

Because I did like him.

I liked him so much.

But I didn't want to think about that.

Unfortunately, if I wasn't thinking about that, then I was thinking about my father. Another man who had turned out to be nothing like I imagined. Those red-stained sheets of paper and that missing piece of the puzzle...

In the end, I drifted into a restless doze, and woke late, feeling groggy and disorientated.

Matilda came when I rang and brought with her a tray bearing a steaming pot of hot chocolate. I sipped at it gratefully, leaning back against my pillows as she pulled back the curtains and laid the fire – not that it looked like I would need it. The light was streaming through the window again, another sunny day.

Serena Fox was engaged. As far as Stefan was concerned, I had agreed to marry him, and in order to dole out the punishment he deserved I was going to have to pretend to be excited about it, to pretend that I actually liked the man. I glanced at Matilda, laying out my clothes.

"Matilda," I said hesitantly. "When you asked me about the prince before, you seemed a bit concerned about whether I was going to be alone with him. Was there any particular reason for that?"

She shifted uncomfortably. "No, miss," she replied, her eyes on the floor.

"Because if there *was* anything … if he had upset you or behaved inappropriately, you could tell me. I'd want you to tell me. I'd believe you, and I'd do something about it."

She lifted her head sharply at that and regarded me with thoughtful eyes. There was a long silence, and she chewed her bottom lip.

"I've not had much to do with him," she said finally. "But there's talk going round the servants' hall. He's been a bit too friendly with some of the maids. Nothing dire, you understand, just suggestive. Free with his hands. There's one girl, Lottie, says he got a bit fresh with her."

"Sounds dire enough to me," I said grimly.

Matilda shrugged. I hated that shrug. I had given that shrug myself. "You know what these house parties can be like," she sighed. "There are a lot of men who think their position gives them certain liberties."

Unfortunately, I *did* know what she meant. While living in the city, I'd come up against my fair share of men who felt they were entitled to take what they liked. I wondered if I would have known about any of it if I'd remained a sheltered society miss. Did Agatha and Cassie know what was going on in their home? Probably not.

"Well, you tell the rest of the girls that if anything happens that they don't like, they can always come to me. I'll do what I can to protect them."

"Yes, miss, but Lord Wynter already said the same thing." Matilda gave me a small smile. "No offence, but I think he's a lot scarier than you."

"You'd be surprised how scary I can be." I grinned at her. Then I pushed back the bed covers. "Now, let's see what this day brings."

"I understand there's going to be a tennis tournament, miss," Matilda said. "Several of the guests are already up practising."

I groaned. Riding and swimming were my sports – tennis was decidedly not. "Save me from organized fun. A tennis tournament? What's wrong with reading a book?"

Matilda tried unsuccessfully to hide her smile. "I've laid out your tennis suit," she said. "At least you'll look pretty as a picture."

I observed the outfit sourly. Of course Nick had been prepared for this. The tennis suit was made of white cotton, with an ivory stripe running through it. There was a straight, light skirt, a fitted jacket, and a white shirt that tied in a bow at my neck. There was also a jaunty straw boater. It *was* pretty; but despite some improvements over the last couple of years, the outfits the ladies were expected to wear were still not the most comfortable or practical for running around and playing tennis. I wondered with a smile what Cassie would turn up in.

As it happened, Cassie was the first person I ran into when I arrived downstairs. She was wearing something similar to her cycling outfit, but in lighter material, a tennis racket in her hand. I eyed her bloomers enviously.

"That's going to make life easier," I said.

Cassie's face scrunched up in a grin. "You have no idea," she said. "The first time I ran around in trousers – it was a transformative experience!"

She linked her arm through mine and we made our way outside.

"I don't mean to be a bad house guest, but I'm really not a talented tennis player," I grumbled.

"I remember!" Cassie chuckled, and I was reminded of the time after Helena and the girl arrived, when we had been thrown into all sorts of activities together. I had been awful then – it was hard to imagine that seven years of not playing was going to have improved matters. "But don't worry about it." Cassie swung her racquet through the air. "No one stands a chance against Percy and me, anyway. Although Agatha is in high spirits." Cassie rolled her eyes. "She's paired up with the prince, and she's actually quite decent."

"Of course she is," I muttered. "She always was, if I remember rightly. Used to enjoy embarrassing me by not letting me win a single point."

"She wasn't anything like as good at riding though, or embroidery, for that matter," Cassie reminded me, clearly trying to raise my spirits. "You were wonderful at that. Do you still do it?"

"I do," I said. "Though it's more of an occupational

necessity, these days. I noticed a piece of mine in the morning room, actually. Agatha passed that one off as her own."

"I remember that," Cassie said quietly. "It was just after your father died. I think Agatha considered it belonged to her because she donated that spool of silver thread that we found."

"It was about the only nice memory I have of her," I admitted. "When you both sat with me that day. It felt almost like having sisters."

Cassie put her hand on my arm, pulling me to a stop. "I hope you feel differently now," she said solemnly. "I hope you know that whatever happens, and whatever you decide to do, I consider you my sister."

Quick tears stung my eyes then. It was painful, this transformation from being alone to having people I trusted, cared about. Like I was being cracked open, broken apart.

I didn't reply to Cassie, but she must have read my emotions in my face, because she squeezed my arm again and then carried on walking, chatting cheerfully about her skills on the tennis court.

When we reached the lawn, we found some of the others waiting. There were comfortable chairs spread out for the audience, and a net had been pulled across to divide the makeshift court.

Helena and Agatha had Stefan cornered, and he was laughing easily at whatever they were saying. The sight of him made something tighten in my chest, and I fought to keep the animosity I felt from my face. Agatha looked delicate and blooming in her tennis dress, and there was excitement in her eyes. I felt Helena's gaze on me as I approached, taking my measure once again.

The dowager countess was sitting in a large cane chair surrounded by plump cushions, a lace parasol in one hand. She looked like a queen, and Nick was standing beside her. I tried not to stare, but my mouth went dry. It could have been because last night had shifted things between us for ever, or it could have been the sight of him in his form-fitting tennis whites, but either way the result was the same. I felt shy and awkward.

"Here's your partner now," the dowager countess called, beckoning me over. "I was just telling Nicholas that I expect the two of you to uphold the family name."

"I'm afraid your grandson has been saddled with the wrong partner, then." I grimaced. "Tennis is not my sport."

"So much the better," Nick replied promptly. "We can get knocked out in the first round and lounge about with a drink instead."

I met his eye, and despite his usual, impassive expression, there was warmth and good humour in his gaze. I felt myself relax.

"I seem to remember you telling me you had a real talent for tennis, thanks to your height," I said.

There was a laugh in his voice as he replied, "It's possible that I exaggerated."

The Bells arrived then, with the colonel and Jack close behind.

"I shan't worry about any competition from you, Wynter." Jack grinned. "Can't ever stand to get your tennis whites dirty. You look very fetching, by the way."

"Kind of you to notice," Nick murmured. "But I'm sure anyone would look fetching next to your rag-mannered style. That poor valet of yours suffers daily."

"And doesn't he let me know it?" Jack groaned. "It's all Lord Wynter this, and Lord Wynter that…"

"A man of exquisite taste, as I have often commented."

"What do you think, Lady Sophia?" Jack turned to her. "As my partner, are you ashamed to be seen with me?" He turned in a circle, showing off his own perfectly presentable suit.

Sophia giggled. "I think there are certainly few who could compete with Lord Wynter on a sartorial front," she said mock-seriously. "I don't think I've ever seen white clothes look so white before. Perhaps his plan is to dazzle his opponents?"

"I think you're right!" Jack waved his racquet accusingly. "Make sure Wynter and Miss Fox are playing in the shade, he'll be absolutely deadly in direct sunlight!"

"Already making excuses for your inevitable loss, Waterford?" Nick quirked an eyebrow. "It's sad, really."

In fact, we didn't even have to play against Jack and Sophia. Our first game was against Agatha and Stefan, and it was clear from the outset that we were outmatched.

Nick had not exaggerated after all. He was a

proficient tennis player and for a while he managed to keep us afloat – those long limbs really did come in handy. I did my best, leaping around, even managing to get in a couple of good shots, but all in all it was a poor showing, and there was one particularly spectacular moment in which I tripped over my own skirts and went sailing over backwards, landing on the ground with an audible thump, the air knocked clean out of me.

I closed my eyes for a moment, and when I opened them, Nick's face hovered in the blue sky above me. He raised his eyebrows.

"Do you think anyone noticed?" I whispered.

Laughter danced in his eyes, and I felt an answering smile on my own lips.

"I'm sure they were all too dazzled by the elegance of my ensemble," he replied.

I burst out laughing then, right there on the grass, and he held out a hand, hauling me to my feet. The others cheered, Jack letting out a loud, ear-splitting whistle, and I bowed.

"I think it's best we concede," I said. "For the sake of my dignity – or what remains of it."

Gracious in victory, Agatha rushed forward, her cheeks pink, her grey-green eyes shining. "Miss Fox, what a tumble!" she exclaimed. "You poor thing, you'd better sit down with a nice glass of lemonade."

"I think you're quite right," I agreed, wincing as I brushed off my skirts.

"Still, a good game." Stefan beamed, coming forward to shake Nick's hand. "A worthy opponent."

"I'm glad you think so," Nick replied evenly.

Stefan took my hand next, looking at me with a significance that I knew was meant for my understanding only. He brushed his fingers briefly over the palm of my hand, a tender gesture that left me feeling queasy. I gave him the sort of shy smile I imagined a secret engagement may produce.

"Miss Fox," Helena called. "Come and sit by me, I've had a drink poured for you already."

With some reluctance I did as I was told.

"I hope you didn't injure yourself?" Helena asked from beneath the wide brim of her hat.

"Only my pride," I said. "I'm afraid I'm useless at tennis."

"Yet I hear that you're a fantastic horsewoman," she said.

"I-I don't think the two skills are really connected," I said, puzzled by this line of questioning.

"No, I daresay you're right," Helena agreed lightly. "Though so often those who are good at one sport are good at many. Take my poor husband, for example. He was a sporting man. There wasn't much he couldn't turn his hand to in that arena. He could ride, shoot, hunt, fish, play tennis, cricket, rugby ... the list was endless."

"He sounds like an impressive man," I managed.

Helena seemed to think this over. "I suppose he was, to some." She looked me dead in the eye. "His daughter was just like you, though; brilliant in the saddle, hopeless at tennis. A difficult girl, that one, always making trouble."

My blood ran cold, as her eyes held mine, luminous, unreadable green pools. "Well, Lady Scott-Holland," I replied, my voice feather-light, "it sounds as though you are not terribly sorry that they are both gone."

"Perhaps you're right, Miss Fox," she agreed silkily. "Though I do hate to sound like the wicked stepmother."

CHAPTER THIRTY-FIVE

That night I lay awake again, tossing and turning. I had spent the rest of the day in fear that Helena, like a coiled snake, was about to strike. My nerves were shredded.

I tried to reassure myself that whatever she might suspect, she couldn't know anything for certain. My relationship and personal history with Nick must be enough to cast doubt on what would be a wild (though accurate) theory. Society had accepted me as Miss Fox, and Helena would be careful about rocking that particular boat.

Still, her words clanged through me and I couldn't sleep. Once more I was chased by anxieties and questions. Only this time I didn't want to worry about them alone. This time there was something that I could do about that.

I told myself it was a stupid plan. Inappropriate, terrible, bound to end in disaster.

But I knew that I was going to do it anyway.

I padded out of bed and put on my dressing gown. Then I headed for the hallway. This was my house, after all, and I was the one who knew its secrets. I also knew which room Nick was staying in. There was no chance that Helena had any idea about the tunnels, I thought idly, as I knocked along the wooden panelling. Most of the upper floor of the house was connected if you only knew where to look.

I knew where to look. After all, I had been a very solitary child with plenty of time on my hands.

I heard the telltale hollow sound under my knuckles and pressed against the corner of the panel. It swung open with a thin creak, and I held up my candle. The space was smaller than I remembered – though actually

I suppose it was more the case that I was bigger. It was dark, and I could see cobwebs.

I didn't have to do this, I reminded myself. But it felt like if I didn't tell Nick the truth now then I might not ever tell him. Here and now, in the inky darkness, I finally had the courage, and that courage might not stick around in the hard light of day. These hours after midnight so often felt that way ... like a time for secrets.

Taking a deep breath, I stepped into the cold, dark space, and let the door swing shut behind me.

The less said about my time navigating the tunnel, the better. It was probably only a couple of minutes, but it felt like longer. As an enterprising child I had carved my own coded directions into the wooden tunnel with my pen knife, and so I was thankfully sure of where I was going. I placed my fingers over one of the small symbols, a moment of communion with the young me, the one who had been left here for so many hours by herself.

When I reached the panel that opened up into Nick's room, I hesitated. Breaking into a man's room in the middle of the night was certainly not the behaviour of a proper young lady.

But that ship had definitely sailed.

Slowly, I pushed the door open. Beyond it was only darkness. Silence.

"Nick?" I whispered. "Nick? Are you awake?"

"Iris?" A startled voice came from the shadows. "Is that you? Where are you?"

I stepped through the door, holding my candle in front of me. "I'm here."

Nick muttered a string of words, all of them unsuitable for a lady's ears, and I realized that he was in bed, though he sounded awake enough. "Do you walk through walls now?" he asked.

I laughed nervously. "Something like that."

"Well, sit down over there by the fireplace," he said, "I'm not exactly dressed for company." He didn't sound angry, only amused.

I sat in the chair, my back to the rest of the room, my candle on the table beside me. There were several more soft curses and thumping sounds, and then he was there, in front of me.

He wore dark trousers and a loose white shirt, hastily buttoned, half-wrong, and open at the neck. His feet were bare, and his hair was rumpled.

I swallowed, a flush coming to my cheeks.

"Yes, well," he said, looking down at himself in the light from my candle. "A bit of notice next time and I can present a more polished picture."

I thought he looked delicious.

He picked up my candle from the table and walked over to the gas lamp on the wall, using a taper to light it and keeping the flame low.

It was enough to illuminate the room in a soft amber glow.

"You really are here," he said, turning to look at me. "I almost thought you were a ghost."

"I'm afraid not," I said, rubbing my hands against my dressing gown. He didn't seem upset by my appearance in his room, but my nerves were jumping all over the place.

"What are you doing here, Iris?" He looked over at the wall panel which had now clicked back into place. "How on earth did you even get in here?" He walked over to the wall and ran his hand over it, obviously mystified, before turning to face me.

"That's a long story," I murmured, tucking a strand of hair behind my ear. "One that I came here to tell you."

Nick leaned against the fireplace. "So that's it. You know it wasn't a trade, telling you all that last night? You don't owe me anything."

"I know that," I said quietly. "I want to tell you. I have wanted to tell you for a long time, but I didn't know how."

"Then tell me," Nick said gently, echoing my own words to him.

I fiddled with the tie on my dressing gown.

"Did you know Lord Scott-Holland?" I asked.

Nick frowned at this apparent diversion from the matter at hand. "I never met him, no," he said. "He died when I was quite young, I think."

I nodded. "You were probably about fifteen or sixteen," I said. Around the time he was falling in love with Lila.

"That sounds about right."

"And when did you first meet Lady Scott-Holland?" I asked.

"A couple of years later, I suppose. Doing the rounds during the London season."

"Did you know that Lord Scott-Holland had a daughter? Lady Scott-Holland's stepdaughter."

Nick's face changed then. His eyes were wary. "The one that Agatha mentioned," he said slowly. "The one who drowned."

"She didn't drown," I said. "She ran away. To London."

The words were out, and I watched them land.

"Iris," he murmured. "Iris Scott-Holland."

His eyes locked on to mine. I couldn't have looked away even if I'd wanted to.

"Yes," I said simply. "Iris Scott-Holland."

"So it *is* you."

"Yes."

He took a step towards me and then stopped. "I wondered, when Agatha mentioned your name ... but then they said that she had died."

I shook my head. "They just let everyone assume. It's

much easier that way. In a couple of weeks it will have been seven years and Iris Scott-Holland really will be dead – legally, at least."

He scrubbed his face with his hands. "And this is your home," he said finally.

"It is," I agreed. "Or it was. I'm not entirely sure."

He looked at me then, his eyes flicking across my face as though I was a book he was trying to read.

"I think," he said heavily, "that you had better begin at the beginning."

I nodded, then felt around for the words to do so. "When I was nine," I said, "my mother died. It was terrible, but I was close with my father. Then, around a year later, he married Helena."

The words felt rusty as I forced them out, but Nick nodded encouragingly.

"At first, I tried to be excited about having a stepmother and two new sisters, but it didn't go well. Helena and Agatha took an instant dislike to me. Agatha made my life unpleasant. She began to tell her mother stories about my behaviour. They were lies, but it didn't seem to matter.

"As far as my stepmother was concerned, I was trouble. I was difficult. My father defended me when he was there, but more and more he was called away by business on the estate. Often, it was up to Helena to decide if I was in the wrong, and when choosing between me and Agatha, there was never a chance I would go unpunished."

Nick made a noise then in the back of his throat, and I glanced up at him.

"It was bad," I admitted. "I was bewildered by it, I suppose. I didn't know what I had done to make them both hate me so much. Then, about a year after they were married, my father had a riding accident and died. My father was an excellent rider. He taught me when I was young, we rode together all the time. I didn't believe it could have been an accident. I thought Helena was involved somehow..." I trailed off. After all, it seemed I had been wrong on that front.

"And then?" Nick asked.

"And then things got worse." I shrugged. "Father's estate was unentailed, and he left everything in his will to his 'daughters' – Agatha, Cassie and me, to be held in trust until we were twenty-one by Helena. I was eleven years old. Twenty-one was an unimaginable age." I cleared my throat. "Helena moved me out of my bedroom to a smaller room near the servants' quarters, *just while she redecorated*, she said, but we both knew that was a lie. She asked if I would be more comfortable eating my meals with Mrs Chambers, the housekeeper, rather than in the dining room with her and the girls, since I had known Mrs Chambers all my life. I *was* actually much more comfortable, but the servants didn't know what to do with me. I don't think Helena did either." I smiled grimly.

"Finally, she began to talk about sending me away – somewhere that would 'correct' my bad ways."

This time there was no mistaking the noise that Nick made. It was low, like a growl.

"Well, exactly," I agreed, smiling ruefully up at him. "I had read *Jane Eyre* and I knew how *that* story ended. When a man came to talk to Helena about my new school, my fears were confirmed. I remember everything about him. He was tall and gaunt, like a skeleton with wicked black eyes that lit up when he spoke about *just punishment*, and *the path to meekness*." I looked back down at my hands. "I was frightened. It was the last straw. I thought Helena had rid herself of my father, and I assumed she wanted to do the same with me. I felt sure that if I went away with that man, that something awful would happen. That I wouldn't come back."

I hesitated for a moment, my voice trembling despite my determination to deliver the facts calmly. That day had been perhaps the most frightening experience of my life. I still had nightmares about that man coming to take me away. I remembered that moment as the one in which I had finally realized that I was alone. Utterly alone.

"And so," I continued briskly, pushing those thoughts aside, "I ran away to London, found work as a seamstress, and there I've been ever since, until the day you walked into the shop."

"How long ago was all this?" Nick asked. "How old were you when you ran away?"

"I was eleven, almost twelve."

"Almost twelve," Nick repeated mechanically.

I nodded.

"And then I appeared, with a plan to bring you here of all places," he said slowly.

"Yes. I was getting desperate. Like I said, it's been almost seven years since I disappeared, at which time Helena can have Iris Scott-Holland declared legally dead, and my share of the inheritance passes to Agatha and Cassie. It seemed like my last chance to try and find some answers, it seemed almost like..."

"Fate." Nick finished my sentence.

"Yes," I said again.

The silence that fell around us was heavy. I could see that Nick was adjusting to these new ideas, could see him matching up all this new information with the questions he had, the things about me that hadn't quite fit before. Now the puzzle pieces fell neatly into place.

"What about Helena?" he asked. "*Was* she involved in your father's death?"

"Not as far as I can tell," I replied. "I was so sure. But something still isn't right with my father's will."

As briefly as possible I sketched out the details of what I had learned since arriving at Holland Hall.

"So, you see," I said finally, "nothing was as I

thought it was. My father wasn't such a hero after all, and Helena wasn't such a villain."

"Not in this, no," Nick said. "But in the way she treated you?"

"I wanted to punish her for it all, just like you with Stefan. By ruining his match with Agatha." I sighed. Sharing everything had left me feeling tired and raw. "I need to try and find out if there really is a page missing from the will. I can't help but think there must have been more to it – that there were certain things my father would have wanted me to have. That he would have protected me better." I hesitated. "Or maybe that's just what I want to believe. Whatever the truth is, however knotted and messy, I need to find it. Only *now* I think that Helena suspects who I really am. I have no idea what she'll do next. I know she can be ruthless; she's like a lit fuse and I'm waiting for the explosion."

Nick was leaning against the fireplace, clearly trying to absorb everything I had told him. That was how I had felt after he'd told me about Stefan. He needed time to let it all sink in. I got to my feet.

"What are you doing?" Nick asked, startled.

"I'm going back to my room," I said.

"Oh," he said. "Of course."

I took another step forward, towards him. "Before I go," I said, "I wanted to ask you something."

He raised his brows.

I plucked up the bit of courage I had remaining. "What you said last night, about Stefan, about history repeating itself. What did you mean?"

"You said that Stefan had been charming you. That you liked him … and I was the one who brought him into your life – just like I did with Lila." There was the briefest pause. "I meant that I didn't want you to get hurt."

"Because … you care about me?" I struggled with the words.

Slowly, Nick nodded.

"Like you cared about Lila?"

Nick cleared his throat. "In a different way to how I cared about Lila."

"I see," I said. My voice was small. Something heavy and crushing settled in my chest.

"No!" Nick exclaimed, and I looked up at him. He

looked angry again. "No! I don't mean... That isn't... What I'm..." He huffed crossly. "Why do I always end up stammering like a schoolboy when I'm with you?"

"I have no idea!" I said, riled by his accusatory tone.

"What I mean," Nick said with elaborate patience, "is that with Lila, I was sixteen. It was an infatuation. Fleeting. In the end, Lila was – and is – my friend. That's not how I feel about you."

"Isn't it?"

"*No.*" I thought the word "no" had never sounded so romantic, so full of heat and tenderness and longing. It made my knees shake.

Still he didn't move from the fireplace, only watched me with a burning intensity.

That was when I realized. After what he'd told me about Stefan's behaviour, about Lila, there was no way that Nick was going to move. What was it he had said to me the night of the ball? *That choice would always lie with you.*

"Oh," I said, taking another step forward so that I was right in front of him. I lifted my hands, placing them on either side of his face. "*Now* I see."

I stood up on my tiptoes and brushed my lips softly against his.

For a moment he stilled, and then his arms were around my waist, and he came away from the edge of the fireplace with a ferocity that would have made me stumble if he hadn't been holding me up. Not that I would have noticed. Even as it was happening, I couldn't believe it was happening.

He was kissing me, and I was kissing him, and we were laughing, and it was heaven. He kissed my lips, my jaw, the spot behind my ear where I didn't know I had needed him to kiss me, and my hands were on his shoulders, my fingers brushed the sandpaper of his jawline, my lips touched the hollow at the base of his throat, where I could feel his heart beating as fast as my own.

Finally, we pulled apart, breathing ragged, eyes wide as we stared at each other.

"Well," he said, attempting to straighten a tie he wasn't wearing. "I hope I have made my feelings plain."

I tipped my head back and laughed, and Nick smiled.

A wide, wicked smile, just for me.

CHAPTER THIRTY-SIX

And just like that, everything had changed.

When I went back to my room I hugged the secret knowledge of what had passed between us to my chest. It wasn't just the kissing – though, *goodness, the kissing* – it was the feeling of having someone on my side. Someone who knew all of my secrets and was still there, next to me. It was a new feeling – or an old one, one I barely remembered.

When I finally fell asleep, I didn't dream at all. I knew nothing of the world until Matilda appeared several hours later, shaking my shoulder gently to wake me.

"Miss," she whispered. "Miss, wake up."

"What is it?" I sat up, suddenly awake, panic beating a loud tattoo in my chest.

"It's Lord Wynter, miss, he asked me to wake you," Matilda said softly. "He wanted to see you before the others were up."

It was music to my ears. The panic stilled inside me as I remembered that I wasn't alone. Today I had Nick.

"We'll work it all out," he had promised me last night. "Together."

When I saw that Matilda was pulling out my riding habit, my spirits soared even higher. Let Helena do her worst – today I felt invincible.

The sun was barely up as I approached the stables, the early morning light pouring across a delicate mist, like rolling clouds of airy tulle. Nick was waiting for me outside, and I felt overcome with an unfamiliar shyness. When I looked at him I saw what everyone else saw: his tall figure, immaculately turned out in a navy-blue riding jacket, dark trousers and shining boots, his inky hair neatly arranged, his easy posture, his sharp cheekbones and strong jaw, those lazy blue eyes and the firm, unsmiling mouth.

But I saw other things now too. I saw the curl in his hair, that made it unruly, and I knew the way it felt, silk between my fingers. I knew how he looked when he smiled, really smiled, and the way the corners of those blue eyes creased. I knew what it was to see them lit with laughter, lit with something else when he looked at me.

It was strange, this intimacy, this way of knowing someone in a different way.

"Good morning," he said.

"*Early* morning," I replied. "I know how you feel about those."

He grimaced. "Yes, terrible isn't it?" He gestured around at the beautiful, gently glowing view. "But I thought you and I had better talk. This seemed the best way."

"Of course," I said, twisting my hands together, momentarily stumped as to how to continue the conversation.

"I'd just like to make sure…" Nick began, "that your recollection of last night is the same as mine. Between the idea of you walking through walls and the really quite excellent ending to the encounter, I woke up this morning concerned it had all been a dream."

"Walking through walls?" I tilted my head to the side. "Lord Wynter, I've asked before and I'll ask again, were you ever dropped on the head as a child? You do have some peculiar ideas."

A smile touched his lips. "Very peculiar, indeed," he agreed. "But I think, this time, entirely correct."

I smiled too. "So, not a dream, then?"

"No." His voice was low. "Not a dream."

We were interrupted then by Jensen, who appeared, leading out both the horses that had been saddled.

I was already moving forward, because there, tossing her head and dancing with barely suppressed eagerness, was Asteria, saddled and ready. I moved towards her, took her head in my hands, and she stilled – just for a moment – long enough for me to rest my forehead against hers. To breathe.

"I can ride her?" I asked.

"Why not?" Nick replied. "She's yours."

Asteria made a noise, as if in agreement. Nick moved

to help me mount, and I placed my foot in his hands, springing up into the saddle, feeling Asteria ripple beneath me like water. I leaned forward and pressed a hand to her neck.

Nick mounted up next on to Felix, and when we were side by side, he turned to me. "Well?" he said. "You two had better lead the way."

It was all the encouragement I needed, and I kept Asteria under tight control as we trotted away from the house. I could feel her excitement, the fragile hold that she had on herself, and I knew that she could feel the same from me. As soon as we possibly could, I glanced over at Nick, a question in my eyes. *Are you ready?* He nodded, and I let my beautiful horse have her head.

Galloping across the park on Asteria's back, I felt a joy that I hadn't known for seven years. We moved as one being, surging across the ground, flying through the cool snap of autumn air. I was dimly aware of Nick riding behind me, but even Felix couldn't catch us, not that morning. We were faster, we were something elemental.

When we finally pulled up, Nick drew up beside me.

My face was wet with tears, but I beamed at him. I felt brand new.

We didn't speak, only walked beside each other for a while, soaking in this world of birdsong and smudgy amber light, in which we were the only inhabitants.

Finally, we reached a dip in the scenery, a quiet bend in the river, where a magnificent oak tree stood, a blaze of firelight orange.

"Here," I said, breaking the silence. "The horses can have a drink."

Nick dismounted first, and he came to lift me down from Asteria's back. His hands were at my waist, and I slid slowly down, until we were standing with barely a hair's breadth between us.

I tipped my head back to look up at him. His hands still rested lightly on my hips. There was a beat. Another. His jaw ticked; the insistent drumming of my pulse filled my ears.

"Goodness," I said. "What does a girl have to do to be ravished around here?"

The words were barely out of my mouth before his lips found mine. We kissed for a long time. Somewhere along the way I lost my hat. Nick lost his as well. The horses took themselves off to drink from the stream. I felt the oak tree pressed into my back. Nick's jacket fell to the ground, quickly followed by his tie. My hair was loose around my shoulders, pins scattered. My hands were inside his shirt, greedy. He kissed me slowly, as if he had nothing but time. I was drunk on the taste of him.

Finally, we drew apart, and I raised a hand to my swollen lips. Nick's hair was rumpled, a pink flush touched his high cheekbones, and his eyes seemed a darker blue. I wanted to kiss him again already. I never wanted to stop. From the way he was looking at my mouth, I would guess that the feeling was mutual.

"We need to talk," I said firmly. Or at least, I tried to say it firmly. It came out slightly wobbly.

He flashed me his half-smile. "You're right, we do." He cleared his throat. "Let's sit down. Preferably with several feet between us, or I can't promise we'll get much discussed."

I laughed, and pulled him down beside me, our backs against the rough bark of the tree. He took my hand in his, his fingers twining through mine. I rested my head on his shoulder. It was nice. For a moment we sat, just like that.

"So," Nick said finally. "I've been thinking."

"A dangerous habit."

"What I've been thinking about is revenge."

"How romantic." I fluttered my lashes.

"You see, you think you're mocking me," he said, tipping his head back, "but you're actually bringing me to my point. I'm very happy, Iris."

I smiled. "I'm very happy too." And I was. In that moment, there with him, I was close to bliss.

"That works out neatly for us, then." His fingers tightened around mine. "I suppose what I'm saying is that we don't need revenge any more, do we?"

I dropped his hand, startled. "What do you mean?"

"Well," Nick said awkwardly, turning to get a better look at my face. "That's how these things go, isn't it? When you find happiness, you let go of the idea of revenge. You realize it's better to find forgiveness and you don't need it any more."

I blinked at him. "Is that how you feel?" I asked.

"You don't need revenge against Stefan? You want to forgive him?"

He shifted. "I don't want anything to come between us."

I snorted. "Nothing's going to come between us. And what could be more romantic than bringing down a villain, together?"

He looked startled. "You mean you still want to stick to the plan? Pretending you're engaged to Stefan? The public showdown? It will make you infamous, Iris."

"What I want is some sort of justice for your friend. I want people to know what Stefan is, for him to be sent home with his tail between his legs. I want to tell everyone how he behaves towards women, and then perhaps that reputation will protect someone from him in the future. I don't want him getting his own way, yet again, sailing through life without a care for the pain he leaves in his wake. If you call that revenge then, yes, Nick, I want it. Very much."

I finished this rather breathless speech and looked up to see a grin spreading across his face.

"You feel that way too?" I asked.

"Yes," he laughed. "I was worried it made me rather unenlightened."

"Then we shall be unenlightened together," I said, settling back against the tree.

"A bloodthirsty pair indeed," Nick agreed.

"You know," I mused, "I thought that by taking Stefan away from Agatha, I was getting some kind of revenge on her and Helena, but now I think I've actually saved her from a terrible, unhappy marriage."

"Probably." Nick shrugged. "Though I think Agatha is a lot more interested in Stefan's title than she is in him."

"Agatha is nothing more than a spiteful cat," I said. "It's Helena who's always been the real driving force. Agatha simply follows her lead."

Nick frowned. "Stefan's not the only one who deserves justice," he said. "The way she treated you, forcing you to run away from your own home. It wasn't right."

"I spent so long thinking that she killed my father," I sighed. "I was *certain*. I based everything on a lie. All the choices I made, every action I took."

Nick seemed to consider this for a moment. "If your instinct was that strong, if you were that sure, then perhaps you *were* right," he said at last. "Everything you've learned could be true, and Helena could *still* have had a hand in your father's death."

I frowned. "If she did, it was nothing to do with his drink. Tookes and Kielty both drank from the same flask and they were fine."

"Maybe she put stronger drink than he was used to in it, or gave him more," Nick said. "Hoping that would lead to an accident."

"I suppose," I agreed, "but it's not a very sure-fire way to kill someone, is it? You'd just have to wait and cross your fingers that eventually it would happen."

We both fell silent at that.

"You know, it was in the woods over there," I said finally, gesturing to the trees over to our left. I had been trying to ignore them ever since we had arrived at Holland Hall. "I don't know where, precisely, but somewhere on the path that he rode every day." That I had ridden dozens of times, hundreds of times. "Perhaps we should ride through them now."

Nick glanced at me. "You don't need to—" he began.

"I know," I said quickly. "But I want to." I realized

that I did want to, that riding that path would be like laying some kind of ghost for me. "If you'll go with me."

Nick got to his feet, and held out his hand. "Anywhere."

CHAPTER THIRTY-SEVEN

In my mind, the Holland Hall woods had become a place of sharp shadows, of perpetual night, where trees rose like skeletons, and thorns tangled underfoot. I imagined them like the brambles that grew up around Sleeping Beauty's castle, thick and forbidding.

The reality was, of course, the opposite of this. The woods were as beautiful as ever – more so, even, dressed in their autumn finery. Nick and I rode silently along the path, beneath an arbour of rustling leaves, drowsy sunlight filtering through the canopy they created.

Everything was still and peaceful. Only birdsong and the sound of the horses' hooves broke the quiet.

"My father used to always take this path down towards the tenant houses," I said. "It's not the quickest way, but he loved these woods." I bit my lip. "At least, I think he did. I'm beginning to feel as though I didn't know him at all."

"You knew him," Nick said. "You just didn't know all of him. You were a child ... it takes a long time for children to know their parents as real, flawed, complicated people. You never had that opportunity."

"I suppose you're right. But I can't help thinking his behaviour towards Helena was unforgivable. And I don't even like Helena!"

"It's hard to witness your hero fall from his pedestal," Nick suggested gently.

"Yes," I agreed, blinking back the tears in my eyes. "I feel angry with him, and I have so many questions that no one else could ever answer, but I still feel his loss." I pressed a hand to my chest. "I still can't believe he's gone."

And somewhere along this path was where it

happened. The words were unspoken, but of course we were both thinking it.

"The path *is* uneven," I said reluctantly. "If he *was* drunk, I suppose he could have fallen easily enough."

Nick pulled up on his horse and jumped lightly down from Felix's back. He held the reins loosely in his hand as he walked a few steps of the path on foot, bending down to take a closer look.

"Yes, the ground is uneven," he agreed. "But no more than, say, the paths out on the other side of the woods, down to the village."

I dismounted and joined him.

"It doesn't seem enough to unseat a half-decent rider, let alone Father," I conceded. "I find it difficult to imagine him being *so* drunk he couldn't avoid a rabbit hole. Not unless his drink had been tampered with."

"Which we know it wasn't," Nick put in. "But you say he rode this path every day? So if someone *did* want to harm him they'd know where to lay a trap."

"A trap," I murmured, looking around us. Yes, this would be the perfect place for that. No witnesses except the silent, solemn trees. A breeze rustled through them then, one that carried untold secrets.

"If I were going to try and cause an accident I would string something across the track," Nick said suddenly, pointing to the trees. "It would be easy enough to tie something around one of the trunks either side."

"It would have to be something he wouldn't see," I said slowly.

"Fishing wire? Were the horse's legs wounded?"

I shook my head. "No, Hercules didn't have a mark on him. Something strong enough to make Hercules stumble but soft enough to break, leaving no mark on him or obvious signs of foul play when Tookes and Kielty found them."

"Perhaps we are grasping at straws," Nick sighed.

"No," I said slowly. "No." My breath caught. An idea came into my mind, one so unthinkable that I almost laughed. And yet ... the pieces might well fit together.

"We need to go back now," I said. "I have to talk to Cassie."

Nick asked me no questions, only helped me into the

saddle, and rode hard beside me all the way back to the house. My mind was turning furiously.

Fortunately, Cassie was an early riser.

We found her in the dining room, where she was making stiff small talk with the colonel, over her tea and toast. She looked almost painfully relieved when I burst into the room, Nick following at a more reasonable pace.

"I'm sorry, Colonel," I said breathlessly. "I need to borrow Cassie for a moment. I'm afraid it's quite urgent ... about preparations for the ball, you know."

Cassie's face crumpled in confusion.

"The ball?" she murmured.

"Yes!" I cried, tugging at her arm, hauling her to her feet. "Ribbons!" I exclaimed, almost at random.

"*Ribbons?*" Cassie's confusion only grew, but the colonel nodded understandingly.

"Female trifles," he said in a low voice to Nick. "Always causing a kerfuffle."

I dragged Cassie away, missing Nick's reply, and made my way to the morning room, tugging a wriggling Cassie in my wake.

"Iris!" Cassie said in a low voice. "What's going on?"

She looked nervously over her shoulder at Nick, who had followed us.

"It's fine," I said. "He knows everything."

"That's *precisely* what I'm always telling people," Nick murmured.

We reached the morning room and I led them over to the far wall and stopped.

"There," I said, pointing at the framed embroidery.

"Your embroidery?" Cassie frowned. "What about it?"

I looked for a moment at the image, the wide, silver moon, high above the twisting river. The light captured in taut strands of silver thread.

"I stitched this, right after my father's accident. Yesterday, when we talked about it, you said that Agatha gave me the bobbin of silver thread to use."

"That's right," Cassie agreed.

"I thought it was hers," I said, a hitch in my voice, "but you said that you *found* it."

"We did find it," Cassie said slowly. "She kept it because it was so pretty. She really was trying to be nice to you for once—"

"Yes, I know," I said impatiently. "That's not important now. What is important is *where* Agatha found it."

Cassie smiled. "It was funny, actually. We found it in the woods, near the path that runs back to the house. We were both convinced at the time that it had been left by fairies ... what have I said?" I could tell from the way she was looking at me that all the colour had left my face.

I glanced at Nick to see if he had made the connection. The grimness in his own eyes told me he had.

How might you bring a horse down? Something strung across the path it always travelled, something light and fine that no one would notice, something that would be invisible to a rider, a rider who had drunk too much, something that would be easy to get rid of afterwards...

I looked at the embroidery again, and this time I felt my stomach turn. All this time it had hung here on the wall.

The murder weapon.

Cassie was still looking at me in confusion. "Iris," she said. "What's the matter?"

I couldn't bring myself to tell Cassie the truth. That her mother was a killer.

"I need to ... go..." I managed. "Sorry, I have to..." I didn't finish the sentence, just lurched through the door.

"Should I go after her?" I heard Cassie ask. "Does she need help?"

"No, no." Nick was reassuring. "I know just what to do."

Nick caught up to me in the hallway and opened the library door, pushing me gently inside. He pushed me down into a chair, poured a glass of brandy and put it in my hand. I just stared at it. I think it was about eight o'clock in the morning.

"Can it be true?" I whispered.

"It's possible," Nick said cautiously. "The pieces all fit together."

"If my father was going to divorce Helena, she would have been desperate enough to do it," I said, certainty edging my voice. "It wouldn't even be difficult, given the state he was in, the way he was drinking. Such an accident *was* probably inevitable. And no one would suspect foul play – they all knew what he was like."

"That's what makes it a clever plan," Nick agreed. "No one would suspect. No one but you."

"And who was going to listen to a grieving child?" I stared into the glass of amber liquid. "There's no proof," I said finally. "It's just a guess."

"It's an answer." Nick crouched down in front of me, wrapping his hand around my wrist. He took the glass from my hand and put it on the table beside me. "One that you didn't have before. We can try and find proof; we can confront Helena."

We.

I managed a watery smile, then crumpled back into the chair. "It's all a lot more complicated than I thought it would be."

I closed my eyes for a moment. When I opened them, Nick was still there in front of me, a worried frown pinching between his eyes. I lifted a hand and rested it for a moment on his cheek. He leaned into my touch.

"For now," I said more firmly, "I think we should keep our focus on Stefan. Once the ball is over, we can decide how to proceed. Because I think I will have to be Iris Scott-Holland again."

"No name can change what you are."

"And what is that?" I asked with a smile. "An infuriating baggage?"

"Heard that, did you?"

"Yes, I thought it was incredibly romantic."

"That bodes extremely well for our future." Nick held out his hand and helped me to my feet. "It's decided, then. We wait until after the ball, and then we'll bring Iris Scott-Holland back from the dead."

"There's going to be a terrible scandal." I bit my lip. "What will your grandmother say?"

"About trading Serena Fox – daughter of a factory owner – for Lady Iris Scott-Holland? I should think she'll throw a party, the terrible old snob," he said fondly.

I was less sure about that, but we already had enough problems to be getting on with.

I straightened my shoulders. "All right," I said. "We concentrate on the ball. After that … well, after that I suppose we'll see how the cards fall."

I looked up and noticed Nick grinning at me.

"If I didn't know better," I said suspiciously, "I'd think you were enjoying this."

He shrugged languidly, a spark in his eye. "I was simply thinking that life with you will never be dull."

"I actually plan to be extremely dull when all this is over," I said primly.

"Better and better," Nick replied promptly. "My grandmother's always trying to get me to give up my rackety ways. Won't she be thrilled to hear about this very dull life you have planned for us?"

CHAPTER THIRTY-EIGHT

Despite the revelations I was keeping hidden, I felt strangely like a weight had been lifted. Knowing that I had been right, that my instincts had not failed me completely, was a relief. Ever since I had arrived at Holland Hall I had felt myself unbalanced by each new twist and turn that had been exposed. Now, I finally felt as if I were on solid ground again.

Thanks to Helena's intense programme of activities, and her determination to keep Stefan and me apart, two days had passed and I had not had to suffer too much time with him. I had settled for casting him the occasional demure glance, and he would wink cheerfully. Once, he had managed to take my hand.

"Not long now, my love," he'd whispered. "On Friday we shall announce our news to the world and then we will have plenty of time to be alone together."

"I can't wait," I lied, through smiling lips.

Now, the night before the ball, I found myself in the drawing room locked in a game of chess with Nick. Stefan was talking to Helena, and Jack and Sophia were chatting in the corner with Lady Bell and the dowager countess.

Stefan was a lot less bothered by Nick and I spending time together since our engagement. There was a smugness in the way he looked at his friend Earl Wynter that made me want to scratch at his eyes. He thought he'd won, and that Nick just didn't know it yet.

As if he ever stood a chance.

Nick's eyes held mine over the top of the chessboard. His gaze dropped, his brow furrowed in concentration. He scraped a hand across his jaw.

I'd never been that interested in chess before, but now I thought it might be the most fascinating thing in the world.

His hands moved towards the pieces, long, elegant fingers scooping up one of his pawns, moving it with confidence. I wanted to knock all the pieces off the board and clamber over it into his lap.

Something of that must have shown in my face because his eyes lit with something wicked, and he touched the collar of his shirt, as though it were suddenly too tight.

"Concentrate," he said sternly.

In the background, Agatha was singing and playing the piano. I forced myself to return my attention to the game – I might be head over heels for the man, but I still wanted to win.

Several moves later I glanced over to the corner of the room where Lady Wynter, Sophia and her mother were being entertained by Jack. He was making Lady Bell laugh, her pinched face softened. Sophia was looking at him as if she was dying of thirst and he was a glass of water.

"Your friend Jack," I said in a low voice. "He's a good man, isn't he?"

"He's a very good man. One of the best, in fact."

I nodded. "I thought so, but I've been getting it wrong lately."

"I shall try not to take that personally." He moved his rook.

"I didn't mean you," I said. My eyes strayed towards Stefan, who was having his ear bent by Helena. The smile he sent me was sweet, a sugared little lie, a boiled sweet laced with arsenic. I looked back at Nick. "I know that you're a good man."

"Not that good," he murmured, in a way that made something clench in my belly.

Now his eyes were the ones darkening as they dropped to my mouth, his pupils dilated. I took an unsteady breath.

"I just want to know if he's going to behave well with Sophia," I said, returning us to steadier ground. "She's in a fragile position."

Nick's gaze slid towards the couple. "You don't need to worry," he said with certainty.

"You know something!" I exclaimed, then bit my lip as several heads turned in our direction.

"Iris," he said quietly, with a lazy grin. "I know *everything*."

"Checkmate," I replied sweetly, sliding my queen forward and pinning his king to the back of the board.

He looked down at the game as though he'd forgotten it existed.

"So now I owe you *two* forfeits," he said.

"That I can collect at any time."

"I'm not sure I can live with the suspense."

"Don't worry," I said silkily. "I have a few ideas how to use them."

His fingers tightened around the chess piece in his hand. "If you keep looking at me like that I'm going to ruin all our plans by kissing you senseless in front of everyone." His voice was low, a rumble in his chest.

I felt heat rise to my cheeks, and I cleared my throat. "Well, I'm glad to hear that things will turn out well for Sophia," I said. "She deserves it."

Helena's throaty, musical laugh filled the room.

"Would that everyone was getting what they deserve," Nick said.

I sighed. It had been the most difficult part of these last two days. To know what Helena had done, and to keep up the veneer of civility. We were like sharks, circling one another now. She knew my secret and I knew hers, but neither of us could act. Not yet.

"I've been thinking," Nick said slowly. "We should take another look at the will."

"The will?" I frowned.

"You said that you thought there was a page missing. If we could find it, then that would be evidence of will tampering, if nothing else."

"That's true," I mused. "Unless she's destroyed it."

"You've looked everywhere you can think of?"

"Yes. Although if my father had two secret hiding places I'm certain there must be more that I don't know about." I grimaced. "It seems that he was really as paranoid as Tookes said..." I trailed off.

"What is it?" Nick asked.

"Probably nothing," I replied. "I just wondered if *Tookes* might know where else we could look. I'd be surprised if any of the house's secrets got by him."

Nick sat back in his chair. "Perhaps we should have a word with Mr Tookes, then."

"More creeping about at midnight," I said wearily.

"Not tonight." Nick got to his feet. "Lady Scott-Holland," he said, striding towards Helena. "I wonder if I might beg a favour?"

Helena looked up at him, a brief flicker of suspicion crossing her face before she arranged her features into something more like that of a gracious hostess. It was clear that she didn't understand the relationship between Nick and me. I could only imagine the questions plaguing her. Did he know who I was? Or was he an innocent dupe? Or did his involvement mean she was wrong? Could she be *certain* that I was Iris Scott-Holland? Whatever the answer, she knew better than to risk alienating one of the leaders of society.

"Of course, Lord Wynter," she said smiling at him.

"I have been asked by Miss Fox's father to see to his wine cellars. The man is building quite the collection, but I fear he is not storing it all correctly. Your own cellars are clearly magnificent, given the quality of the wine we've been enjoying these last weeks. May I ask who chooses the wine?"

Helena eyed him narrowly. "The butler, Tookes," she said. "I'm sure he would be happy to give you a tour of the cellar. Both of you," she added, her eyes darting towards Stefan, who was grinning good-naturedly.

"That is most generous of you," said Nick.

I tried to keep my face emotionless as she tugged on the bell.

"Tookes," Helena said, once the butler arrived. "Would you show Lord Wynter and Miss Fox to the wine cellar? I believe they have some questions for you."

"Of course, Your Ladyship." Tookes bowed.

We followed the butler down the stairs and through to his office, where he used a key to open another door that led to the wine cellars, which were enormous, dark and cool.

Tookes' eyes slid towards me, but otherwise there was nothing at all to give him away when he turned to Nick. "In what way may I be of assistance, my Lord?"

"It's fine, Tookes," I said. "Lord Wynter knows who I am."

Tookes looked between us. "I see," he said. "Lord Wynter is the friend who helped you to come here."

"He is."

Tookes drew himself up to his full height. "In the absence of Lady Iris's father, I hope you won't be offended, sir, if I ask what your intentions are."

"Tookes!" I exclaimed, flushing to the roots of my hair.

"Completely honourable," Nick said promptly, submitting meekly to the butler's interrogative stare. "I'm in love with her."

"*Are* you?" I asked.

"Hopelessly."

"Oh."

Tookes watched this exchange with interest. "In that case," he said, breaking through the tension that threatened to smother us all, "I would imagine you're not here to ask me about the wine cellar."

"No," I said unsteadily. "Tookes, I need to find a copy of Father's will – I think there's a page missing in the solicitor's copy. Do you think there's one in this house?"

He frowned. "I don't know," he said, but something shifted behind his eyes.

I supressed a groan. "If *anyone* knows, Tookes, it's you."

There was a beat. Tookes exhaled. "Lady Iris," he said finally. "Your father was a complicated man, but he was always good to me. Before he died, I made him certain promises and I still consider myself to be bound by them."

"You know that I wouldn't ask you if it were not very important." I turned to him, my eyes pleading. "I think I'm entitled to the truth. I'm his *daughter*!" The words burst out of me, full of anger and frustration.

Tookes released another long sigh. "Wait here," he said at last, and then he disappeared back through the door to his office.

Nick placed a hand on my trembling arm, letting me know that he was with me.

Tookes returned, holding a small wooden box in his hands.

"Your father gave me this," Tookes said. "Not long before he died. He made me swear not to look inside it, but to keep it somewhere safe. I don't think he intended to leave it with me, but then he had the accident." Tookes shrugged awkwardly. "I've been wondering whether or not I should give it to you ever since you turned up, but I could see you were hurting and I didn't want to stir things up any more for you. Besides, I gave your father my word.

"I've never looked inside, but as I've said to you before, I don't think your father was quite in his right mind at the end. I think if you want to look in it then you should have the choice."

With those words he retired from the room, swift and silent as a shadow.

I held the box in my hands. It wasn't locked, just closed with a small brass catch.

"Only Tookes could keep an unlocked box full of secrets for seven years and not open it," I said.

"Are *you* going to open it?" Nick asked.

I nodded. "I can't be afraid of the truth any more."

I took a deep breath and opened the box. Inside were lots of small sheets of folded paper. I pulled the top one out and opened it.

Papa,

I loved going to the casil with you and playing at being a nite. Espeshully when we slayed the dragin! I hid all my sweets from Mrs Chambers in my pilow case. Don't tell her, it's a secrit!

Love from
Iris

"Oh!" I exclaimed softly. "They're notes. Silly notes I used to write him." I shuffled through the papers, dozens of little scraps of nothing. "I can't believe he kept all of these."

"There's something else in there," Nick said.

He was right. Underneath the notes was a thick sheaf of paper, carefully folded. I knew what it would be before I opened it.

"His will," I said. "Written in his own hand."

"He would have written it out to send it to the solicitor to prepare properly," Nick murmured.

I unfolded it, smoothing the sheets out. Nick leaned

towards me, my eyes rapidly scanned the words written there.

"Well," I said finally. "That certainly clears a few things up."

CHAPTER THIRTY-NINE

The next day was the day of the ball.

There was palpable excitement about the place. The whole house was a hive of activity, new staff had been brought in, and there was an endless stream of tradesmen arriving, hammering away behind closed doors. There were flowers everywhere, and I knew that the cook had been working for days to prepare all the food.

I had been hard at work too. It had taken every moment I could snatch, but I had finally finished my dress. It was exactly as I had imagined it, and I felt a thrill as Matilda helped to slip it over my head, and the heavy silk glided down my body.

The pearly cream silk was overlaid with tulle to form a full skirt. A low-cut square neckline, fitted bodice and small cap sleeves created a pleasingly simple shape, but the rows of glass beads that hung from the sleeves caught the light, like tiny stars. The gown itself was embroidered in silver thread, a pattern of silver stars, that only revealed itself when the light played across it. It gave the dress an ethereal quality. I knew I had done my job when Matilda's breath caught.

"Oh, miss," she said, her eyes wide. "I've never seen anything like it. It looks like magic. Like it was stitched by fairies!"

It was the best thing I had ever made. I thought with a smile about how furious Madame would be if she knew she had let it go.

Matilda piled my hair on top of my head, and I wore my mother's crescent moon hair pin, the one Cassie had kept for me. It was as if it had been made just for this occasion. I draped her silver shawl around my shoulders. I wore no other jewellery. I didn't need to trick anyone tonight. Tonight I would simply be myself, and everything I wore spoke to that. I left Serena Fox's wardrobe behind in her room.

By the time I had finished getting ready I could hear an enormous amount of noise coming from downstairs. The dowager countess had told me that she would come and collect me from my room, but that we would be making a fashionable entrance this time – there was to be no invitation for drinks. Helena wanted her guests to have the full experience of a grand ball, with all the ceremony it entailed.

She had no idea of the experience they were going to get.

I looked in the mirror. Cinderella, off to the third and final ball. Tonight Nick and I would play our hand. The diamond pin gleamed in my hair.

"Do you need anything else, miss?" Matilda asked.

"No." I smiled. "Thank you, Matilda, you've been wonderful these past two weeks. I don't know what I would have done without you."

Matilda flushed, pleased. "Thank you, miss." She twisted her hands in her skirts. "If you find yourself looking for a lady's maid again, I hope you know I'd be very interested in the position."

I held her eye in the mirror for a long moment. "I may well take you up on that," I murmured. "Now, go and have a good time, I know there's a party below stairs as well tonight."

Matilda whisked away, a smile on her face that I attributed to the handsome footman I had heard her mention.

When the knock finally came, I felt a nervous flutter in my stomach. This was it.

I opened the door and found that the dowager countess was not alone. Nick leaned negligently against the door frame, frighteningly beautiful in a dark evening suit.

When he saw me, however, he moved away from the door in an involuntary action and his eyes widened. He opened his mouth, as though to speak, but no words came out.

The dowager countess chuckled and rubbed her hands together. "My grandson, rendered speechless at last."

Nick, visibly gathering his wits, cleared his throat.

"I can't disagree," he said. "You look..." He trailed off here, but the look in his eyes made it clear that there was a compliment in the silence.

"Yes, yes." His grandmother batted her hand at him. "The girl is a beauty all right, but if we don't get to the ball then no one else will be able to comment on it. A dress like that shouldn't be shut up here." She began to move down the corridor, Nick and I following. "These things start later and later nowadays," she grumbled. "I've been twiddling my thumbs in my room for an hour just to make sure that we arrived late enough to make a splash."

Nick offered me his arm and I took it. "I convinced my grandmother to let me come and escort you both," he said in a low voice, while the dowager countess continued her tirade against ballroom etiquette. "How are you feeling?"

"Nervous," I admitted.

"You know that you don't have to do this," Nick replied. "I would understand if it was too much."

I shook my head. "We've come so far." I managed a smile. "I'm looking forward to seeing Stefan squirm."

"Ghoul," Nick laughed.

"If I'm a ghoul, then you're a ghoul."

"Very true."

"What are you two wittering about?" The dowager countess turned on us, at the top of the stairs, her hands on her hips. "I hope the pair of you are going to behave yourselves at this party. Falling in rivers, haring around on horseback, secret shooting contests... Oh, yes." She fixed us with a quelling look as Nick and I stood, our mouths open in shock. "There's not a lot that gets past me."

"Let's hope there are a *few* things," Nick muttered.

"I'm not hard of hearing either," she said sharply, before turning to descend the stairs.

Downstairs, Helena had outdone herself. The house looked spectacular, primped and polished and lit by hundreds if not thousands of candles, softly flickering, giving the place the hazy air of stepping into a dream. Coming through to the ballroom was like entering a fairy bower, greenery twisted across the ceiling, and flowers hung in long ropes above our heads. The smell was heady – roses and something fresh, sweet and green.

An enormous orchestra played on a stage suspended on a platform, level with the balcony that ran around the room, where guests congregated for a bird's eye view of the festivities.

The room thronged with people, all in dazzling finery. The long windows had been flung open, allowing a gentle breeze to enter, and there were waiting staff circulating with wide silver trays laden with champagne saucers, or tiny delicacies. I saw Nick's gaze lock wistfully on to a tray full of cherry tarts.

Heads turned as we entered the room. I kept my chin high, taking small, even steps. People fell away from us. I think it was the dress – Matilda was right, it had some magic in it.

Stefan appeared, fairy-tale handsome in a formal military suit that must have been part of the royal livery. A row of medals shone on his chest. The smile on his face as he looked at me was smugly possessive. He reached out his hand and I placed my own on top.

In a parody of our first meeting he swept me straight on to the dance floor and into a waltz.

"You are so beautiful," he said, his breath hot against my ear. "A true princess."

We danced and I felt like a tiny doll, spinning inside a jewellery box.

This time Stefan didn't have to stick to the rules. Tonight we were to announce our engagement and so he could monopolize me as much as he wished. My hand was clamped to his arm, and he steered me around the room, showing me off. I smiled graciously, accepting the compliments strewn at me like flowers at my feet.

The night wore on, and I saw Helena and Agatha watching me. Agatha, beautiful in pale pink, seemed to realize that the game was over. The look she treated me to was one of undisguised hatred. I had stolen something from her. I wondered if she would ever understand what I had actually saved her from.

Helena was harder to read.

"My dear, how lovely you look," she said, while Stefan stood tall and proud beside me. "Such a handsome pair."

I saw her glance linger on the silver pin in my hair,

the tightening around her lips, the flare in her eyes of something knowing and dangerous.

I didn't care. I wanted her to know. Let her stand there, certain of who I was and knowing that she couldn't touch me. I would be dealing with her soon enough.

But, for now, I needed to concentrate on Stefan. Tonight I would be pulling the mask away, letting everyone see who he really was.

A man appeared, dragging Stefan away, and I felt my breathing ease. "There you are!" Sophia appeared, flushed and happy. "I haven't been able to get near you tonight. Everyone is talking about you and Prince Stefan."

"Never mind about me and Stefan," I said. "What about you and Mr Waterford?"

Her whole face lit up, as though a match had been struck. "Oh, Serena," she sighed. "He's *wonderful*."

"I think he feels the same way about you," I laughed.

She blushed. "He says he does," she admitted. "Though I can hardly believe it."

"I can," I said sincerely.

"How glad I am to have come to this wretched party

and met you all." She pulled me into a swift, surprising embrace.

I hugged her back, just for a moment. I hoped that soon there would be a way for Sophia to become friends with the real me. Everything was about to change.

I fixed a smile to my face as Stefan returned, taking possession of my hand again, swirling me through the crowd. I danced again with him, then with Jack, who wanted to spend the whole time talking about Sophia, then with Percy, who looked as though he was counting his steps and gave me that sweet, rueful grin every time he stepped on my toes.

All evening Nick and I were apart, yet I always knew where he was. I felt his presence in every room, just out of my eyeline. It was as if we were tied together by some invisible thread, as if I could feel the tug of it wherever he moved. I was sure that he felt the same.

The minutes crawled by, but finally, *finally*, the time came.

"I have asked the orchestra to stop after this song," Stefan said, "to let me make our announcement. Are you ready, my love?"

I looked at him steadily. "I'm ready."

The last notes of the song died away, and Stefan stepped forward.

"Ladies and gentlemen, may I please have your attention?" His voice was commanding, deep with the entitlement that comes of always being listened to. The crowds instantly fell silent, though a hum of expectation thrilled around the room. The dance floor cleared, and Stefan stood in the middle.

"I have a very happy announcement to make," Stefan said, an unfettered smile on his face. "I am pleased to tell you all, to share with you the news, that Miss Serena Fox has agreed to become my wife."

The ballroom burst into spontaneous applause, and Stefan held out his hand to me. I stepped forward, into the space that he occupied, but I didn't take his hand.

"I hate to contradict you, Your Highness," I said, my voice ringing out loud and clear. "But I'm afraid there has been a mistake. There will be no wedding."

Stefan froze, a look of confusion flashing across his face. "Serena!" he exclaimed. He smiled, but his eyes darted confusedly. "Now is not the time for a display of your British humour."

An awkward rattle of strained laughter ran around the room.

"I'm not laughing," I said, looking him straight in the eyes, holding his gaze, daring him to look away from me.

I saw the exact moment when the joviality fell away, when the barely repressed anger and self-interest rose to the surface.

"I wouldn't marry you if you were the last man on earth," I continued, the words carrying around the room with startling clarity. This place really did have excellent acoustics. "Not after all that I've learned about you. The way you treat women. You have left a string of ruined reputations behind you, destroying the lives of good women who thought they could trust you. You are a cad and a lecher. In this house alone I know that the maids fear being left on their own with you. Is that the behaviour of a prince? Is that the behaviour of a good man?"

I glanced around at the shocked crowd and my eyes found Cassie's. She stood frozen, eyes wide, a fruit tart held halfway towards her open mouth. A smile grew on her face as our eyes met. She nodded. It was almost as if I could hear her cheering me on. I might have known that my sister would be firmly on my side. I turned back to face the prince.

Stefan's face was ashen now, fury burned in his eyes. If I hadn't been swept up in my own performance, I would have been frightened.

Instead, I carried on. "You should be ashamed of yourself, and I hope your grandmother teaches you the lesson you sorely need."

"I— You—" Stefan took a step forward, but the dowager countess of all people materialized beside me.

"Well, Stefan," she said crisply, "I can't say that I'm surprised to hear this. Your grandmother told me she had her own suspicions about your behaviour, and I'm afraid that what I have to report to her will be damning indeed. If what Miss Fox says is true, I think it is certainly time that she brought you to heel."

With that the spell broke and the silence that had overwhelmed the room shattered. The thrill of gossip –

better than anything they could have hoped for – filled the air.

I watched the disapproving glances at the prince, the news carrying like wildfire. My words had rung true and the dowager countess's friendship with the queen seemed to seal the matter. Stefan would find no bride in England. In fact, I'd be surprised if he ever came back.

Stefan stood bewildered, unsure of his next move. He glanced appealingly at Helena, who gave him a cool glance and turned her back.

Nick appeared at my shoulder.

He held out his hand. "Shall we get out of here?"

I didn't think I had ever heard sweeter words.

CHAPTER FORTY

Nick and I retreated to the library. I was breathing hard, as if I had just run a race.

"We did it!" I exclaimed, flinging my arms around him.

"*You* did it!" He spun me around before setting me back on the floor. "You were spectacular."

"Did you see his face?" I said. "When he realized it was all falling down around him, all his careful plans?"

"I did." Nick nodded. "I only wish Lila could have been here."

"It will never be enough," I said, "but it's a small act of revenge for what he took from her. And at least others will be warned. No more hiding behind that Prince Charming facade. Thanks to your grandmother the news will be all over town before the week is out."

Nick wrapped his arms around me and I rested my head against his chest, hearing the reassuring, steady beat of his heart beneath my ear.

"Thank you," he murmured.

"How very moving." A frozen voice came from behind me. It was a voice I knew all too well.

I turned to find Helena standing in front of the door, her features sharpened by barely concealed rage.

She stepped forward, the movement rigid and controlled.

"I knew you would bring me nothing but misery, Iris Scott-Holland." She spat the words. "I knew it from the moment I laid eyes on you, all those years ago. The way you had your father wrapped around your little finger."

I stood, tall and unyielding, as she confronted me with a truth I had tried for so long to keep hidden. I *was* Iris Scott-Holland. Nick was right – I always had been.

And it seemed that this particular battle was not about to wait any longer.

Fine with me.

"I never wanted to make your life harder," I said, stepping away from Nick so that I could face her alone. This was my fight, after all. "I was just a child, grieving for her mother."

"From the start you were always between us," Helena snapped. "It seemed as though you were his only concern, outside his bloody horses. But I was his wife. His *wife*. He should have put me first. We might have had a chance had it not been for you."

"I know that you killed him."

The words spilled into the room, sucking all the air out of it. Helena's face grew still; her eyes became watchful.

"I don't know what you're talking about."

"It must have been easy to get him to drink more. He was cruel enough to force you to fill his flask for him," I said softly. "Easy to top it up a little higher, a little more often."

Helena's gaze didn't leave my face.

"You knew the route he rode every day, knew the state he would be in by the time he reached the wood. Knew that no one would question an accident. His drinking was no secret ... well, not from anyone but me, I suppose. It wouldn't have been complicated to tie something across his path, to wrap something around the trees, something taut and strong, something light enough to be invisible. Did you creep out later to remove the thread yourself or did you have someone else do it? Did you do it that night? Did you make sure he was dead and then leave him there?" My voice trembled here, and I brought it back under control.

"Whatever it was, you made a mistake. You dropped the bobbin of silver thread, left it behind in the woods for Agatha and Cassie to find."

Helena started at that. I had thought her face was leeched of colour already, yet now it seemed to turn paler still.

"You have no proof," she whispered.

"No." I shook my head. "But you and I know the truth. So in this room, let's hear it." There was silence. "Give me that, at least."

She took an agitated step back, her hands clutched compulsively at her full skirts. She seemed to age right in front of me, her shoulders hunching.

"You have no idea what it was like," she said finally, her voice raw. "What *he* was like. Manipulative, paranoid. He wouldn't let me leave the house or see anyone. You can't know the fear I felt. He began to talk of divorce. Divorce! It would ruin me. He claimed he was going to reveal I had a string of lovers. A total fabrication. I don't know if he even believed it, or if he only wanted to be rid of me, to hurt me. It would have been in the papers, it would have been everywhere. I had nothing of my own. Nothing. If he had gone through with it, my daughters would be lost. Destitute."

I could hear the fear in her voice, the panic. Despite everything she had done, I felt for her.

"And so you took matters into your own hands," I said. "Then, when you were sure he was dead, you removed a crucial page from his will."

Helena recoiled. "How did you— How do you—" Even if I hadn't found the original copy, this would have told me that I had been right all along. She might as well have announced her guilt.

"The page in my favour," I said steadily. "Tookes heard you arguing about it. It was never supposed to be an even split at all, was it? Cassie and Agatha were to be left small bequests outlined at the bottom of the missing page. *They* were the ones who were to have their money held in trust by you, not me. My father left me everything: the house, the money, the jewellery, the horses. All to be held in trust by a lawyer until I turned eighteen. But you couldn't have that, could you? Not when it could be altered so easily and without my father knowing a thing. All you had to do was add an 's'. 'To my daughter, I leave the entirety of the estate', became 'to my *daughters*'. By making sure that the pages ended and began where they did it was easy enough to remove the one you didn't want anyone to see, after Father had signed it all.

"But to do that you must have had help. The will had to be laid out just right so that you could make the change when you needed to." My mind went to Mr Fortescue's office, to the visible softening in his features when he spoke of Helena, to his efforts to dissuade my father from a path that would lead to her ruin. "The solicitor, Mr Fortescue, seems very enamoured of you."

"You seem to have it all worked out," Helena said sourly, refusing me a straight answer.

"I *will* be able to prove it, Helena," I said quietly. "I have my father's original copy of the will."

She flinched. I had her.

"How well do you think Mr Fortescue will stand up to questioning?" I pressed then. "Do you really think he would risk his reputation and livelihood for you?"

"Who will believe a word from your lips?" Helena hissed. "After that stunt you pulled tonight with the prince, after tricking society into thinking you're some heiress called Serena Fox? They'll eat you alive. No one will stand by you."

"I will."

The words came quietly, and I saw them strike Helena like a blow. She had forgotten that Nick was here; he had done such a good job of stepping back and leaving me to my confrontation that he had all but disappeared into the shadows.

There was no ignoring him now. He stepped forward,

next to me. "I will stand by her," Nick said coolly. "And believe me when I tell you that society will listen to what I have to say."

The door swung open then, and the dowager countess strode in.

"And they'll listen to me," she said, her eyes snapping as she looked the three of us over and we gaped at her. "I can't believe I'm reduced to listening at doorways like a servant," she added, shaking her skirts out in a frustrated gesture.

"No one asked you to do so, Grandmother," Nick said. "I have the matter in hand."

"Oh, do you?" his grandmother said sarcastically. "Well, Lady Iris. You have both myself and my grandson in your corner. What would you like to do?"

It really did seem that Lady Wynter knew everything that went on.

I glanced at Helena. Her spine was rigid, her chin high, her posture fierce, elegance even in defeat. She knew as well as I that the Wynter family name carried enough weight to ruin her.

I thought of Cassie, of her bright, confident plans for

her future, of the security that my father's fortune gave her, allowing her to be herself, an incredible woman. My sister. I had already decided what I would do, and I knew it was the right thing.

"There's no proof Helena killed my father," I said. "Perhaps it was an accident. Perhaps he fell because he was drunk. We'll never know. I am going to be Iris Scott-Holland again. I want my home back. But I will not contest the will."

Helena took a sharp intake of breath.

"On the condition that you and Agatha leave and don't come back. Agatha is about to turn twenty-one. I will arrange for a third of the estate's assets to be transferred to her, as well as your allowance. I don't want to see you at Holland Hall again."

"It seems an *extremely* generous offer to me," Lady Wynter said pointedly. "One that only a fool would refuse. And you are no fool, Lady Scott-Holland."

"No, Lady Wynter, I am not that," Helena agreed. "Yet I do not see how I can salvage a life for my daughter and myself if we are to be banished from our home."

"Don't you?" The dowager countess raised her

brows. "Personally, I can see the pair of you making quite the splash on the continent. You're still young, Helena. Perhaps you will even marry again."

A sneer flashed across Helena's face. It seemed the idea of marriage held little appeal for her these days. Still, I could see the idea settling in her mind. The possibility.

"Very well," she said rigidly. "It seems that I have no choice. I accept your offer."

"Good," I said, suddenly tired. "And for what it's worth, I promise to do my best to help Cassie live the full and happy life she deserves. She will always be a sister to me."

Helena treated me to one last long, wordless gaze, and then she swept from the room.

CHAPTER FORTY-ONE

"Well!" the dowager countess sighed heavily. "That's quite the tangle that the pair of you have managed to get yourselves caught up in. I suppose it shall be up to me to smooth everything over as usual. I assume" – she paused here to fix Nick with an interrogative look – "that you intend to marry the girl?"

"I'd rather ask her that question myself, thank you," Nick replied, a smile in the words. I felt myself flush bright red. "She hasn't even told me she loves me yet."

"Hmmmph," his grandmother exclaimed. "Well, don't wait too long. There's—"

"—the succession to consider," Nick finished her sentence. "I know, I know, Grandmother, but I was actually striving for something a bit more romantic."

"What I was *going* to say was that there's every chance the chit will turn you down. Seems she's got some brains, this one."

I laughed, and it was like the air suddenly flooded back into my lungs. Was it really possible that all of this had happened? That Stefan had been exposed? That I finally knew the truth of my father's death, and Helena had been turned out of my home? Was my life of the last seven years with its secrets and hiding over? I was reeling.

"Now," Nick's grandmother said bossily. "You two should return to the ball. Make sure everyone knows that you're head over heels for one another. Society loves a good love story." She glanced at us and sniffed disapprovingly. "You shouldn't have too much trouble making them believe it."

"Certainly," Nick agreed, holding out his hand to

me. "A relief to know we can leave everything in your capable hands, Grandmother. What a knack you have for turning up at just the right moment. You know, Iris," he mused, "I wonder if we've been wrong about this fairy godmother business from the start. It seems there might be one involved after all."

"Yes," I agreed. "I half-expect Lady Wynter to wave her magic wand, and have society believing that Iris Scott-Holland never went away."

The dowager countess sniffed again, but this time she couldn't conceal the smile that curled in the corner of her mouth. For a moment I saw the resemblance between her and the grandson she clearly adored.

"I shall do my best. Now, go on with you," she said, shooing us from the room. "I need a moment to catch my breath."

"I know just how she feels," I said to Nick as we wandered hand in hand down the corridor. "Shall we go back through the gardens? I'd like a bit of fresh air, and some quiet before we go back in there. You know people will have an awful lot to say."

"Of course," Nick agreed. "We don't have to go back

at all if you don't want to, whatever my grandmother says. It's been a big night. A lot has happened. How do you feel?"

"I don't really know," I admitted. "Overwhelmed, I think, as if most of my feelings are far away and I can't quite get at them. It doesn't feel real, after all this time, for the truth to be out. Everything is changing again, but I think it's good. I'm happy. I'm glad that you're here."

He squeezed my hand. "I'm glad too."

We made our way outside. A huge wave of noise and light drifted from the open windows. It seemed that the party had degenerated into something more debauched by now, that some revellers had begun to make use of the secluded shadows that the garden offered. It must be after midnight, and as we walked along the side of the house I noticed several discarded bottles sticking out of the topiary. An ornate silver ice bucket stood on one of the wide stone stairs, and Nick leaned over, pulling out a bottle of champagne.

"Now all we need are some glasses," he said.

"Don't be such a snob," I said. "We can drink from the bottle."

It was then that a figure loomed menacingly from the darkness.

"Stefan!" I exclaimed.

He stopped in front of us. "Thought you'd seen the last of me, I suppose?" he said, the words slurred. He swayed towards me and I could smell the alcohol on his breath. "But you and I have unfinished business."

At first I thought he was talking to me, but then I realized it was Nick that he was addressing.

"Name the time and the place." Nick's voice snapped through the air, cold with fury. "It's long overdue."

"How about here and now?" Stefan said. "The *lady* here can watch me beat you to a pulp."

He reached out and grabbed my arm.

That was his mistake.

I had no knife, but I curled my hand into a fist, thumb wrapped carefully around the outside – just like I'd been taught. I'd learned quite a few lessons during my time in the city.

As my fist connected with Stefan's nose there was a disturbing crunching noise, and I felt the warm cascade of his blood running over my knuckles.

Stefan made a sound that was something like a whimpering dog and stumbled backwards.

"My nose," he cried thickly, his hands cupping his bleeding face. "You've broken my nose!"

"*That*," I said, "was for Lila. And for Lottie, and for every other woman who has been mistreated by terrible men like you."

Stefan looked torn for an instant, and I braced myself, but then, with a noise of disgust, he turned and lumbered off into the shadows, still clutching his face.

There was a moment of silence.

"I'm sorry about that," I said, turning to Nick. "I really should have let you be the one to thump him."

The grin that spread across Nick's face was the one I knew he saved for me, the one I wanted to see every day for the rest of my life.

"No need for me to get my hands dirty, my love," he said, taking my own fingers gingerly in his.

I grimaced. Not only was my hand spattered in Stefan's blood, but I could tell that my knuckles were going to be horribly bruised.

"Here," Nick said. "Sit down."

I sat on the step and he pulled off his jacket, dropping it around my shoulders. Then he grabbed the ice bucket.

"Drink this," he said, holding out the champagne. I took it in my good hand and swigged, straight from the bottle. The silver bubbles slid down my throat.

Next, Nick removed his waistcoat.

I raised my eyebrows. "I don't think that is *quite* the public display of our affections your grandmother had in mind," I said. Still, my eyes lingered on the fine white linen of his shirt.

Nick tutted. "*Try* to keep your mind from the gutter, Iris." He picked some of the ice from the ice bucket and wrapped it carefully in his waistcoat, then he held the bundle gently to my swollen knuckles.

"Oooh." I winced. "That is going to leave a mark."

"My poor little prize fighter," Nick murmured, coming to rest his arm around my shoulders. I slumped back against him in relief.

"That was quite the adventure," I said.

"It was. I'm looking forward to this dull life you promised me."

"I'm in love with you too, by the way," I said. "In case you didn't already know it."

"Hopelessly?" Nick smiled.

"Actually, I'm feeling quite hopeful." I wiggled my fingers. "We slayed a lot of dragons together, you and I. What do you think happens next?" I twisted to look up at him.

His blue eyes shone in the moonlight. The sound of the party faded in the background as I stared at him. His mouth curled at the corner.

"Well, I'm no expert," he murmured, "but I *think* this is the part where we live happily ever after."

And then he kissed me.

ACKNOWLEDGEMENTS

First thanks *must* go to my three collaborators, Louise, Gen and Sophie. Not only did we dream up this book together but even when it was knotty and full of gaps I had so much fun working on this with you, and even in the darkest night I felt ALMOST optimistic that it was all going to be ok! Thank you, especially, for coping with the wildly tight turn-arounds and for taking my scrambled thoughts and making them shine. I really love this book, I would like to live inside it, and that's because of you. I appreciate you all so much and I LOVE making books with you.

Huge thanks to the whole team at Scholastic, especially to the magnificent Lauren Fortune, human sunbeam, Harriet Dunlea and new pal Bec Gillies. Thank you to Jamie Gregory for working his magic on the SO beautiful cover. Thank you to Jenny Glencross for smoothing this whole thing out and for being so kind.

Thanks to the whole TEAM of people online who frequently astound me with their outrageous levels of support. It means so much to me every time you comment or send me a message. Writing a book is mostly a solitary thing, and it feels so strange to think that there are other people who are as excited as I am about this book being made!

Thank you to the writers who I hugely admire who have all said such nice things about my books, and encouraged me beyond measure: Sarra Manning, Louise O'Neill, Alice Broadway, Ella Risbridger, Laini Taylor, Maria Kuzniar, Lucy Powrie, Lauren James, Keris Stainton, and Katherine Woodfine.

Thank you to the booksellers, the librarians, and the teachers who put their whole hearts into their work and help my books find their way to the readers who will love them.

Thank you to the late, great Sarah Hughes who supported me from my very first book. I'm very sad that she couldn't read this one. I hope she would have liked it.

Thank you as always to my family and friends for their support. I love you all too much to be succinct about it so I'm not even going to try to write it all down here. I just hope you know how grateful I am.

Thank you most of all to Paul and Bea – the only people I have seen for a year and one of you isn't even a person. Even in a pandemic, you are my big joy and I love you.

Laura Wood is the winner of the Montegrappa Scholastic Prize for New Children's Writing. She has a PhD from the University of Warwick studying the figure of the reader in nineteenth-century literature. She is also the author of *A Sky Painted Gold*, *Under a Dancing Star*, *A Snowfall of Silver*, *Vote for Effie*, *Effie the Rebel* and the *Poppy Pym* series.

lauraclarewood.com
Follow Laura on Twitter – @lauraclarewood Instagram
– @lauracwood

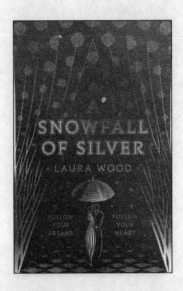

In the Autumn of 1931, eighteen-year-old Freya Trevelyan runs away from her home in Cornwall to follow her dream of becoming an actress.

When she is invited to join a theatrical company about to head out on tour, Freya thinks the path to success is clear, and, amidst all the glamour and bustle of stage life, she finds - for the first time - a place to belong. But can reality ever live up to her expectations? What if her life - and falling in love - turn out to be nothing like she planned?

"Irresistible... gorgeous escapism"
Guardian